The Eighth Day Brotherhood

Brotherhood

Alice M. Phillips

BLACK ROSE
writing™

D1414238

ISBN: 978-1-61296-737-0
PUBLISHED BY BLACK ROSE WRITING
www.blackrosewriting.com

Printed in the United States of America
Suggested retail price $15.95

The Eighth Day Brotherhood is printed in Adobe Caslon Pro

To Ben, my companion amid the gargoyles of Notre Dame.

The Eighth Day Brotherhood

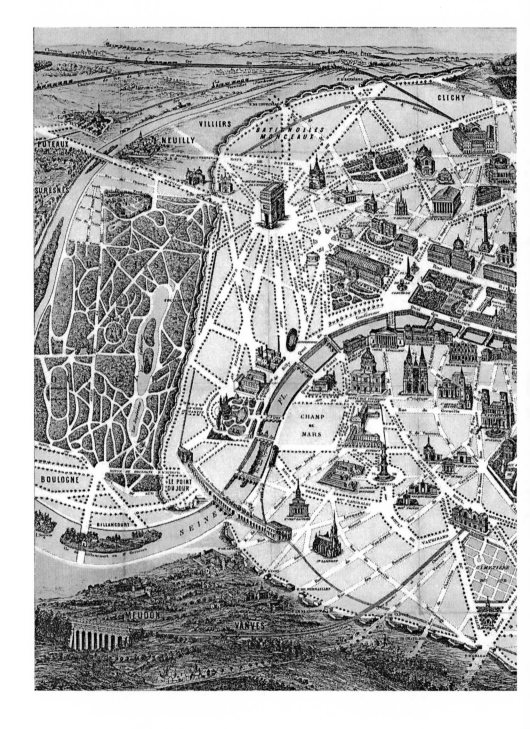

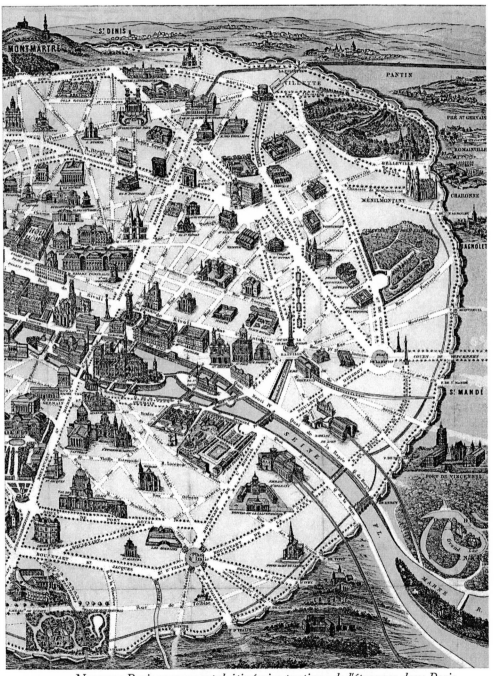

Nouveau Paris monumental: itinéraire pratique de l'étranger dans Paris.

Paris: Garnier frères, 1878.

August 1, 1888

"And God saw the light, that it was good: and God divided the light from the darkness. And God called the light Day, and the darkness he called Night. And the evening and the morning were the first day."

—Book of Genesis

One by one, white feathers were grafted to the young man's mottled skin with melted wax. Supple limbs were lifted from the stone slab, bound with thin ropes like marionette strings, and fastened to a skillfully carved wooden framework. Muscles were slashed and bones were snapped to mimic the impact of falling from a dizzying height onto a rocky shore. The Messenger, holding a fire iron with a twisted shaft ending in a red-orange smolder, insisted on melting out the man's eyes himself.

Another press of the chloroform-soaked cloth to the dying man's lips silenced his attempts to scream. The sound quickly faded to a murmur, allowing the eight men to continue their work without the distraction of extraneous noise. On this evening, the first night of fulfilling the prophecy, their light was dim and their surroundings were stifling, but soon their formidable sculpture would be exhibited for all of Paris to admire.

The self-appointed Messenger of the Eighth Day Brotherhood peered into the handsome face of the stranger he had selected to become his Icarus. His slender hands worked diligently, his eyes ice-bright. Occasionally, when particularly satisfied with his work, he flashed his white teeth in a wolfish grin. The smooth flesh stretched over his sharp features suggested he was not much older than his reluctant model for the First Day sculpture.

At least the young man had stopped twitching. He remained motionless and silent once the Messenger finished removing his eyes. Black-tinged blood diluted by viscous fluid oozed from the sockets, emitting a sickening stench.

In the façade of everyday life, the Messenger was best known as a painter. Tonight, however, marked his first masterpiece in sculpture: a living model, work of art, and necessary sacrifice combined into one magnificent composition.

The Messenger dismissed his seven assistants with a low mutter and a flick of his wrist. As the men crept away, he reached out to arrange a few sticky strands of dark hair over his model's face. How fortunate was this young man, to have been selected for such a noble purpose! His chosen model would become the first creation of the Eighth Day Brotherhood, and also its finest, the Messenger knew, since he had overseen the sculpture's intricate design and execution himself. His carefully selected muse would be resurrected in the spirit world and guide the Brotherhood into a higher state of existence: the new Creation.

Once he finished adjusting the final touches on his masterpiece, manipulating every detail with his deft fingers, he commanded his fellow artists to assist him in transporting the Brotherhood's creation to its intended location before dawn. He was impatient to supervise the model's final placement and position. The Messenger's gleeful smile widened. Everything was falling into place, just as the spirit world had promised him. Soon the sun would rise upon the First Day.

The artist's hand moved across the page of his sketchbook, slowly at first, then faster as he lost himself in the mesmerizing act of drawing his model. He was oblivious to the smears of graphite staining his knuckles as he shaded her face, to the heat and stench of sweat in the crowded auditorium, and to the sharp glances from the man seated next to him when the scratch of his pencil was distractingly loud. In his drawing, the young woman drifted in midair with her head tilted to one side, eyes closed, and wore a long white gown, like a sleeper suspended in space.

Claude often felt as if he had slipped into a trance himself while watching her. The red-haired girl was of slight build, her limbs birdlike and delicate, blue veins visible beneath nearly translucent alabaster skin. Her eyes were closed while she writhed and quivered on the low wooden stage. Her feet were unsteady in her macabre dance, and her thick hair became a fiery mist around her face. One of her convulsions finally shook one strap of her chemise from her bare shoulders. Something in Claude's stomach twisted, making the young artist retreat into the dreamy miasma of his own mind. Instantly he was alone with her, saw only her, once their gaslit surroundings faded from his captured gaze.

She will be perfect.

Again she thrashed her head from side to side, making coils of red hair caress her shoulders. Her body exuded a haunting grace despite her erratic movements, her sinuous limbs stirring in an uncanny dance like a marionette on taut strings. Claude knew he had found his muse.

What color are her eyes?

A harsh male voice shattered Claude's reverie. "As you can see, gentlemen, Mlle. Finnegan's hysteria is an unusually advanced case."

Released from the woman's spell, Claude's consciousness snapped back to the demonstration auditorium of l'Hôpital Sainte-Geneviève and the black-suited doctor who had spoken. He realized he was holding his breath, and slowly exhaled into the moist air he shared with dozens of other curious men.

"This patient may endanger herself and others while in such an agitated state," continued Dr. Jacques-André Veyssière. "However! After many years of working with her, I have succeeded in bringing her hysteria episodes under control. Please observe."

Claude shoved a lock of dark hair out his face and watched intently, his sapphire eyes wide while Dr. Veyssière demnstrated his signature technique. The physician was an elegant but severe-looking middle-aged man with slick black hair receding from his domed forehead. His dark eyes were intelligent but often unreadable, his nose aquiline, his face angular.

Dr. Veyssière raised his large hands to the young woman's flushed face. She moaned softly and opened her eyes.

Claude leaned forward in his uncomfortable seat for a closer look. *Green. Or are they blue?* The wooden chair creaked sharply, and Claude froze as the woman's gaze flickered over him for a brief moment. *Emerald green.*

"There now, mademoiselle," the doctor said gently. Facing her, he slipped his fingertips beneath the tangled hair around her temples and pressed them firmly against her head, forcing her to meet his gaze before

11

addressing his audience again.

"Like the great physician Franz Anton Mesmer, I have been gifted with the ability to project my energy into my patients' bodies and cure the imbalances that plague and torment them. This energy, or magnetic fluid, as Mesmer called it, I draw from the very cosmos. I draw upon the sun, the moon, and the stars. Yes, gentlemen—I manipulate the magnetic fluid of the celestial bodies themselves!"

The physician's voice had grown louder and increasingly theatrical. Two muscular ward attendants quietly approached the mesmerized patient from behind, wheeling a rickety gurney. They reminded Claude of wolves circling their prey, waiting hungrily for her to weaken and fall.

The young woman's convulsions had calmed, but she still struggled slightly when the doctor tightened his grip, pressing his palms against her cheekbones, digging his fingertips into her scalp. He raised his voice further when he continued speaking. "Now, by concentrating my energy—" He leaned his forehead against the shuddering woman's, challenging her furious glare with his own. "—I free this unfortunate woman from hysteria."

He withdrew both hands at once like a magician releasing a dove, and with a final shiver the woman collapsed into the waiting arms of the ward attendants. She released a long breath and remained still, her eyes shut and her face as serene as if she were enjoying a pleasant dream. One attendant replaced her chemise over her shoulders and grasped her beneath her arms. The other robust man wrapped her long grey skirt around her ankles, and together they lifted her onto the gurney.

"Now, you observe that the patient is quite docile," the physician was saying in a lower voice. "She will remain so until her next hysteria episode. These little fits often occur in female patients with a history of trauma and suffering, and they can be triggered by environmental…"

Claude was no longer listening. He was watching the two attendants arrange the woman's body on the gurney, their faces as expressionless as marble statues while they buckled three leather straps across her torso. Then, with a piercing squeak of wheels, they maneuvered her through a wide swinging door at the back of the stage.

Claude watched her disappear back into the sanitarium, reminiscent of Ophelia drifting downstream. First her pale face with its wild halo of red hair slowly vanished across the threshold, then her frail body, and finally her small bare feet, slightly tinged with grey dust from the dark wooden floor. Then she was gone.

Claude was dimly aware of closing the worn cover of his sketchbook and rising to his feet along with the rest of the audience, which mostly consisted of elderly doctors and younger medical students. They quickly surrounded the mesmerist and began to congratulate and question him in loud voices, eager for his attention.

"How are your methods different from those of M. Charcot at the Salpêtrière?"

"Is the patient in a trance? How long will she remain magnetized?"

"Are you willing to teach your healing technique to others, Dr. Veyssière?"

"Can we observe Mlle. Finnegan's progress at your next demonstration?"

The questions flew past Claude's head as he slowly pushed his way through the perspiring crowd towards the physician and climbed the few steps of the demonstration stage. The fervid audience dispersed at last, and Claude approached Dr. Veyssière. He could not help noticing that the doctor's heavy, muscular hand did not appear to be that of a miracle worker, nor did it seem like a hand that deserved to touch the angelic woman's body.

"Well, young man?" asked the doctor, raising a dark eyebrow. "Did you find my demonstration enlightening? I am Jacques-André Veyssière, and you are—?"

Claude realized he was staring blankly at the man's flinty, chiseled face. He shook the stupor from his brain and bowed politely to the doctor. "Forgive me, Monsieur. My name is Claude Fournel. I want to ask about the—the patient," he mumbled. "Mlle. Finnegan, I mean."

"Oh! She will recover quite soon. She typically remains in a trance-like catatonic state until she has another hysteria fit—"

"No, I mean, who *is* she?"

The doctor narrowed heavy-lidded eyes that had already scrutinized Claude's dusty black suit, paint-encrusted hands, and unkempt dark hair. "I have never noticed you attending my demonstrations before," he said. "You are not a medical student, I presume?"

Claude lifted his chin towards the taller man and tried, but failed, to look imposing. "I am an artist," he said boldly. "Studying at the atelier of Alexandre Baltard on the Rue de l'Abbaye to become a great p—"

"A great painter. Of course," the doctor finished sardonically, glancing at Claude's sketchbook. "Another art student who needs Finn to 'model' for you, correct?" His lips twitched into a derisive smile.

"Finn?" Claude murmured. The unusual name swam through his mind, which began to blur back into dreaminess.

The mesmerist's eyes darkened. "Margaret Rose Finnegan is my patient, and she is a very sick woman. I will not just sedate her and wheel her out for any artist who wants to paint her. Frankly, young man, I have grown quite weary of so-called artists and poets and other bohemian lowlifes invading my scientific demonstrations to ramble at my colleagues and I about dreams and madness and whatnot and leer at unfortunate women in their chemises. Is that clear, M. Fournel? I suppose if you were a respectable Salon painter or a prize pupil at the École des Beaux-Arts whose reputation preceded him, but—an independent atelier student, are you?—I am afraid I cannot help you. Good day." He spun on his heel and strode resolutely towards the swinging door.

"Please, Monsieur," Claude begged. "My intentions with the lady—with Mlle. Finnegan—are strictly professional. My work is quite modern but rooted in sublime history and myths. I considered applying to the École des Beaux-Arts but instead chose to study with the distinguished master—"

"Shall I summon my attendants, or can you find your own way out of my sanitarium?" interrupted Dr. Veyssière, turning around sharply to focus the black chasms of his eyes on Claude's desperate gaze.

Claude fell silent with a sigh. The doctor continued his stride, shoved the swinging door aside, and disappeared.

The artist turned listlessly in the opposite direction and withdrew from the auditorium to the main hallway. The heavy door shut slowly behind him, and he resisted the urge to cast one last glance through its narrow glass window towards the stage where Finn had stood. With his sketchbook under his arm, he stormed out of l'Hôpital Sainte-Geneviève and into the Parisian August heat.

Rémy Sauvage glanced up from the book of poetry he was reading at his bookshop counter to greet the three customers who had just entered, but held his tongue when he recognized their uniforms.

Detectives from the Préfecture? thought Rémy with an inward scowl. *They must be here to ask about the Rosicrucians again.*

He stood, straightened his eccentric garb—a forest-green velvet jacket and a jewel-toned silk scarf—and adjusted the black ribbon loosely restraining his long ivory-colored hair. A lanky man in his mid-thirties, Rémy's pallid hair, still-youthful features, and outdated clothing made his age difficult to determine. He forced a pleasant expression onto his face, keeping his gaze bright and expectant below straight eyebrows that almost made him appear haughty. His eyes were a gold-flecked green that faded to brown in the middle, the color of medieval parchment, as if they had consumed too many rare books and were starting to turn the shade of decaying pages.

Rémy reached for his cane with bejeweled fingers. The cane's silver pommel resembled one of the architect Viollet-le-Duc's recent designs for the balustrade of Notre-Dame cathedral: a snarling gargoyle leaping from its perch on a miniature gothic tower. The bony creature's wings lay flush against its curved back, the coil of its serpentine tail providing a convenient grip for one's hand. Purchased from an antiques dealer near the Louvre, the cane was decorative rather than necessary, but Rémy had on rare occasions needed to draw the hidden blade that descended from the ornate tower into the ebony shaft.

"Welcome to *Le Jardin Sauvage*, the finest source of rare and occult books in Paris," he greeted his visitors with a bow. "How may I assist you, messieurs?"

Rémy took pride in the fact that entering his shop was akin to stepping inside a Gustave Moreau painting. Orientalist lamps, Symbolist paintings, and alchemical diagrams adorned the peacock-green walls decorated with brushed-gold patterns, while the dark-paneled bookshelves were heavily laden with occult tomes, swatches of jewel-toned fabrics, and small oddities carved in ivory. Rémy, however, also assumed that this sublime experience of life imitating art was lost on his current group of visitors.

An unsmiling lump of a man with intelligent dark eyes, thinning black hair, and a meticulously trimmed mustache stepped past the two younger officers. His intense gaze quickly surveyed the bizarre selection of Rémy's bookstore, which offered everything from Symbolist poetry to demonology, and then settled upon Rémy. "Inspector Marcel Percier from the Préfecture de Police," he introduced himself curtly. "I am looking for Rémy Sauvage, the owner."

Rémy leaned on his cane. "You have found him."

Percier tilted his head like a curious bird. "You have an accent."

"Yes—I come from Lyon. I relocated to Paris over a decade ago."

The policemen began shuffling through the shelves, flipping through books and browsing like any other inquisitive customers.

"I know." The inspector studied Rémy's expression as he continued speaking. "Rémy Sauvage. You attended seminary in Lyon but you were never ordained. Was that a personal choice, M. Sauvage?"

"I asked too many questions," Rémy replied testily, watching the policemen hasten their search through his shelves. "Anyway, I don't see—"

"Or did it have something to do with the church's distaste for your interests and—your preferences?"

Rémy readjusted his grip on his cane, but said nothing.

"Then you moved to Paris. Educated at the Sorbonne. According to one of your former professors, you took a particular interest in ancient literature, art, and the occult." Percier raised an eyebrow. "Then what? *You* tell *me*, M. Sauvage."

Rémy swallowed. "Then I worked with rare book dealers until a friend convinced me to start my own trade a few years ago—"

"Would that 'friend' happen to be Stéphane Desnoyers?"

"I—" Rémy stammered, taken aback. "Why are you here? Is he in some sort of trouble?"

"M. Sauvage, we have been conducting some interviews around this neighborhood, and we understand that you are, shall we say, a close friend of M. Desnoyers, correct?"

Rémy felt struck by a sudden dizziness, shortness of breath, and a flutter of panic. "Yes," he replied cautiously, unconsciously tapping his ring on the silver pommel of his cane. "He works in my shop a few hours per week, and rents one of my rooms in the apartments upstairs."

"Indeed," Percier replied with practiced incredulity. "May I ask where you were at dawn this morning?"

"Asleep. I have not seen Stéphane—M. Desnoyers—since yesterday evening. He also works as a model for painters at the École des Beaux-Arts and various ateliers, so he keeps odd hours. Please, Inspector, what is this all about?"

Percier fixed his level gaze on Rémy's widened eyes. The inspector's sharp, wary features and close-cropped hair reminded the bookshop owner of Jacques-Louis David's later portraits of Napoléon.

"M. Sauvage, I am investigating the murder of Stéphane Desnoyers, whose body was found shortly before dawn this morning at the Panthéon. With all—this—in your possession—" Percier's sweeping gesture indicated the occult paraphernalia surrounding them. "I thought you might know something about it."

"Murder?" Rémy retreated back into his chair at the bookshop counter. His body felt drained of all vitality, leaving only the chill of despair and disbelief. "Why?" he asked weakly, yet even he was uncertain what exactly he was asking. Why would he, Rémy, know anything about Stéphane's death? Why would he—why would anyone—murder the only person he had ever loved? *Why*— He shook his head, wondering when he would awaken from this nightmare.

The inspector observed the drastic drain of color from the bookshop owner's face. "Due to the circumstances in which we found the body," he explained slowly, "I'm afraid anyone with occult connections must become a suspect. You claim that M. Desnoyers posed for artists. Well, his final job seems to have been modeling as Icarus."

Rémy's empty but questioning eyes met the inspector's piercing gaze.

Percier continued speaking. "The thing is, the 'artist'—the murderer—mutilated him and turned his body into a sculpture while he was still alive. He was given Icarus's wings. The white feathers were attached to his skin with wax."

Rémy closed his eyes for a long moment. He had heard enough.

"Furthermore, strange letters or symbols were carved into his forehead. Possibly an occult reference." Percier produced a folded piece of paper with the numbers "1:4-5" written on it in black ink. He showed it to Rémy, who shook his head, still dazed. "M. Sauvage, I will not ask you to return to the Préfecture with us. M. Desnoyers's family has already identified the body."

A vacant nod.

"We need the name of every artist for whom M. Desnoyers recently modeled. Can you provide us with that much?"

Rémy shrugged, suppressing a sob.

Percier ignored this display of sorrow and turned away, but then paused. "One more thing, M. Sauvage. I thought that, with your interests, you might have some insight into why someone would commit this atrocity. It is clearly the work of a madman."

Rémy struggled to regain his composure before replying. "I—do not recognize those symbols. They could be anything. A Bible verse. An alchemical equation. A cabalistic code. A reference from a book."

"A book such as this?" Percier held up a copy of *The Mystic Rose* by Stanislas de Guaita. "What do you know about the Rosicrucians?"

Rémy shrugged listlessly, listening to the flutter of pages as the policemen began unceremoniously dropping books into piles on the floor. The inspector had doubtlessly ordered them to search the bookstore's obscure tomes for the symbols carved into Stéphane's skin. "The Rosicrucians are fellow occultists. Many are artists and writers, like that poet whose book you are holding. They visit my shop regularly, bringing me work to sell or trying to track down a rare item. Some of them are my finest customers. They seek a higher existence through deciphering mystical and divine secrets in religious texts. They are not murderers."

"Inspector!" One of the officers, a bright-eyed young man with sand-colored hair and a thick mustache, held up a rectangular package wrapped in brown paper and twine. His feet awkwardly straddled a pile of discarded books on the floor as he turned, and he was perspiring from the heat and from the effort of his search.

"Yes, Alain?"

"What about these?"

Percier nodded at him to proceed.

"That is nothing," Rémy insisted, as Alain tore into the package. "Only some mythology books an artist named Antoine Barre ordered months ago, but he never picked them up. I heard he left Paris to spend a year studying in Rome, so I have saved them for him."

The young officer froze and looked at Percier, letting the wrapping drift to the floor. "Antoine Barre? Inspector, isn't he the artist who—"

"Disappeared. Months ago." Percier said. "And I seriously doubt we will find him in Rome."

"*La mythologie dans l'art ancien et modern* and—*Mythologie iconographique*," Alain read on the books' spines. He shrugged and began flipping through the pages.

"Alain, let's borrow those. For investigative purposes. Or evidence." Percier turned to Rémy before the bookseller could protest. "M. Sauvage, something profane is happening in this city, and I intend to discover what it is." He moved as if to leave, but then paused and stared intently at Rémy. "I may have more questions. Do not attempt to leave Paris. Do you understand?"

Rémy listened to the sounds of the officers' continued investigation for a moment before he glanced up at Percier's stony face with red-rimmed eyes. "Stéphane Desnoyers. Let me see him," he demanded.

Percier ruminated for a moment, removing his hat to wipe his forehead with his handkerchief before nodding in agreement. "If you insist. His remains were taken to the closest hospital that could accommodate us. In this heat—well, you understand. His body lies in the morgue at the Sainte-Geneviève sanitarium."

Claude was awakened by a man's calloused forefinger rudely jabbing him in the face.

"Claude, is that you? *Claude?*"

The finger touched his forehead and flung aside a dark lock of tousled hair.

"Aha! I thought I might find you here. You missed your painting lesson today, and your history tutor still charges me whether you show up or not, you know."

Claude vaguely registered the scrape of chair legs on the worn parquet floor as the black-clad figure took the seat across from him, jostling the café table as he sat down.

"*Look* at me," the man ordered.

Claude forced open his eyes, his long dark lashes making their lids appear heavier, and looked drowsily across the table at the scowling man's sunken grey face. "*Bonjour*, M. Baltard," he mumbled.

Claude vaguely remembered striding through the narrow streets of the Latin Quarter towards the Pont des Arts, his gaze seeking solitude in the cobblestones, hardly glancing up at the familiar sights of his usual wandering explorations of Paris. Soon he felt the breeze from the Seine and stumbled into the decadent comfort of his favorite café, intending to disappear into the strange and distant worlds inside his head.

Alexandre Baltard ignored his student and foster son's forced formality. "If you want me to teach you how to paint as skillfully as your father did, you had better start showing up to the studio on time. Don't squander your life, Claude. Your father's legacy is the *only* reason you are not still enrolled in a proper school and sitting in class at this very instant. Well, that and the fact that the instructors claimed you spent more time staring at the murals in the lecture hall than actually paying attention, not to anyone's surprise, I'm certain."

Claude shrugged, having heard all this before, and stared at his surroundings. The Café Hugo had been renamed for the writer whose death three years prior still left a void in the heart of Paris, and aspiring artists and poets often found solace within its solemn interior. Deep red walls extended between the gothic details carved into the wainscoting and the heavy ceiling beams. Black and white etchings of gargoyles, medieval ruins, and characters from Hugo's novels hung on the walls behind dusty glass in simple frames with delicate gilded designs that were gradually flaking away.

Baltard continued to rant. "And stop wasting your money on bottle after bottle of wine before you have even made a name for yourself. Fortunately I'm managing your inheritance until your birthday. Your father, may his soul rest in peace, assumed you'd have *some* sense by the time you turned eighteen, I suppose." He grabbed one of the dark glass bottles from the café table and gave it a gentle swirl. "Empty! Hmmph!" He let the bottle slip back to the table with a *thud*, slightly startling Claude.

Baltard narrowed his eyes, fixing his foster son with the same icy blue gaze he employed for critiquing Claude's paintings. "What's going on, Claude? Are you upset about that murder at the Panthéon? If so, you're taking it worse than anyone I've seen yet today. Did you know the victim?" he asked, lowering his voice at the last question.

"Murder? No." Claude stared past Baltard's unshaven face to that of the dancing gypsy girl in a painting on the café wall. "Today I found my Salomé. She's the muse I have searched for my entire life as an artist. I found her and lost her within the space of a few minutes."

When Baltard did not reply, Claude looked back at him, and saw that the older man was regarding him with a slow shake of his head.

"*That's* why you swallowed two bottles of wine on a Wednesday afternoon?" It was more of an accusation than a question. "Any of my models can pose as a dancer carrying a saint's severed head—and would enjoy it, too." He shrugged and watched an elegant young woman with a black parasol stride past the café window. "Calais makes a fine Salomé, as you know," he said in a calmer tone, picturing his favorite model and longtime mistress. "You can draw her when she's not posing for me."

20

"Monsieur, you don't understand—"

"Isabelle! Coffee!" Baltard abruptly shouted to a young barmaid who was idly adjusting her flaxen braids. He turned back to Claude, muttering something under his breath about this new generation of Romantics. "Is that her?" he asked irritably, gesturing to the table. "Not your best work, but I see the appeal of the lady."

Claude looked down and saw his open sketchbook. Amid a miniature labyrinth of meandering lines and a broken pencil was a small portrait of a young woman with wild hair. He had forgotten he had drawn it. "Margaret Rose Finnegan," he said dreamily.

Baltard sniffed. "What a name. Sounds Irish."

Claude shrugged. "I don't know."

The barmaid slid two cups and saucers onto the precarious table. She looked skeptically at the sketchbook, then at the younger artist. "We're not taking drawings as payment today, Claude," she said with a faint smile, one hand on her hip.

"Don't fret, Isabelle, he'll pay for that wine in more ways than one. Here." Baltard reached into his vest pocket and fished out a few coins for the barmaid, who thanked him and returned to her counter. "Drink," he ordered, pointing to Claude's cup and lifting his own. "So, where did you meet your *femme fatale*?" he asked before taking a sip.

Claude pulled the cup of filmy black liquid towards himself. "A hypnosis demonstration at Dr. Veyssière's sanitarium."

Baltard almost choked on his coffee, burning his tongue. "The Sainte-Geneviève? That notorious asylum near the Panthéon? Claude, *please* tell me she was just a visitor. No? Someone's wife, then? No? Heavens, boy, a *madwoman*? You're even more of a fool than I thought."

Claude sighed. "The doctor will never let me see her again." He rubbed at a graphite smudge on his hand with his threadbare coat sleeve.

"Well, at least the doctor has some sense." Baltard sipped his coffee. "Hypnosis demonstrations and madwomen. Hmmph! We studied from professional models when I was your age, when your father and I were at the École des Beaux-Arts. What would he think if he were alive today?"

Claude decided not to anger Baltard any further by mentioning Dr. Veyssière's chiding him for not attending the École des Beaux-Arts. He knew that Baltard coveted a teaching position at the prestigious art school, but his style was considered out of fashion. Claude sulked and closed his sketchbook.

"I am sorry, Claude, but you should consider yourself lucky if an unattainable lunatic is your biggest problem." He pulled a crumpled copy of *Le Petit Journal* from the pocket of his black coat and tossed it onto the table. "Haven't you heard? Take a look at this."

Claude clumsily unfolded the newspaper and clamped its edges to the table with his elbows. The headline swam slowly into his vision:

DREADFUL MURDER AT PANTHÉON
VICTIM'S CORPSE A MACABRE WORK OF ART

He tried to read the corresponding article, but his eyes refused to focus on the miniscule text. He leaned his head in his hands and shut his eyes, but that only made the dizziness worse. He groaned. "What happened, Monsieur?"

Baltard swallowed a sip of coffee and grimaced. "A young man, an artists' model, was kidnapped and turned into a sort of living sculpture. For as long as he managed to survive, at least. He was no one I know—Stéphane something. Probably one of the Montmartre crowd." Baltard cast a nervous glance around the café and leaned closer to his student. "I dare say, this is rather incredible, isn't it, Claude? Using the human body as a work of mythological art, I mean. It's a shame that the 'artist' felt the need to torment and murder the poor soul, but there is something intriguing about the idea, don't you think? Just don't tell Calais I said so. She's rather shaken up, being a model herself, after all. It sounds dreadful. *Look*." He jabbed a finger at the wrinkled page. "The man's eyes were burned out of his head."

"Like Icarus staring into the sun," Claude muttered, without looking.

Baltard raised an eyebrow. "Exactly. How did you know?"

Claude shrugged and attempted to read the article again. Slowly his mind latched onto the sickening details: a handsome young man's body mutilated and burned alive. His eyes cruelly seared from his head. Wood and feather wings grafted to his body with melted wax. His figure lightly draped in ragged strips of singed fabric. The numbers "1:4-5" carved into his forehead. His body suspended in a cruciform position between the central columns of the Panthéon façade and abandoned there, a silent witness to the sunrise.

"The police cut him down this morning," said Baltard after a moment.

"It is always a shame, the death of a beautiful youth. Yet I would wager that such a death made him, well—immortal. He will be remembered as the boy who briefly lived and died as Icarus. Not such a tragic end for an artists' model."

Claude glanced up and saw Baltard's eyes glistening with what he feared was admiration. His own imagination abruptly presented him with images of bleeding, empty eye sockets and lacerated skin seared with candle wax, all left to rot in the blazing August sun. He slammed his fist on the table, splashing coffee out of his cup. "Well, maybe Calais will be next!"

"What?" Baltard snapped out of his reverie.

"With the murderer still loose in Paris, perhaps more people will have the privilege of becoming 'immortal' by being slaughtered. Do you want to see Calais's blood all over the Panthéon?"

"Of course not! Calm down, Claude, stop shouting. People are staring…"

"I don't care." Dishes rattled precariously as Claude grabbed his sketchbook and shoved himself away from the table, nearly overturning the rest of the coffee onto Baltard's lap. "I am returning to the atelier to paint something worthy of the Salon," he said in a calmer tone. "I cannot remain in my father's shadow forever. Nor in yours."

Baltard's halfhearted protests fell upon deaf ears as Claude stumbled outside into radiant daylight. The afternoon sun assaulted his eyes, filling his mind with visions of Icarus falling to his death, followed by fleeting images of fiery red hair and ivory flesh. His head throbbed with sudden, searing pain. He flung one arm upward to block the light.

Am I going mad? Is Baltard mad? Is everyone mad in this wretched city?

His scuffed boots carried him across the street to the Seine, where he leaned his elbows on the stone barrier and stared at the hypnotic reflected shapes on the glistening water. Bile rose into his throat and he remembered that he had not yet eaten today.

He tore his gaze from the river to study the cyclopean architecture that dominated the opposite riverbank: the massive former palace of the Louvre. Now that it had been transformed into an art museum, the French government kept promising that soon it would become the world's finest. For now, however, all of Paris was bustling about next year's Exposition Universelle, either raving excitedly about or lamenting the skeletal iron tower and other controversial modern structures that had been rising in the city's western horizon for the past year and a half.

If Claude could paint a masterpiece by next year and exhibit it at the exposition, the entire city—no, the entire world—would recognize his talent. He would receive government commissions. His paintings would be displayed in the Louvre. He would be a famous artist like his father, whose reputation had barely faded since consumption claimed both of his parents less than a decade ago. He would no longer feel like a passive observer of his own life, with only painting and books to stir his passions.

At that moment, the sunlight relentlessly glinting off the Seine became promising rather than painful. Claude resolved that he must paint his masterpiece, the canvas that would launch his career, in time for the exposition of 1889. To accomplish this, he needed an ideal muse to present to the world as he forged a new generation of Romanticism. He needed to paint Margaret Rose Finnegan. His art and his ambition would accept no other muse.

Baltard's concerned voice and lumbering footsteps hurried towards him from the direction of the café. "Claude! Come away from the river. Your father would never forgive me if I let you throw yourself into the Seine. I am sorry, Claude. You're right. What happened to that Icarus boy is dreadful. Sickening. Calais felt the same way. I am returning home to her now." Baltard extended his hand. "Come along, Claude."

Claude shut his eyes and let the warm breeze soothe his wine-flushed face. "The woman I saw today—I need to paint her for the world's fair, Monsieur. Even if I have to find her window and set up my easel in the middle of the street. Even if I have to steal her away from the sanitarium myself."

His instructor sighed. "That imagination of yours has always been your blessing and your curse." He let his arm drop heavily to his side. "I felt the same way about Calais when I first laid eyes upon her at the colonial exposition. I knew I needed her as my muse. Years later, I still would do anything for her. But a *lunatic*, Claude?"

Claude, transfixed by the water, did not respond.

Rémy felt like a shade entering the underworld.

He descended the stairs to the morgue of l'Hôpital Sainte-Geneviève and walked in silence through somber corridors, following the black shape and domed head of Inspector Marcel Percier.

An odd conductor of souls, Rémy thought idly. A blank haze still clouded his mind while the scent of formaldehyde taunted his senses, challenging his stunned state of shock and denial. He needed to see what the murderer had done to his lover despite every rational part of his mind screaming in protest, telling him to remember Stéphane as he had last seen him: alive, silhouetted in the bookshop door and smiling as he waved farewell, then stepping out to model for a painting class at the École des Beaux-Arts.

"Prepare yourself. His body is in here," said Percier in a gruff voice, keeping an eye on Rémy. The younger man was aware that he was still a suspect. No display of grief would change the sharp-eyed inspector's mind about that.

The coroner, a bald man with doughy features, greeted them with a solemn nod. He did not question the purpose of their visit to his subterranean realm, and immediately made his way to the covered table with an uneven gait.

Not even the cool cellar temperatures and chemical odor could completely suppress the putrid scent of decay emanating from the corpse under the white sheet. An odd wooden framework entangled with ruined white feathers and coils of bloodstained rope was arranged on a nearby examination table.

"We removed the wings," the coroner explained slowly, noticing Rémy's curious glance at the apparatus. "But some of the feathers were—attached to the skin."

Rémy pressed his handkerchief to his nose and mouth with one hand and gripped the staff of his cane with the other, the knuckles bone-white beneath his gloves. He stepped closer to the covered body, fear and dread rising with each step and each pulse of his accelerated heart that it would indeed be Stéphane lying beneath it. The coroner gripped the edge of the sheet and flipped it back, exposing the mutilated face of Stéphane Desnoyers.

Uttering a faint cry into his handkerchief, Rémy was certain that his platinum hair had just turned completely white. Stéphane was barely recognizable, his dark eyes now empty sockets surrounded by charred skin and dried blood. Yet Rémy knew it was him. He knew every freckle and faint scar on Stéphane's flesh, which was now riddled with much crueler marks. Rémy's gaze kept returning to the narrow lines carved into the center of the forehead—1:4-5. He peered closer at them.

Percier noticed Rémy interest in the marks. "Considering those symbols, and his relationship with you, M. Sauvage, you understand why we are considering an occult connection," the inspector said, not quite achieving the gentler tone he reserved for family members identifying their loved one's remains. "We've begun compiling sources, every occult text and epic poem we can find, and exploring the possibilities. So far, nothing has shed any light on the case. Do you recognize the reference or the meaning of these numbers?"

Rémy stared at Stéphane, then at the contours of the stained white cloth for a long moment after the coroner mercifully concealed the corpse's face again. Rémy then emitted a soft, joyless laugh. "Perhaps it is the very simplicity of the thing which puts you at fault," he muttered, as if talking to himself.

Percier stepped closer. "What did you say?"

Still staring blankly at the white-shrouded face, Rémy dismissively shook his head at his companion's ignorance. "It is a line from a detective story by the American writer Edgar Allan Poe, *The Purloined Letter*. Baudelaire's translation—"

"And?"

"Genesis," he said, nodding once at the now-hidden symbols on Stéphane's forehead.

"Pardon?" Percier's expression grew slightly alarmed. He wondered if the sight of Stéphane Desnoyers's corpse had indeed shattered Rémy's mind—and if the occultist's grief was genuine after all.

"'Shed any light,' you said," Rémy continued. "Genesis. Book 1. Verses 4 and 5. The reference is quite obvious."

"Of course we thought of the Bible," Percier insisted. "It was the first source we investigated. So far, nothing we've found makes sense."

Rémy blinked, then looked up at Percier as if seeing him for the first time. "I cannot remember the exact verse, but it comes from the creation story, of course. The division of light and dark." Rémy's hand hovered over Stéphane's covered face. "Icarus flew too close to the sun. The blinding light burned his eyes from his skull. The heat melted the wax sealing his feathers

26

to his wings. He fell into the sea. Into darkness," the occultist added quietly. A distracted expression crossed his features. He turned away and walked towards the door, moving as slowly as a somnambulist.

"But what does it *mean?*" Percier called after him, tightening his stranglehold on the already warped brim of his hat. "A murder like this could be the work of a religious fanatic, yes, but I am not yet convinced. In such a case I imagine we'd find some sort of message at the crime scene, perhaps a madman's prophecy or warning, alongside the victim's body—"

"I believe Stéphane's death *is* a warning, Inspector," Rémy interrupted. "If we are finished here, I will see myself out." His voice was distant and flat as he strode away, idly twisting his cane in his hands while lost in thought. "Genesis," he repeated. "The creation of light and darkness." He paused on the threshold of the morgue's examination room, gripped the doorframe with one hand, and glanced back at Percier with an ominous look. "That was only the First Day."

Alexandre Baltard's home on the Rue de l'Abbaye was undoubtedly the domain of a bachelor with a penchant for the exotic. The painter often expressed his dreams of traveling to warmer climates to paint the mysterious veiled women, spectacular architecture, and azure skies that enthralled his imagination. However, he only made it as far as the northern coast of France and, to the south, the city of Algiers in northern Africa. Although Baltard had returned from the latter destination praising its warm weather and brilliant colors, he was dismayed to find that so many other westerners had gotten there first. The once-alluring foreign city had been transformed into a tourist-infested extension of Europe.

Claude grew up learning from and admiring Baltard's collection of travel oddities and antiques, some of which he used as props while composing his fantastical paintings or arranging his occasional still lifes. The various sculptures, jewelry, daggers, bones, and carvings of strange animals were displayed prominently throughout the house.

Being of a somber nature, as befitted a Romantic painter, Baltard preferred darker colors for his home décor. Claret red wallpaper and ebony wainscoting decorated the parlor and dining room, with forest green hangings and imposing furniture in his library. Dark mahogany railings framed the main stairwell that complemented the worn burgundy carpet in the gilded hallway.

Occasionally Calais's touches could be seen in a vase of bright flowers on the dining room table, a canary-yellow scarf left on the divan, a petal fallen from the flowers she pinned in her hair, or her softly rounded face in Baltard's paintings in his atelier.

Most of the paintings in gilded frames that decorated the walls of the main floor were gifts from fellow artists in Baltard's circle. His friend Vincent Morel's medievalist scene of *Saint George and the Dragon*, a triptych in a gothic frame designed by the artist himself, hung prominently in the main hallway. The saffron walls of the dining room displayed an imaginary landscape inspired by Khmer temples and orientalist fairies, a gift from a reclusive artist named Léon Fable.

The colors brightened as one ascended the floors of the house. The halls remained a dusky gold with a watered-silk pattern, but dark wooden doors opened to reveal bright and airy rooms, save for Baltard's master bedroom. He preferred to keep the heavy curtains drawn upon the midnight blue and grey-draped bedroom, but had finally stopped complaining years ago on the days when Calais insisted on opening the drapes to allow the light inside and enjoy the view of the English-style garden behind the building, where everything was overgrown and vine-covered to appeal to the resident artists' aesthetic sensibilities.

In the same hallway was Claude's room, much smaller than Baltard's, but comfortable enough for a young man with little interest in material possessions besides poetry books and paintbrushes. He had shied away from making many friends in school, and often retreated here afterward. The walls were painted ultramarine, and when Claude was younger he often imagined himself to be an adventurer in an undersea vessel such as Captain Nemo in the *Nautilus* or other heroes from the Jules Verne novels he enjoyed reading as a child.

Next to his nightstand was a small wooden chest filled with a few belongings he inherited from his parents, including his father's palette. The rich oil colors on its surface had dried into a rough topography of stains long ago. Claude also kept his father's antique duelling pistol with its silver-chased side panels, etched barrel, and one remaining bullet. Wrapped in black mourning crêpe at one side of the chest was the small leather-covered case containing his parents' wedding daguerreotype. They sat side by side with gently clasped hands, gazing benevolently at him from their brass frame despite their rigid pose, the gleam in their pale eyes forever captured by the photographer's chemicals and the plate's reflective surface.

Several of Claude's paintings were displayed around the house, mostly small canvases that Baltard replaced and rearranged from time to time as Claude's style and skill matured. Claude's work ran the gamut of mythological subjects and biblical heroines, but Baltard seemed most impressed when Claude incorporated something original into his scenes and conjured images from his dreams.

Claude liked to believe that Baltard, for once, felt proud of his student and foster son on the day he hung one of Claude's imaginary vistas next to one of his own paintings in his atelier. It depicted an undersea palace populated with nereids and sirens, painted in ethereal shades of emerald and teal. Claude's fantastical and delicate architecture, overrun with seaweed and crumbling under the weight of barnacles and shells, was based on photographs of India and Cambodia that he had studied in the illustrated travel magazines. It was akin to one of the undersea realms Claude imagined visiting as a young boy while falling asleep in his deep blue room, imagination merging with dream while he slipped into the weightless and infinite illusions of sleep.

Calais had her own little room. She had requested the one with marigold walls, shabby but charming furniture painted with roses, and a white-curtained window seat where she could enjoy the sun. The Tahitian native did not care for expensive gifts or glittering jewels. Instead, she valued simple beauty and uplifting light.

The few other members of the household staff occasionally grumbled about Baltard's 'housekeeper' having her own retreat, and a lavish one at that. Yet they did not envy her long hours posing for Baltard in his studio during the winter on top of her usual duties. Besides, they had to admit, Calais had settled nicely into her role and managed the household quite efficiently. Other guest rooms, rarely used, were scattered in small rooms on the second floor, including one jade-colored room for ladies and a darker green room for gentlemen.

A second staircase in the back hallway led to Baltard's luminous two-story studio. The spiraling iron structure always reminded Claude of climbing the tower of a cathedral. Ascending to the atelier from the heavily ornamented lower floors was akin to entering a dream world of floating resplendence. White curtains drifted delicately in the breeze from the tall windows. They resembled diaphanous clouds within the space of the sapphire-blue walls, most of which were hidden by gilded frames and large canvases. Each painting provided a mesmerizing portal into a scene of mythological intrigue, a hallucinatory fantasy, or a *tête-à-tête* with an alluring siren.

This morning, Baltard's atelier echoed with the percussion of young men arranging their paintbrushes and easels for the day's lesson, each vying for the workspace with the ideal view of their assigned subject. By evening, the vast square room was silent, and only Claude's easel was occupied.

Claude lingered in the corner of the studio opposite the iron staircase, intending to paint, but managed only to slouch on his wooden stool and glare straight ahead as if transfixed by the blank canvas. Tonight he found he had little inspiration now that no model or muse graced the Persian carpets and multicolored silk pillows arranged on the raised platform extending along one wall.

Not wanting to waste the jewel-toned colors mixed on his palette, he scraped his brush through a shade of ultramarine and lifted it to the canvas. He sketched a dark wing with sweeping brushstrokes, then idly extended the lines of the feathers into wispy flames.

A creak of stairs and a rustle of silk alerted Claude that he was no longer alone in the atelier. He did not look up at the dusky-skinned young woman wearing a rose-colored gown who approached him quietly and peered at his canvas.

"You are painting in a new style, Claude?" she asked him in her rich, accented voice.

"*Bonsoir,* Calais." Claude replied dully.

"Alexandre wonders if you will come down to dinner."

Claude shrugged. "I will eat later."

Calais tilted her head and laid her small hand on Claude's shoulder. "What is it, Claude? Alexandre has been in a foul mood all evening. Did you two have another disagreement?"

Claude looked up at her then, his listless gaze meeting the beautiful Tahitian woman's concerned dark eyes. He noticed that Calais wore her thick black hair halfway down, not attempting to hide the silver strands that were beginning to appear, and a rose matching her dress was pinned into one curled lock. He turned back to his canvas and dabbed his brush in vermillion paint to outline the flame-like wing.

"Today I found the woman I need to model for me," he replied. "But I fear she is unattainable. She is locked away in an asylum, the Sainte-Geneviève."

Calais drew back. "The Sainte-Geneviève? Claude—"

"I *know*. I've already heard it from Baltard."

"Claude." She squeezed his shoulder before withdrawing her hand. "Alexandre is concerned about you. You know that."

"And that is why he keeps *me* locked away, always studying, always painting?"

"He thinks—it is what your father would have wanted."

Claude gazed around the studio with an exasperated sigh. His eyes lingered on the familiar large canvases obscuring the walls. Several of these paintings were Baltard's unsold Salon entries, more of them rejected than accepted in recent years. Baltard knew that his star in the art world was fading, but his Romantic visions of tragic myths, fallen angels, and fatal beauty still attracted quite a following among the dream-obsessed Symbolist artists and poets.

Claude's favorite of Baltard's paintings was *Hades and Persephone*, an enormous vertical canvas that greeted visitors at the top of the stairwell. Baltard had painted the vaporous mouth of the Underworld directly at eye level. Hades soared overhead in an ebony chariot while the viewer stared into the ominous pit that twisted underground at a sickening angle. Hades appeared young and robust in his black armor with gilded trappings, although a silver helmet with fiery plumes and skull-like eye sockets concealed his face. The god clutched the reins of his chariot, which was drawn by two phosphorus-eyed black steeds with one hand, and violently embraced his reluctant bride with the other. Persephone, clad in a translucent white gown, stared intently into the hellmouth as Hades plunged into his domain of the Underworld. Flowers tumbled from Persephone's hands and from her flowing golden hair, adorned with painted rubies and pearls. Baltard had signed his name in red in the lower right corner.

Claude remembered his pride in being one of Baltard's students when he saw *Hades and Persephone* exhibited at the Salon of 1886, but critics had called it 'gothic' and 'tasteless.' Still, the painting was well-received among those with lingering Romantic sensibilities. Claude was secretly pleased that it had not found a buyer, and had instead been returned to Baltard's atelier where he could study its masterful technique.

For a moment his imagination replaced Persephone with Finn in a white lace nightgown being spirited away by Dr. Veyssière, while the rumbling earth opened into a nightmarish pit of wailing souls below her feet.

"Baltard has his muse," Claude said abruptly, shaking off the disturbing vision. "He has you. I do not understand how he expects me to follow in my father's footsteps, or in his, without a muse of my own."

"But—she is mad, Claude? And you have your imagination. I have seen you paint directly from your dreams."

"The doctor says she suffers from hysteria," Claude admitted. "And dreams are not enough. Although I begin to wish they were," he muttered.

Calais sniffed. "Anyone can get rid of a pesky female relative by claiming she has hysteria. If a girl is not insane before she goes into the Sainte-Geneviève, she might be when she comes out. The stories I have heard from other models. Some of them, their mothers and sisters have disappeared into that place…" Calais shuddered and shook her head sympathetically. "It sounds like a nightmare."

Claude flung his paintbrush into the easel tray, sending a ruddy splatter across the lower half of the canvas. "If you saw her, Calais, you would understand. I have never seen anyone like her."

Calais remained silent for a moment. "Did Alexandre ever tell you how he stole me away from the colonial exposition?" she asked.

Claude glanced up at her sharply. "He said he met you in Calais, which is why he calls you that."

She laughed softly. "He calls me that because he could never pronounce my real name, but what he told you is only half the truth. My younger sister and I became part of a touring exhibition after missionary explorers brought us to Europe. A diorama of our fishing village was built so tourists could stare at us during carnivals and world's fairs, as if we were strange animals. That is when I first saw Alexandre. He came back again and again with his sketchbook and his pencils to draw pictures of me in the ugly dresses the missionaries made me wear." She smiled, causing gentle lines to feather around her eyes. "The last day of the fair in Calais, Alexandre had a carriage waiting when the workers were dismantling the colonial village. So I went with him. I knew he was much older than me, but—he had kind eyes." Calais's smile faded. "I also knew that if a wealthy man had not bargained with the exposition's owners to 'adopt' my sister the day before, I would not have gone. I would never have left her. But I shall see her again someday. Do you think so?"

She looked expectantly at Claude, who nodded. "I truly hope you shall," he said.

Calais touched Claude's thin shoulder again. "I have been Alexandre's muse ever since. Fortunately, I have learned to love him, along with the quiet boy who became his foster son. I guess what I am trying to say is, perhaps it is fate, how an artist finds his muse. If there is a way to get yours out of the asylum, then I know you will find it."

"*Merci*, Calais." Claude reached up to cover her hand with his own. "You know, I have always considered you a sister to me. We practically grew up together, didn't we?"

She shrugged and laughed. "Enough flattery. I am old enough to be your mother. I suppose we did, though. Except we were always on opposite sides of the easel." She gently pulled away. "Come down to dinner, Claude," she called over her shoulder. "The roast chicken is getting cold." Calais strode back towards the winding stairs to the dining room, a rosy apparition on the spiral staircase.

Rémy Sauvage had been plunged into a nightmarish trance in which familiar surroundings seemed foreign and strange. He had the sense of moving underwater, as if everything was happening in slow motion. Somehow he drifted out of the morgue where Stéphane's corpse lay under the white sheet that seemed impossibly bright in his memory, like a terrifying specter he would be able to see from any room in that grim asylum if he dared turn in its direction. Inspector Percier was far behind by the time he wandered through the main hall of l'Hôpital Sainte-Geneviève, passing a severe-looking doctor speaking to several tearful visitors, and continued on his way through the main doors.

Rémy tried not to look at the Panthéon when he emerged onto the street, but the cyclopean monument was as inescapable as his own despair. It was one of the buildings that represented the tumultuous struggles and revolutions of French history, and it had been converted from a church to a secular building and back again countless times. He was not close enough to the front portico to see if the central columns were still stained with

Stéphane's blood.

He tried to avoid looking up at the carvings of famous Frenchmen receiving laurel wreaths from the draped allegorical figure of France on the Panthéon's pediment, where disproportionate portraits depicted a range of geniuses from philosophers to military heroes. He now felt only distaste for the words emblazoned below the pediment in capital letters: *Aux grands hommes la patrie reconnaissante.* To the great men, the grateful homeland. Rémy had nothing but respect for the eminent dead entombed in the monument's crypt, but it sickened him that Stéphane had been hung from the building like a grotesque offering. This was not the modern Paris those honored men would have wanted.

Somehow he managed to walk home without wandering in front of an oncoming carriage, and found himself standing at the door to his bookshop, unable to remember how he had arrived there. He twisted the key in the lock and opened the door, keeping the sign turned to 'closed.'

Except for the aftermath of the policemen's rummaging, the shop looked the same as always. Books and scrolls filled every nook and pigeonhole. Dark shelves were crammed tightly with occult tomes, artifacts, and religious texts. Antique maps, small Symbolist paintings, and alchemical diagrams adorned the gilded blue-green walls, while jewel-toned carpets hushed his steps on the wooden floor.

Yet shouldn't the shop look different now that Stéphane was gone, and would never set foot in it again? Shouldn't the entire atmosphere have changed? Rémy slid into his chair and stretched his long legs beneath the bookshop counter.

He was not ready go upstairs to the apartment where he would be faced with memories and relics of Stéphane: strands of his dark hair ensnared in a comb, his best pair of boots shined and empty at his bedside, his fingerprints lingering on the wine glass he touched only yesterday—

Rémy covered his face with his hand and wept, his body racked by violent sobs. When he could finally force himself to stand and ascend to his apartment, the pain at experiencing its new and sentient emptiness was worse than he expected. There was nowhere he could turn without seeing traces of Stéphane. He paced the rooms they had shared, filled with the decadent art, kaleidoscopic fabrics, and exotic objects they had selected on their outings and travels.

Rémy lost track of time as twilight approached. Unable to eat, he went to bed early. Unable to sleep, he contorted himself in and out of sweat-dampened bedsheets. One particular thought had latched onto his subconscious. He knew he had to face the possibility that he, Rémy, had brought this tragedy upon Stéphane and himself. Was the killer someone who had visited Rémy's shop and seen Stéphane there? Rémy was well-known in the neighborhood for his occult expertise. Had some religious fanatic, aware of Rémy's arcane knowledge and also of his clandestine relationship, taken matters into his own hands to purify the city and drive the heathens and sodomites out of the Latin Quarter?

Rémy flung aside his tangled bedsheets and began yanking open furniture drawers, searching through Stéphane's possessions. Inspector Percier had requested a list of all the artists for whom Stéphane regularly posed, but Rémy would be even more thorough than that. He would investigate every artist, every scholar, and every thrill-seeking student whose name was signed on his ledger or written in Stéphane's appointment book.

He shoved damp locks of pale hair out of his face and dug deeper into Stéphane's dresser drawer, finding only a few volumes of Baudelaire that Rémy had given him and a Bible with a black cover, embossed with a decorative gold cross and serpentine vines.

Unlike Rémy, Stéphane had kept his faith, but he always listened with interest when Rémy rambled on about ancient civilizations, alchemy, and esoteric beliefs. He lacked his companion's education, but often surprised Rémy with endearingly odd questions and observations while he lay awake at night, starting at shadows on the ceiling and rubbing limbs stiff from hours of posing for artists.

What if you haven't found the Philosopher's Stone because it isn't visible to human eyes?

Do you think there are secrets written in the tangled shadows of barren trees upon snow?

If silver is what allows us to capture spirits in photographs, will different elements show us other creatures not of this world?

Stéphane's voice lingered in Rémy's mind while he turned the Bible slowly in his hands, gently touching the frayed, worn edges of the cover, and set the heavy book on his nightstand.

He suspected that the investigation depended on himself now. He could tell that Percier was no fool, but if the inspector and his officers had overlooked the obvious connection between Icarus and the book of Genesis, how could they be astute enough to find Stéphane's murderer? Rémy would have recognized the mythological link sooner if he had not been so grief-stricken.

Rémy froze as another terrifying idea disrupted his thoughts. It would have been difficult for one man to commit the atrocity that had happened to Stéphane. Percier mentioned that the victim most likely had been 'prepared' elsewhere, and later suspended on the portico of the Panthéon like a macabre sacrifice. How could one man have transported and bound the corpse between the columns quickly enough to escape without being noticed? Stéphane's build was slight, but muscular, and then there was the added weight and bulk of the wooden wings and wax-coated feathers. The murderer, Rémy realized, was not working alone.

Rémy was unaware of having angered any of the religious cults or black magic societies with whom he had traded and studied. He regularly encountered eccentric people with secretive purposes in his line of work, but no one whom he had ever considered capable of murder. Mostly his customers were fraternal groups of artists and writers who believed they would be the ones to decode a biblical mystery, discover the Philosopher's Stone, or achieve a sense of brotherhood by wearing ornate robes and inventing rituals as creative outlets.

He grabbed Stéphane's Bible from the nightstand and flipped through its gossamer pages to the book of Genesis. Indeed, the verses 1:4-5 chronicled the division of light and dark and the creation of night and day. Meanwhile, the fall of Icarus in his reckless journey towards the sun came from ancient Greek mythology.

Rémy knew the reference was all part of some demented puzzle, a riddle he had to trace through ancient myths and legends, but the pieces did not quite yet align. He did notice, however, that his grief at losing Stéphane was turning to rage, simmering like the contents of an alchemist's crucible and sharpening his mind. Whoever had abducted and tortured his lover to death might soon be back for Rémy.

Stéphane had perished at dawn, so Rémy determined he would not sleep tonight. He threw on his dressing-gown and glided downstairs to the shop for his ebony cane and its hidden blade. Sooner or later he would have his revenge. When the bloodthirsty fiends came for him, he would be ready.

The Messenger was exceedingly pleased by the success of last night's sculptural creation and séance. The spirit world had related its secrets to him alone, a clandestine truth he shared with a chosen few. Soon they would vanish from this world and be reborn into an artists' paradise where saints and mystical beings walked the earth again. Their rituals would unlock its hidden door. There was no need to feel remorse, he often reassured his brothers, when the lives they released from this world would experience a resplendent immortality.

The Messenger was also pleased that each member of the Eighth Day Brotherhood had studied anatomy and had a strong stomach. They were gathered around the now-limbless body lying on the table, watching with reverent intensity while the Second Day artist positioned the bone saw in the center of the young woman's head and began to slice. The Messenger interrupted only to command that the sacrifice's eyes remain open to witness the sunrise.

The artist made a vertical incision along the central division of the woman's long, golden hair, and the narrow crevasse was soon flooded with blood. He continued forcibly to draw the serrated blade down through the rest of her torso. The artist and those assisting him saw the inside of her skull, then her neck. He needed to saw harder when he reached her breastbone, digging in with a soft grunt and rolling up his shirtsleeves when he began to perspire in the humid air.

Finally, the ribcage was severed. Then there was only soft skin and slick viscera until he encountered the spine and the pelvis, but at last the body was sundered. The two halves lay on the table, lurid and exsanguinating. After a nod of approval from the Messenger, the artist positioned the saw for the horizontal cut.

"Fine work, Brother," the Messenger said, praising the Second Day artist once that loyal follower finished his task. The artist laid the bone saw next to the other surgical tools and wiped his forehead with the back of his hand.

Besides his prowess in the studio, the Messenger knew that the Brotherhood's séances were his true opportunity to shine. When it came to communing with the 'other side,' his dear mother had taught him so well. Until her own heart gave out, she made her fortune as the celebrated spiritualist medium known as Orris d'Ombre, contacting departed souls for the consolation and entertainment of the Paris elite.

In the end, it was her legacy that convinced most of the Eighth Day

Brotherhood's members to join his cause. When he invited his colleagues to participate in séances at his home, they saw the phantoms materialize with their own eyes. They were captivated by the myriad translucent figures in his photograph album. They felt the caresses of phosphorescent and disembodied hands. They heard ghostly voices and watched in amazement while ectoplasm emanated from his lips.

Mother had been such a striking figure, the Messenger thought fondly, while she transmitted messages from the deceased, majestically seated at the red-draped turning-table in her darkened parlor. She slipped effortlessly into her trances, her head of thick silver hair tilted back, her thin wrists emerging from the black lace cuffs of her mourning gown to grip the hands of the séance participants seated at either side of her. She insisted upon wearing only mourning gowns after her husband died. She had worn the black gowns as long as her son could remember, and had been buried in her finest.

Growing up in her macabre household and studying her occult books, the Messenger knew that some of her talent had inevitably passed on to him. She taught him to commune with the spirits and heed their wisdom. Now they were everywhere, impatient for his attention. They transmitted their messages with unseen voices, through automatic writing and drawing, and by tapping subtle sounds upon the turning-table. He had earned their favor under her motherly guidance. He had learned all of her tricks and techniques that were sometimes necessary for convincing skeptics of the truth. Now his home was a mausoleum of her memory. The Messenger took his mother's lessons and the spirits' messages to heart. He continued to listen while the spirits guided his hand in assembling the new Creation.

The Messenger turned away to slide his thin fingers into a pile of costume jewelry arranged like glittering entrails on a silver platter. "Now, gentlemen, let us adorn her with strands of pearls. Only the most beautiful ones for our aquatic-born goddess, don't you agree? When our work is complete, we shall begin the séance."

August 2, 1888

And God made the firmament, and divided the waters which were under the firmament from the waters which were above the firmament: and it was so. And God called the firmament Heaven. And the evening and the morning were the second day.

—Genesis 1:7-8

L'Hôpital Sainte-Geneviève, a former abbey that had retained the austerity of its Romanesque architecture, was a long, rectangular structure in the Place du Panthéon. Its three floors had been intermittently renovated over the years, but none of the hospital's former directors had changed its purpose and structure as radically as had Jacques-André Veyssière.

The renowned mesmerist had controlled the hospital for nearly twenty years, transforming it from a public hospital into a private sanitarium and experimental research facility. He had commissioned the building's modern touches, such as gaslight and limited electricity, new operating rooms, a Mansard roof and cupola to hide the medieval structure's decaying barrel-vault, polished wooden floors, and an auditorium. He had also given the hospital its questionable reputation.

The patients at the Saint-Geneviève were predominantly unfortunate women whose families wanted to dispose of them or forget about them: young women whose fathers had not managed to marry them off, middle-aged women whose husbands desired a younger mistress, and old women whose children could not or would not care for them. The rumor in Paris was that Dr. Veyssière would declare anyone mad for the sake of having new test subjects who would not be missed by their families. The physician had published numerous articles and treatises about his magnetic powers and hypnotic cures, yet the patients who entered the Saint-Geneviève were rarely released except into the cemetery occupying a bleak corner of the asylum's garden courtyard.

The patients lived on the uppermost floor of the building. The female population was housed in strict separation from the smaller men's ward, except on the occasion of the sanitarium ball held annually at Christmas. The Saint-Geneviève had its own pharmacy, kitchen, laundry, chapel, carriage house, and morgue. It was its own microcosm within Paris, its own functional city of the allegedly insane.

Margaret Rose Finnegan had eaten almost the same meal for breakfast every morning for the six years she had lived within the thick stone walls of l'Hôpital Sainte-Geneviève: a bit of bread, sometimes with butter or *confiture*, if one of the other girls did not snatch the food out of her hands first. Finn always held her tongue. She had quickly learned from fighting with the other patients in the past that there was a beating in it for both of them, plus extra chores in the laundry room or the scullery.

Finn sat at the long wooden table in the dining hall with her few friends, nibbling with birdlike anxiety at a morsel of baguette she clutched between the fingertips of both hands. She rarely directed her gaze to the other end of the table to meet the other girls' sneering looks if they caught her staring.

She knew that some of the other hysterics in her ward envied her for the seemingly privileged position she held at the Sainte-Geneviève. After all, she was Dr. Veyssière's star patient. She was the one whose hysteria convulsions curious gentlemen came to observe, and who was allowed out of the ward to be put on display at hypnosis demonstrations.

Those young women would not be so jealous if they knew the truth. Finn no longer hated them as deeply as they hated her. She lost the motivation to truly hate anyone years ago. She no longer even despised the doctor.

Her friend Marie, sitting next to her, poked Finn in the arm with a bony finger. "That boy was looking in your window again," whispered the emaciated blonde. "Did you see him this time, Finn?"

"What boy?" Finn asked, her soft voice expressionless.

Marie rolled her eyes and kept her hands in her lap. To her nurse's dismay, Marie was refusing to eat again today. "My room is right next to yours," she answered in a singsong voice, teasing good-naturedly. "I saw him through *my* window. He has messy black hair, and a rather sweet face. He's the boy who has been circling the building all morning. I think he's trying to find a way in." Marie giggled. "Maybe he's mad, too, and Dr. Jacques will sign him right in if he asks! But he keeps stopping and staring at your window, Finn, when he passes by. I thought he was looking at me, but he never waves back when I wave at him."

Finn swallowed a mouthful of dry bread and reached for her cup of water. "Oh. That boy," she said listlessly. "I've seen him at the demonstrations. Yes. He was there this morning when I was brushing my hair by the window. I assumed he was waiting for someone else. What could he want with me?"

"What all men want," drawled Violet, the moody brunette seated across from Finn, her sharp elbows slung onto the table. "Eh, Finn?" It was Violet, the only other patient who spoke English, who had given the Irish girl her nickname. "At least, that's all my dashing soldier boy wanted before he had me signed off as a lunatic and abandoned me in here," she added, then tore off a chunk of baguette with her sharp teeth.

Marie giggled again. "Maybe he wants to steal you away, Finn. You are like a princess in a tower," she said dreamily.

Finn glanced at her nervously. "Stop it," she whispered as a ward attendant passed behind them. "He might hear us."

Violet sniffed. "Your admirer isn't too bright, at any rate." She licked the crumbs from her fingertips, then fixed her jaded gaze on Finn's worried face. "Doesn't he know you belong to the doctor?"

The Desnoyers lived in a narrow building in the Marais, located amid the remaining medieval streets that Baron Haussmann's urban renovations of Paris had overlooked.

In the dingy lobby, Rémy found the elderly concierge sleeping in a stained chair that had once been a pale shade of pink, wearing a drab blouse and skirt that nearly blended in with the peeling paint. He reached down to shake her gently by the shoulder and rouse her from her nap. A few *sous* convinced her to lead Rémy up several increasingly humid floors of winding stairs to the rooms rented by Stéphane's parents and older sister.

Rémy assumed that his three-year relationship with Stéphane had been a clandestine one as far as their families were concerned. He and Stéphane had met none of each other's relatives during their time together.

He began to reminisce on bittersweet memories of the day they first met at the Salon. He had been wandering through the galleries, his critical eye darting from one canvas-laden wall to another, when a Symbolist rendition of *Endymion* stopped him in his tracks. He had been too captivated by the model, a young man with silken dark hair sleeping serenely among imaginary foliage, to even notice or remember the name of the artist, but he assumed that someone as beautiful as this moonlit subject could only exist within a painting.

As it turned out, Rémy's guess was not far off. He encountered the very model who had posed for *Endymion* when he wandered into the next room of the Salon. The young man was evidently unaccustomed to public recognition, lowering his dark eyes and smiling softly when passersby commented that he looked familiar, but the reality of his striking presence nearly made Rémy forget that he was surrounded by thousands of other paintings by internationally renowned artists.

In Rémy's current reality, however, he was rapping on the warped door of an miserable household in mourning. The concierge shuffled back downstairs as soon as a thin woman in a drab black gown answered his knock. She had silver streaks in the curls of her dark hair, and her skin was moist from shed tears settling into the fine lines around her eyes.

"Madame Desnoyers?" Rémy's throat was bone-dry. Likewise clad in black, he respectfully bowed and removed his top hat, slightly alleviating some of the August heat. "I am terribly sorry for your loss. My name is Rémy Sauvage, private investigator. May I come in?"

The woman looked him up and down with her red-rimmed eyes. Then she nodded and invited him to enter with a subtle gesture and a creak of worn hinges as the door swung open wider.

Rémy's gaze surveyed the apartment once he stepped inside. The room was sparsely decorated, lived-in, but clean, with a few framed engravings of popular paintings on the faded beige walls. An honest laborer's household. Rémy understood why Stéphane so often sent his family generous amounts of the money he earned from his long hours working as a model and as Rémy's assistant at the bookshop.

Mme. Desnoyers was watching him, wringing her withered hands. "Have you discovered anything about my son's death, M. Sauvage?" she asked softly. "About why this—terrible thing was done to Stéphane?"

Rémy opened his mouth to reply but turned abruptly at the sound of a door opening at the opposite side of the room, revealing a tall gentleman with sunken features. Decades ago, Rémy recalled, Stéphane's father had helped build the *grands boulevards* and worked on demolishing medieval Paris to make way for the modern city. Indeed, his sickly grey skin seemed never to have shaken off the last of the dust and rubble of the centuries-old buildings that had fallen to progress. Rémy noted that Stéphane must have gotten his dark chestnut hair from his mother and his svelte but athletic build from his father.

"We have already spoken with the police inspector," M. Desnoyers mumbled, trudging to a corner table to grasp a bottle of cheap wine with tense fingers. "We have been to the morgue and seen—"

"As have I," Rémy said, a little too quickly.

M. Desnoyers collapsed into a chair and rubbed his purple-shadowed eyes. Like Rémy, he obviously had not slept well. "At least they took him to the Saint-Geneviève and not the city morgue," he grumbled.

"Yes, I suppose in a case where the body is identified—" Rémy paused, feeling too sick to continue. Another result of Haussmann's renovations, the Paris Morgue located behind Notre-Dame cathedral displayed unidentified corpses to thousands of curious visitors every day. The thought of Stéphane's body exposed to gaping voyeurs while street vendors profited from his death was too lurid to abide. "He deserved to be treated with dignity," Rémy said, lowering his voice. "I am not affiliated with the Préfecture. I am a private investigator. I have come to offer you my services in finding your son's murderer."

"I cannot pay you," Stéphane's father replied gruffly. He let the bottle slide from his hand onto the floor upon realizing it was empty. "Burying my son will nearly ruin us as it stands."

"I ask nothing in return," Rémy assured him. "Please do not trouble yourselves with Stéphane's burial. I shall make the arrangements," he offered, cursing himself for not having thought of it sooner.

Stéphane's father regarded him curiously, an expression of relief flashing across his features before darkening to one of suspicion. "Who sent you here, M. Sauvage?" he asked gravely. "What is your fascination with my son's death?"

"I require your assistance with some information," Rémy said, avoiding his questions. "Can you tell me everyone you remember associating with Stéphane, at the École des Beaux-Arts or elsewhere, or any private studios that hired him to model?"

Mme. Desnoyers shook her head. "I know he worked at a bookshop in the Latin Quarter, and lived in the apartments above it, but we never met the owner. Nor did we meet any of the artists who asked Stéphane to model." The faintest of smiles brightened her strained features. "We saved every Salon review he sent us. I could tell he was proud when a painting he posed for won a prize, or when a critic wrote about his character in the painting as if he were a skilled performer playing a role. Which he was, I suppose, my Stéphane, although he always pretended he had such a small part in the artists' successes."

"May I see those papers?" Rémy asked eagerly.

"If you wish." Mme. Desnoyers glanced in her husband's direction. "They're in the drawer—"

Still keeping a wary eye upon Rémy, Stéphane's father reluctantly stretched out his arm, pulled open a shallow drawer in the small water-damaged table beside him. "Here." He settled back in his chair and stared into the distance, his gaze empty and his fingertips drumming slowly on his weathered lips.

Rémy strode to the table and lifted a fluttering handful of yellowed Salon review clippings from the drawer. "Yes. These will be helpful," he muttered, shuffling through a few pages. "Do you have anything else that might help with the case?"

M. Desnoyers seemed not to hear him, but his wife was shaking her head. "Nothing," she replied. "Stéphane had no enemies, as far as we know. We could never afford to attend the Salons, but we saw the engravings made from the paintings," she added. "He told us stories about working for some of the great Legion of Honor painters. They all wanted to paint my son." Another faint smile. "He was such a handsome young man." She laughed darkly. "Sabine, his older sister—she resembles her brother, of course, but she sometimes complained that everyone thought Stéphane was more beautiful than she was."

"Is Sabine at home? May I speak with her?"

Mme. Desnoyers shook her head. "No—she's not home. She's taking Stéphane's death worse than any of us. She wanted some time alone and stepped out for a walk." Suddenly she crumpled into a rickety wooden chair.

"Why would anyone—"

Rémy found himself at her side, one hand still clutching the papers, the other hand resting upon her trembling shoulder in a gesture of mutual comfort. For a moment all he could see was bloody feathers and blackened eye sockets. Then he heard a door slam as M. Desnoyers retreated into the bedroom, as if he were ashamed to be seen mourning the death of his only son. For his part, Rémy was thankful that the grieving mother did not look up to see that he, too, was attempting to restrain his tears.

Rémy pulled away from her and stepped slowly to the door. "May I borrow these clippings?" he asked. She nodded, and Rémy slid them carefully into his coat pocket. "I shall return them, and I shall solve this case, I promise you. I am sorry to have disturbed you and your husband at a time like this. *Au revoir*, Madame."

"It's you, isn't it?" she asked abruptly but gently.

Rémy paused, his hand lightly grasping the door handle. He could not bring himself to meet her searching eyes. "Madame?"

"Your name, Monsieur. Stéphane told us he was working at a bookshop called *Le Jardin Sauvage*. He said that the owner was a brilliant man who seemed, well, not quite of this era," she said delicately. "He was deeply fond of you."

Rémy bowed his head. "The shop's name was Stéphane's idea, Madame," he said after a moment.

"M. Sauvage," she replied, her voice suddenly resolute. "I know you are not what you say you are. I also know that you mean well. Find him. Find whoever did this to my son."

"Madame, I shall—" Rémy twisted the door handle, escaped from the airless room into the grimy hallway, and shut the door on the wretched household behind him. He could not bear to look back.

Marie was right. The raven-haired boy *was* watching her window. His tired, pale face lingered wistfully between the iron bars of the sanitarium gate for several minutes, then disappeared only to reappear soon afterward, in about the time it would take to circle the sanitarium. There was something furtive about his movements, and Finn assumed he did not want Dr. Veyssière or the ward attendants to notice him.

Finn's third-floor window overlooked the garden courtyard behind the building, and she had memorized every detail of the view by now. This was the window from which Finn watched the seasons change, with the weather as her sole indicator of passing time. Fall was wet and rainy, stripping the trees to skeletons and the sky to a colorless void. In the winter, her soft breath fogged the glass while she peered out at the snow falling upon the courtyard and watched it turn gradually to filth and slush. Shrubs, topiaries, and bowers graced the courtyard in the spring, their obsessively trimmed shapes an extension of Dr. Veyssière's compulsive desire to control everything he touched. Red and white flowers unfurled like angry fists. Then summer brought black flies, unbearable heat, and urban noise through her open window.

Finn's room in the hysteria ward was on the north side of the sanitarium, facing away from the Panthéon. In clear weather she was allowed outside for fresh air in the narrow courtyard below. The courtyard had a short, curving path between several flowerbeds and two large oak trees. A carriage house was constructed in the northeast corner, where Finn could watch the Sainte-Geneviève's old grey horse and enclosed black wagon depart at odd hours of the night and day, and return bearing new patients. Finn had ridden in it once, trembling with fury and straining at the stained canvas and creaking leather of the straitjacket she had been forced to wear upon her arrival.

Thorny dark rosebushes climbed the asylum walls, while other patches of earth bore medicinal flowers and herbs. The simple headstones of the small cemetery occupied one corner of the courtyard, populated by patients whose families refused to claim them even after death. Occasionally a new grave appeared or fresh flowers decorated the gradually sinking mounds of the existing ones.

Her view would be a pleasant one were it not entirely walled in with drab grey stone. The stone wall and surrounding architecture almost completely blocked her view of the city of Paris beyond her confined existence, save for the roofs and spires of the tallest buildings. She could see the wrought-iron gate where the dark-haired boy watched her. The dismal walls also served to shield the courtyard from the eyes of curious passersby unless, like the stranger below, they peered through the bars of the gate.

Today Finn's window was open to allow the breeze inside for what little it could do to alleviate the summer heat, but its vertical bars prevented even the slenderest asylum patient from escaping. She disliked this time of year, when the stench of the asylum was worst and some of the male attendants grew bolder about becoming more familiar with the female patients.

Finn had gotten to know all of Dr. Veyssière's henchmen. Some were cool and detached, only working to take home a paycheck. Others, the men closest to Dr. Veyssière, carried out the doctor's every command and would do anything he asked. Those were the men she feared. She knew how quickly they would turn upon her if they all were not under the doctor's watchful eye, and if she were not his so-called star patient. They were the ones who exacted the harshest beatings. They were the ones who never questioned the doctor when he tested new surgical and chemical experiments on unsuspecting patients, whether the treatments were related to their particular diagnosis or not.

Finn swept her copper hair to one side and leaned on the windowsill, taking a quick glance back at the door to her small room. As always, it remained locked from the outside, but she knew the ward attendants' routine like clockwork. Soon the observation panel in the center of the door would slide aside with a scrape of rusted metal. Then beady eyes would peer inside while a ward attendant confirmed that Finn was occupying herself with nothing besides slowly being driven truly mad by boredom and isolation during the interminable hours in which she was not doing her chores or being 'treated' by the doctor in the hospital auditorium. She had been exhibited on the sanitarium's stage long enough to barely remember the gilded Palais Garnier where she performed as a ballet dancer rather than a hysteric.

The opera house was also where she met Jacques-André Veyssière.

Nearly a decade ago, Finn's father set his heart upon becoming an artist. He left his family behind in Dublin while he journeyed to Paris to continue his lessons, dreaming of the École des Beaux-Arts and Salon fame. He sent for his wife and two young daughters once he finally began earning a meager living as a portrait painter. Finn, her mother, and her younger sister Brigid left Dublin for Paris, only to watch her father die of cholera in a squalid Montmartre apartment soon afterward, leaving them with nothing but his debts.

Finn's mother tried to earn them a living as a seamstress as she had done in Ireland, although immigrant life seemed to pose new obstacles and expenses daily. Her daughters pleaded to return to Ireland while helping her sew, and she promised they would go home as soon as she had saved enough money for the voyage. Mrs. Finnegan finally agreed to model for artists, although modeling jobs came less frequently as her features grew tired and her hands raw from endless sewing.

The women remained in the garret in Montmartre, selling what they could of her father's belongings until they had little to remember him by. Food was purchased on credit until the shops refused to serve them any longer. Neither the broken windows stuffed with rags, nor her father's remaining belongings burning in the stove, kept out the winter chill.

Finally, out of desperation, Mrs. Finnegan scrubbed her daughters' faces clean and plaited their red hair. Then, without a word, she took the girls by the hand and hauled them to the spectacular new opera house of Paris to try out for the ballet. Her older daughter passed the audition.

At first, Finn was confused. These strange movements were not the dances she had learned as a young child in Ireland. Eventually she understood, however. She was there to attract a patron. Her beauty and grace must catch the eye of a wealthy man who would support her and her family. Her mother never uttered the threat, but Finn knew she feared that otherwise her daughters would end up in a brothel or on the street.

Dr. Veyssière was the first to notice Finn at her debut performance on the stage. He loved watching her dance, he told her afterward. He loved how the spotlights made her red hair resemble flames, how her ivory skin matched the angelic white of her lace costume, and so on. He began attending her rehearsals. His dark, hulking figure always seemed to be lurking in the wings. Finn forced herself to smile and pretend she was pleased and grateful to see him. Her family needed the money. He was their ticket back to Ireland.

At fourteen, Finn was offered the chance to advance from the ranks of the *petit rats* to the corps de ballet. She always wondered if she would have achieved this or not, for the day of her audition was also the day that Dr. Veyssière appeared in her dressing room while she was alone.

Wealthy patron or not, Finn refused his advances. Over time, her rage at what happened afterward and at the doctor himself had faded to despair, then at last to apathy. She once hated her mother, too, for signing that piece of paper that allowed Dr. Veyssière to lock her away immediately in the Saint-Geneviève, but gradually she understood that an immigrant woman had been powerless to intervene when a respected doctor had diagnosed her daughter with hysteria. After months of pleading to see her family, Dr. Veyssière informed Finn that her mother and sister were dead. They had not survived the winter, he claimed. She refused to believe him. Either her family was too ashamed to visit her, or the doctor intended to keep them apart until he was the only person upon whom her life depended.

Brigid would be nearly fifteen by now, she thought, older than Finn when she had been committed to the Saint-Geneviève. She held onto fleeting memories of running along the coast with her sister, Brigid with misty rain glinting on her hair the color of dark rosewood, her perpetually windblown locks slipping loose from her braids. She was lively and sociable, always flitting about with artless energy in contrast to Finn's graceful stride and tendency towards quiet moodiness. Brigid wept after she had not passed the ballet audition. Finn now wished she could tell her how fortunate she had been. She hoped that her family had found their way back to Ireland at last.

Finn's shabby green steamer trunk containing her few possessions was delivered to her room soon after her arrival. Wrapped carefully within the folds of her shawl, she found her mother's rosary. The translucent horn beads, dyed deep red around a heart-shaped center of warped metal, were Finn's last relics of home. Sometimes she still prayed silently in bed, letting the beads slip through her fingers until she fell asleep. More often, however, she ruminated while holding the chain up to the raking light of her window, imagining the beads as drops of blood.

Finn grew accustomed to asylum life over the years: its odd company, daily routine, punishments, and ambient sounds of weeping, screaming, beating, restraint buckles jingling, and wild laughter pealing. The one sound that still flooded her heart with sickening dread was that of the key turning in the door of her cell, especially at night. At least she had learned to dissociate while the doctor had his hands on her. She would stare at a particular spot on the ceiling and invent stories featuring herself as a vengeful warrior-goddess, escape into her favorite Irish myths and legends, and visualize happier times before she came to the continent. Afterward, the doctor muttered words she was beyond hearing and left her 'medicine' on the bedside tray. Finn drank the tonic gladly. Bearing his child would only bind her to him indefinitely.

Dr. Veyssière often told her how lucky she was to be under his protection, since destitute girls like her usually ended up selling themselves on the street. Between the straitjackets, the experimental therapy, and the doctor's nocturnal visits to her room, Finn often suspected that she had indeed lost her mind, or at least herself, somewhere along the way.

49

She looked out of her window and sighed, wondering how long she had been dwelling on her past and whether the boy skulking below had noticed the stormy expression that crossed her otherwise passive features. He was still there. When she turned her face towards him, he lifted his hand and waved shyly at her.

Finn was aware that she did not know much about men. Few suitors at the opera had the chance to notice her before the doctor rose like a sinister shade from the underworld and claimed her, but she thought she recognized the type: a romantic, a dreamer, a man who probably called himself an artist or a poet or an anarchist, who believed himself in love with a mad girl whom he glimpsed from afar. If that were true, thought Finn, then the two of them truly were on the wrong sides of the asylum wall.

She smiled faintly and waved back nevertheless. She did not believe in Dr. Veyssière's mesmerism, which was all an illusionist's act to her, but she sensed that this young man's consciousness seemed attracted to her as if by some sort of magnetic pull. Finn realized that she felt strangely drawn to him, too. She waved again, her slender fingers and loose hair catching the breeze, and wished she lived in a fairy tale where she could toss him the key to the gate with a graceful gesture and unfurl her hair for him to climb.

Calais flung open the door to Baltard's library without knocking. "Alexandre? What is this about not allowing me to leave the house?" she demanded sharply, her pretty features marred by a cross expression. "I was just talking to the cook. She says you have forbidden me even to the flower market and back?" She fell silent when she noticed Baltard's face was drawn and serious, the stubble around his trimmed beard giving his flesh a greyish tone. "Alexandre, what is it?" she asked in a gentler voice.

The painter was sitting at his desk, solemnly writing a letter until he looked up at his mistress. "I intended to tell you myself, Calais. Do you remember the dreadful murder that happened yesterday?" he asked. He set down his fountain pen and removed his reading glasses, laying them carefully on the desk.

"Of course. How could I forget?"

Baltard gathered the morning newspaper from his desk and spun the front page around so that Calais could read the headline. She stepped closer.

"He has killed another model," he said. "A woman this time, Hélène Laroche. I knew her, Calais. She modeled for me before. As long as someone is murdering artists' models, I am not letting you out of this house. I should not even let you out of my sight." He leaned his elbows on the desk and rubbed his sunken eyes.

Calais, half-listening, held the newspaper in trembling hands. Baltard had taught her his language, but there were some words she did not recognize in this article, and she was uncertain she truly wanted to know their meaning.

The journalist described a modern Venus, a beautiful young woman with long reddish-blond hair and Botticelli eyes, who had been dismembered, beheaded, and cast into the Medici Fountain in the Jardin du Luxembourg. Her remains were found draped in pearls and shells. The numbers 1:7-8 were carved into her forehead with a knife or scalpel. The chief inspector on the case, Marcel Percier, suspects that the symbols refer to the book of Genesis in the Bible. Percier also speculates that the murderer has a certain level of artistic and medical knowledge, may be associated with a religious sect, and wishes to communicate a yet unknown message to the city of Paris.

Calais dropped the paper to the desk and swept behind it in a swirl of saffron-colored silk to embrace Baltard around his shoulders. "I am sorry about Hélène," she whispered.

Baltard had resumed scratching his pen slowly across the page. "I am writing a letter of condolence to her parents. I will post it myself."

Calais paused a moment before replying. "You know I dislike being caged, Alexandre," she said quietly.

Irritably he dropped the pen to the desk. "I'm not caging you, I'm protecting you. Promise me you will not leave this house until the police find this madman."

"Very well." Calais pulled away, letting her hands fall slowly from his tense shoulders. "I promise."

Claude slipped unnoticed into the afternoon hysteria demonstration with the rest of the men in the eager crowd. He brought his sketchbook again, attempting to carry it surreptitiously under his arm. He sat in one of the polished wooden chairs at the back of the auditorium and tried not to draw any attention to himself, making the scrape of charcoal on his paper as quiet as possible.

He focused his attention solely on Finn, ignoring the doctor's practiced explanation of her hysteria case and his mesmeric prowess for healing her. Several times her distant gaze seemed to settle on his face, although she made no indication that she recognized him.

This morning he had discovered which of the upstairs windows belonged to his muse, and felt his stomach flutter when she finally noticed his shy presence and waved a delicate hand at him. Claude was determined that they would be together soon.

What Dr. Veyssière did not know was that several pages of Claude's sketchbook were dedicated to the Sainte-Geneviève itself. He had drawn a map of the perimeter and as detailed a floor plan as he could manage of the *rez-de-chaussée* and upper floors of the asylum. Determining the layout of the ground-floor areas accessible to the public was simple enough. For the third floor, Claude sketched the same outline of the building, but was certain of one thing: which room was Finn's. He had seen other girls' melancholy faces peer through identical windows on the same floor, so he assumed those rooms were the patients' living quarters.

Yet, in Finn's presence, Claude could draw only her. This time when she ceased her convulsions and collapsed into the waiting ward attendants' arms, he was certain that her emerald eyes slid open momentarily and looked straight at him.

Despite the heat, Rémy wrapped his green coat tighter around his thin frame and tentatively approached the crowd of Parisians surrounding the Medici Fountain, attempting to make himself as inconspicuous as possible.

The Medici Fountain was secluded by a screen of trees and foliage, and was typically a place dedicated to courting lovers. Several mythological sculptures graced one end of the small rectangular pool. The two marble figures, the river spirit Acis and the sea nymph Galatea, lounged together in post-coital languor in a sheltered grotto. Above the two lovers, the bronze giant Polyphemus—Galatea's jealous suitor—prepared to dash a boulder down upon Acis's head. Today, this third sculpted figure seemed even more sinister.

Rémy had hurried to the Jardin du Luxembourg as soon as he heard the news. Slowing his step, he attempted to blend in with the mob of excited yet horrified onlookers who pointed and whispered while steely-eyed policemen guarded the perimeter.

He was on his way back to his bookshop after his meeting with Stéphane's parents, emotionally drained but determined to continue his investigation by studying the Salon clippings in his pocket. He was oblivious to his surroundings until he saw the newspaper headline proclaiming that the killer had struck again.

The police had removed the young woman's remains from the fountain early that morning. The calm water was still tainted red, and the low wall of stone urns still bore traces of her blood.

Rémy knew that he was still a suspect. Leaning on his sword cane beneath one of the trees surrounding the fountain, he attempted to peer closer at the scene through the gap between the heads of a heavyset gentleman and a middle-aged woman pretending to shield her eyes from the grisly sight.

Inspector Percier noticed him anyway. The policeman eyed him coldly and strolled over to him, ignoring questions from the press and the rest of the intrusive crowd.

How many such faces had leered at yesterday's spectacle at the Panthéon?

"I came as soon as I heard," the occultist told him softly, although his tone was more exhausted than calm.

"You were not in your bookshop this morning," Percier replied curtly. "I think you may have been correct about the book of Genesis, M. Sauvage."

"I went for a walk. I needed to clear my head." It was partly true. "I only saw the headline when I returning home. My heart is with the victims' families." Rémy reached into his pocket and handed Percier a folded piece of paper. "From Stéphane Desnoyers' appointment book. The list of artists for whom he posed."

"Appointment book? I will need to take a look at that myself," Percier said gruffly, but he nodded his thanks and accepted the list. He glanced back towards the fountain with a tired exhale. "I have just been informed that the victim was another artists' model. Her name was Hélène Laroche. Did you know her?"

Rémy felt guilty about the relief in his voice when he replied that he did not know Hélène Laroche. So the killer had not specifically targeted Stéphane and himself after all. The madman simply sought artists' models or youths of exceptional beauty. Yet, he chided himself, feeling more certain of his own safety must not alter his determination to bring the murderer to justice.

The inspector was momentarily absorbed in the list Rémy provided. "Hmm. These are all fairly well-known artists, are they not?"

Rémy nodded absently and glanced at the fountain. "The firmament and the division of the waters," he muttered. "The Second Day of Genesis."

"Precisely. And apparently Mlle. Laroche was known for her resemblance to a Botticelli painting of Venus."

"The goddess who emerged from the sea," Rémy pondered.

"Of course. M. Sauvage, I stationed several officers to watch the Panthéon overnight. Then, at sunrise, I hear about a murder victim found in a fountain at the Luxembourg gardens. The killer—or killers, as we suspect—chose a different location in the Latin Quarter. Are you quite certain you know nothing more than you admit about the crimes occurring here in your neighborhood? I don't suppose the missing artist has turned up? No one suspicious has entered your shop? No one associated with the Rosicrucians or another religious cult?"

Rémy shook his head. "No one, Inspector, but I shall inform the Préfecture immediately if I see anyone suspicious."

"Please do." Percier's dark eyes never left Rémy's impassive face. "We must anticipate where the next murder will occur, considering the fact that the Third Day in Genesis is the creation of plants and trees. Every man under my command will be stationed in the Latin Quarter tonight, especially the parks and gardens, but I can certainly spare one to keep an eye on your bookshop." The inspector abruptly turned away and strode back into the chaos at the roped-off fountain, and Rémy understood that he was being watched.

The Messenger was intensely proud of his successes thus far. The spirit world was pleased with him, and pleased with the Brotherhood. Soon their efforts would bring about the Eighth Day! They would awaken from hypnotic sleep, and the divine entities they had created would welcome and guide them into a new world, where myth and magic would be restored to these artists deserving of their secrets.

Each of the eight artists initiated into the mysteries of the Brotherhood had painstakingly designed his own day of creation. The Messenger led them with Icarus. The Second-Day artist offered his vision of Venus. He was even permitted to direct the artistic steps of her creation once the Messenger approved the design. The latter could not have been more pleased with the model: a true embodiment of a goddess on earth.

The Brotherhood's art and exploits graced the front page of every Paris journal, and they were probably featured in international newspapers by now. Their message was being received, but it would be understood only by a chosen few.

The Messenger adjusted his black gloves. He was impatient to assist the Third-Day artist with the Brotherhood's most ambitious sculpture yet: the figures of Hades and Persephone. The model for Hades was a young man with swarthy features. Persephone was a petite blonde, once a youthfully exuberant model.

The lord of the Underworld was now bloodless, his body drained of every sanguine drop by a syringe. The dead had no pulse, and no lifeblood running through their veins. They adorned Hades in regal black costume armor and cropped his hair short until he resembled a dark-hearted Roman emperor.

Persephone was more complicated. The lead artist needed a little guidance from the spirit world, transcribed by the Messenger, regarding her creation. Together they severed the woman's small hands and replaced them with lovely bouquets of flowering branches tied to her supple wrists. They sealed her nose and mouth with flowers and placed luscious petals over her eyes. They tied roses into her river of golden hair while she slowly suffocated. Both figures would be bound together within the thorns and brambles of winter.

The Messenger stepped back and admired their work. Tilting his head, he directed the arrangement of the bodies, wrapping the man's dead limbs around those of his eternal bride, indicating how he wanted them posed at the destination site. The Messenger always insisted upon adding the final touch himself, and carved the prophetic numbers into their foreheads with a gleaming scalpel.

At last he turned his gaze heavenward, his face ecstatic, his luminous eyes glistening. Soon the Sun would rise upon the Third Day.

August 3, 1888

"And the earth brought forth grass, and herb yielding seed after his kind, and the tree yielding fruit, whose seed was in itself, after his kind: and God saw that it was good. And the evening and the morning were the third day."

—Genesis 1:12-13

Viewed from the outside, the greenhouse of the Jardin des Plantes in the fifth *arrondissement* resembled an airy glass cathedral, an iridescent palace of blue and violet-swirled panes linked together by delicate tracery: the ideal place for an ethereal winter garden. The public gardens were often a pleasant escape from the noisy and crowded boulevards of Paris. On this particular morning, however, a milling crowd of policemen stationed at the entrance and their sharp scent in the summer heat dispelled any sense of wonder that a typical visitor to the garden might have experienced.

The uniformed crowd parted for Inspector Percier, who made his way to the crime scene at the heart of the greenhouse. He truly felt as if he were navigating through a jungle while he stepped through the garden, brushed aside low branches of tropical plants, and shouldered his way through another crowd of policemen, a few of whom held their handkerchiefs to their faces against the heightening stench of decay. "What have they done to them this time?" he demanded, then stopped in his tracks when he saw the bodies.

The policeman at Percier's side removed his hat and scratched his sweaty head. "Killed another man and a prostitute, Inspector," he answered.

Percier looked down at the notes loosely clasped in his hand. "Rosalie Dumont was an artists' model, Alain," he said quietly. "Not a prostitute."

The younger man turned away to cough and replaced his hat on his head.

"Same thing, isn't it?"

"Show some respect, Alain."

"Yes, Inspector."

Percier barely registered Alain's reply while he stepped closer to the victims. The scenario both enraged and intrigued him. The Genesis killer— as he, or they, had become known in the newspapers—had arranged the corpses so that the man was seated on a tree stump as if enthroned. His body was propped up with a wooden framework similar to the structure of the Icarus wings. A woman in a bloodstained white gown and floral wreath knelt at his feet with her upper body draped across him and her head resting on his lap, half-hiding her suffocated face. The flower-bound stumps of her hands dangled over the opposite side of his legs. The murderer had achieved their precise poses by winding dry vines and thorny plants around both bodies.

"Persephone pleading to return to the living world," Percier pondered aloud. "Alas, too late for this poor girl." He leaned closer, peering at the numbers carved into their foreheads. 1:12-13. "Genesis verses. God created plants and seeds on the Third Day. We know the killer has a pattern. But what is he trying to tell us?" Percier crouched down. "Look at this. Not a drop of blood left in this man's body, appendages severed from the female victim, yet hardly a trace of blood on the ground. Again, the victims were killed elsewhere, transported here, and carefully arranged. And—" Percier looked up at the glass ceiling. "They were posed to receive direct sunlight at dawn."

"Seems like this murder was planned long in advance. Maybe months or years," Alain observed.

Percier nodded, only half-listening while he stared at the crime scene and committed every detail to memory before writing furiously in his black notebook.

"Shall we have the victims taken to the Sainte-Geneviève with the others?" another officer asked. "The morgue at l'Hôpital de la Salpêtrière is closer."

"The Sainte-Geneviève," Percier insisted. He intended to gather all his evidence in one location until the victims' families claimed their departed, despite the public's morbid clamoring to see the spectacle of their bodies displayed at the Paris morgue. Besides, Dr. Veyssière had been most cooperative in allowing the Préfecture to borrow his hospital's facilities.

"Inspector?"

"Yes, Alain?"

"There's something else. We interviewed the botanist, the one who found the bodies early this morning. He says that those vines around the victims' bodies have never been grown here in the greenhouse." Alain checked his notes. "Says they're hardy enough to withstand the winter."

Percier studied the corpses while his mind calculated the new information. He began thinking again of Rémy Sauvage and his extensive mythological and occult knowledge.

"Also, Inspector," Alain continued. "I've been doing a little research of my own. I know a bit about mythology. Seems like the perpetrator deliberately used winter vines for the god of the Underworld."

Percier glanced at him. "What are you thinking, Alain?"

"Well, the victims are intended to represent Hades and Persephone, right? Hades wanted to marry Persephone, so he carried her off to the Underworld." The younger man's eyes rolled upward while he tried to recall the tale. "And—then Persephone's mother Demeter, a fertility goddess, was so bereft that she caused winter to reign until Persephone returned. When she returned to her mother, it was spring again."

"I know the story." Percier looked back to the figures. "Evergreen vines in midsummer, then," he mused. "He wants to show us that Persephone has been taken to the Underworld."

The young officer remained silent for a moment. "Inspector?" he said at last.

"Yes, Alain?" Percier did not look up from his pen and notepad.

"I wonder if Mlle. Dumont's mother will feel the same way," he said, nodding once at the mutilated corpse. "Same as Demeter, I mean."

"Worse than that, Alain." Percier continued writing, his voice distant. "Her daughter will not return to her in any season at all."

Claude paced the studio for hours, fidgeting with props and considering all the roles he could play. He could pose as a building inspector evaluating the Sainte-Geneviève's structure, a family member seeking a lost relative, or a wigmaker needing a particular shade of red hair. In the end, he decided that the most obvious disguise also would be the most convincing.

Holding an awkward parcel of supplies under one arm, Claude stood at the asylum's courtyard gate and caught his breath before reaching out to loudly rattle the iron latch, catching the attention of a tall ward attendant leaning against the shaded wall of the carriage house. Claude prayed that the man would not recognize him from the audience of Dr. Veyssière's demonstrations or from his previous skulking around the asylum, and resisted the urge to pull the brim of his rumpled black cap even further down over his eyes to hide his face.

The guard noticed the black sliver of Claude's form peering through the close-set bars of the courtyard gate, not recognizing him but taking an immediate dislike to a presumed curiosity-seeker nevertheless. "No visitors at this entrance," he called. When Claude refused to budge, he loped towards the gate and pointed him in the direction of the street. "No visitors. Move along."

"Forgive me, Monsieur," Claude replied. He intended to affect a flustered tone, but his voice only sounded nervous. "I have come about the painting."

"What painting?" The guard was unimpressed.

"The painting Dr. Veyssière has commissioned of himself and his famous case study. He invited me to draw some preliminary sketches of a particular female patient to make certain I capture her likeness in detail. One with red hair." For a fleeting and terrible moment, Claude wondered if a hysteria patient could model without being hypnotized. He shook off the thought, reassuring himself that he could find a way to paint his muse. He shifted the awkward bundle in his arms to show the guard he carried nothing except an unwieldy drawing board, several sheets of thick paper, and a handful of brushes and pencils bound in an old leather case.

"Dr. Veyssière never mentioned any portraits," the guard replied. "Only one red-haired patient comes to mind, the Irish girl, and she's the doctor's star patient." He glared at Claude, leaning close enough for the artist to catch the smell of chemicals and sweat in his black clothes and dusty brown hair. "So, you had better prove you have permission from Dr. Veyssière before I let you anywhere close to her."

"Star patient?" Claude blinked innocently. "I beg your pardon?"

The guard rolled his eyes. "His favorite. The one he always uses to demonstrate his hysteria cure and prove he's a more powerful healer than Mesmer himself. He can calm her right down by hypnosis alone. She goes from having a fit to going completely limp when he's done. We have to carry her out of the auditorium."

Claude nodded, keeping an earnest expression in his blue eyes. "Of course. All of Paris is well acquainted with Dr. Veyssière and his miraculous techniques."

"All right, then." He scowled and unlocked the massive iron gate, letting it scrape open just wide enough along the cobblestones to allow Claude to struggle inside with his art supplies. "The doctor's usually in his office at this hour, down the hall from the auditorium."

"I am grateful for your assistance, Monsieur." Claude took a quick glance around the courtyard and strode towards the pair of iron-hinged wooden doors nearest the gate.

"Wait. What time is your appointment?" the guard called after him.

The visitor turned with a bewildered expression. "Appointment? Monsieur, my apologies again, but Dr. Veyssière requested specifically that I not disturb him while he works, and to use the service entrance closest to the ward. Am I in the right place?" he asked, gesturing to the doors.

The larger man shook his head. "If you don't have an appointment, go to the reception desk at the main entrance, make one, and come back later," he replied firmly, then moved to grip Claude's arm with a thick hand and drag him back towards the alley.

"Please, Monsieur. I would loathe having to tell Dr. Veyssière that one of his loyal assistants is the reason that the painting of himself magnetizing and healing his star patient in the auditorium of the Sainte-Geneviève cannot be finished in time for the world to admire at the Exposition Universelle! I only wish to bring even more prestige to this renowned institution."

The guard relaxed his grip and sighed wearily. "Very well." He jerked his head towards the service entrance, then followed Claude to the door while he retrieved the keys from his belt. "Go past the storerooms and the dispensary. The patients are upstairs, with the hysterics' ward on the third floor, but the attendant on duty will tell you the same thing I did. No access to the ward without Dr. Veyssière's permission. For your own good." He chuckled while unlocking the heavy door to let Claude step inside. "You never know what those girls will do."

He slammed the door shut before Claude could reply. Claude heard the bolt slide into place behind him and realized that he, like Finn, was trapped in l'Hôpital Sainte-Geneviève until the guard released him. He would deal with that later. For now, Claude could hardly contain his excitement. He knew from observing the sanitarium from the courtyard gate that the demonstrations were finished by this hour, and that Finn had been returned to her room. Judging from her seemingly alert appearance at her window, she recovered quickly from her trances.

Claude stepped quietly through the sepulchral corridors of the storeroom hallway. His makeshift maps would not help him with this unknown part of the asylum, but the layout seemed simple enough, and at least he knew where to find the stairs. He climbed from the *rez-de-chaussée* to the first floor, trying to look confident as he approached the guard on duty: another muscular young man with pugnacious features who could easily overpower someone with Claude's slight build.

"*Bonjour*, Monsieur." He grasped the brim of his cap in an awkward greeting. "I have come to work on a painting commissioned by the doctor, who requested that I include a portrait of a girl on this ward who possesses radiant copper hair." He glanced down the stark hallway of the ward, flinching slightly at the sound of a sudden scream followed by a dull thudding noise amid soft weeping and chattering voices that presumably spoke to no one in this world. Claude thought he could perceive a few coherent words amongst the din of female voices and the creaking of leather straps as patients' bodies strained against them, but his heart was pounding too loudly in his ears to be certain. *This place is enough to drive anyone mad.*

The attendant seemed unmoved by the asylum's ambient noise. He probably listened to it all day, Claude realized, but he doubted that he could ever harden his own heart against such distress.

"Right. Mlle. Finnegan. First room on the right." A puzzled expression crossed the guard's face. "Dr. Veyssière's allowed you to see her? Alone? Where's your letter from the doctor, then? All visitors need permission before being granted access to the ward." The attendant glanced down at Claude's hands, seeing that the visitor carried only an armful of art supplies.

"I—must have dropped it," Claude replied, halfheartedly patting his pocket. "But Dr. Veyssière is so eager to see my sketches and approve the composition," he pleaded, thankful that the heat provided an excuse for the beads of sweat cascading down his face. He was struggling to breathe in the humid air tinged with pungent chemical odors, and the increasing nausea did nothing to calm his nerves.

"If I don't see the doctor's signature, I don't open the patients' doors," the guard said sternly. "Especially not *that* girl's."

Claude had been hoping that the situation would not come to this. He sighed as he dropped his drawing materials, drew his father's duelling pistol from his pocket, and aimed for the guard's heart. "Unlock the door. Let her go."

The guard guessed correctly that Claude had never challenged anyone to a fight before in his life. He laughed and lunged at the slighter man, intending to pin him to the floor and disarm him, but Claude slithered out of his grasp and lashed out with the pistol. The heavy firearm clubbed the guard across his face, drawing blood, but the man remained standing.

"Let her go," Claude insisted, leveling the pistol. His raised voice had agitated the patients in nearby rooms. The unseen women began either wailing louder or laughing harder. Claude truly could not tell which.

The guard slicked his finger through the blood on his cheekbone, examined the damage, and grinned at Claude. "And then what?" he demanded, rubbing his bloody fingertips together. "How far do you think you'll get? The doctor is a powerful man. If you even make it out of the asylum, with or without the girl, he'll have every policeman in the city looking for you within the hour." He leisurely began strolling towards Finn's door. Claude kept his distance. "Remember my face, boy. I'll be seeing you in the men's ward before too long. You're obviously mad." He turned the key in the lock. "Finn? You've got a visitor," he called to the young woman inside.

Claude managed to concentrate on the situation at hand, not allowing himself to get distracted by the thrill of being in Finn's presence without the uneasy dynamic of the hospital auditorium. He pointed the pistol at the attendant while taking a quick glance around her small, drab room. The only furniture was a small wooden table, a sagging mattress covered in institutional white sheets, and a battered green steamer trunk at the foot of the bed.

Finn had been gazing out her window, as usual. Upon hearing the scuffle outside her door, she turned sharply towards the noise, wide-eyed, frozen in place while the key turned in the lock and the bolt slid back. Her heart sank when she saw the guard, but then she recognized the visitor: the boy with the raven hair. She was shocked that anyone had risked his life and freedom to rescue her from the Sainte-Geneviève. He was either extremely brave or extremely foolish.

"Come with me," he pleaded. His tone was urgent, but his eyes were gentle, despite the weapon grasped in his thin hand, pointed at the guard. "I know you're sick, but I'll help you, however I can. I'll never hurt you."

The guard was laughing cruelly again. The young woman glared at him with hatred, and Claude jabbed the pistol against his spine. "Get inside," he ordered the man. "You'll take her place. Face the wall." He offered his hand to Finn, intending to wrench her out of the guard's reach before he tried anything.

Finn made her decision. The young man's expression was one of mad desperation, but his eyes, a watery shade somewhere between blue and grey, shone with adoration and kindness. She accepted his hand.

Claude drew her to him and slammed the door shut behind them, locking the man inside and wrestling the keys from the lock. The ward attendant was already at the window, screaming for help.

"The guard in the courtyard will hear!" Finn cried.

"Perfect. He will be out of our way." Claude guided her quickly but gently back down the hall. The imprisoned guard shouted and pounded his fists on the door, further agitating the hysteria ward's patients. Claude momentarily wished he could release them all. He fled down the stairs with Finn to the service entrance and stopped at the door, clasping her to him, feeling both of their nervous heartbeats. "Wait here," he whispered.

Finn understood. The guard patrolling the courtyard had already unlocked the door, but he rushed inside only to run past Claude and Finn lurking in the shadows. The two fugitives slipped outside. Claude's heart sank when he saw that the gate was locked once again. He stopped short, still gripping Finn's hand, while the guard trapped in Finn's room shouted at them from above, raising the alarm. He scarcely noticed that Finn was fumbling with the ring of keys that Claude had taken from the ward attendant.

"It's this one," she said, grabbing the ring and wrapping her small hand around the heaviest key. "Hurry!" She dashed towards the gate and twisted the key in the lock.

Claude pocketed the pistol and followed, praying silently that he would be the only one punished if they were apprehended. The gate creaked on its hinges as Finn struggled with the iron door. Claude drove his shoulder into the bars, and together they shoved it open and slipped through into the empty street behind the sanitarium.

Once again Claude took Finn's small hand in his and fled. Finn, her dove-grey skirts flying and her hair a defiant red banner streaming behind her, ran away with Claude without a single glance back at the hospital that had been her home and prison for the past six years. The sanitarium seemed to seal itself behind them like a sepulcher, and the sounds of alarm created by their escape faded to silence as they vanished into the Latin Quarter.

Elsewhere in the Sainte-Geneviève, in an office with marble busts of medical personalities from Asclepius to Mesmer and polished cabinets laden with medical books, glass bottles, and plaster *écorchés*, Dr. Veyssière conversed with the Messenger of the Eighth Day Brotherhood. The Messenger lounged in one of the dark leather upholstered chairs that faced across the desk from the doctor. He wore his ever-present smile, a smug Mephistopheles paying a visit to Dr. Faustus.

"You seem pleased with yourself, Étienne," said Dr. Veyssière. He closed the file he had been reading before his expected visitor arrived.

The artist smiled. "I am most proud of my work. Proud of the Brotherhood. I grow impatient to witness the Eighth Day. Don't you, Doctor?" he slid a wilting rose out of the crystal vase on Dr. Veyssière's meticulously organized desk, and began plucking at the blood-red petals with his long fingers.

The doctor nodded. "Of course."

"We have accomplished so much, and it is only the Third Day of the new era of Creation. Soon we shall escape from this false world and ascend above the filth and stench of this modern city." He curled his lip. "Now it is a matter of days until we regain Paradise by completing what God began. Doctor, you may not be one of the artists in the Brotherhood, but with your gifts of magnetism, your chemical knowledge, and your surgical skill, your honored place is with us nevertheless. I cannot thank you enough for your assistance." The Messenger laid the crumpled flower on Dr. Veyssière's desk. "I trust you remain loyal?"

"Of course, Étienne." Dr. Veyssière furrowed his brow and blinked away the faint flicker of concern in his eyes. "You know very well that I owe everything to you for proving that there's more to this spiritualism craze than I previously thought, especially when combined with my own capabilities. I shall be there tonight—"

A knock at the door. A breathless, elderly nurse flung it open, agitating the black folds of her nun's habit. "Pardon the intrusion, Doctor, but a patient is being kidnapped! It's Mlle. Finnegan. A man is trying to escape with her. He pretended to be a portrait artist and threatened the guard with a pistol—"

"Finn?"The doctor stood, imposing fury darkening his sharp features.

"Yes, Doctor! Look!" The nurse pointed frantically out the window facing the enclosed courtyard.

It was true. The flame-haired beauty was disappearing through the gate with a dark-haired young man.

A low growl rumbled in the doctor's throat as he recognized the intruder. "That art student from the demonstration!" he spat. "Sister, notify the police! They must bring her back and apprehend that young man—"

"No. Let them go," the Messenger interrupted in his languid voice. "A man of your reputation would not want to make a scene, especially over an escaped patient, would you, Doctor? No police, either. Besides, I know that man. He is no dangerous criminal. His name is Claude Fournel. Alexandre Baltard's adopted boy. He will be easy enough to find." He gazed at Dr. Veyssière with a smile and a slow blink of ice-blue eyes. *"Trust* me."

The doctor sighed angrily and glared at the iron gate of the courtyard through his window. "Sister, return to your duties and tell the ward assistants to remain here for now," he commanded through clenched teeth. "We shall recover Mlle. Finnegan later."

Dr. Veyssière's staff had learned never to question their employer's orders. The bewildered woman nodded and left, closing the office door behind her.

The doctor continued simmering. "You had better be right about this, Étienne. That young woman is the one I want with me—at the end."

"Then we have plenty of time," the Messenger replied with a shrug and an expression of mock offense. "Have I ever misled you, Doctor? You shall be with Mlle. Finnegan in the end, somehow or other. I promise you that." He stood and stretched his lean body. "Well. I shall take my leave, since I suppose your hysteria demonstration is cancelled this afternoon? Pity. I do so enjoy watching you work your magic on your patients. Oh! Before I go, I don't suppose you have an extra dose of that marvelous white powder? I seem to have been losing a bit of sleep lately. It should help me stay alert, don't you think?"

Dr. Veyssière unlocked one of his desk drawers, pulled out a small glass vial filled with the desired substance, and handed it over.

"Thank you, Doctor." The Messenger curled the vial into his lithe fingers and strolled to the door. "I'll see myself out. *À bientôt*."

Finn's pulse still pounded in her ears. Paris was more crowded and vibrant than she remembered. Claude had taken her hand and pulled her along on a disorienting chase through the winding streets of the Latin Quarter, occasionally glancing back over his shoulder with wild eyes to see if Veyssière's men had followed them. She ran past a walled medieval castle, caught glimpses of gothic towers, and stumbled on the cobblestones while trying to avoid the café tables, sleek carriages, and vendors' carts. The bustling avenues and striking vistas were almost overwhelming, but preferable to the view of stone walls and barred windows.

Soon the narrow streets gave way to the Seine. Finn's eyes widened upon seeing the river and the city beyond it again, but Claude abruptly plunged her into a place called the Café Hugo. He guided her to a table in the back corner where she could catch her breath at last, rubbing her sore hand where Claude had gripped her.

"I'm sorry—if I hurt you," he said breathlessly, nodding at her hand. "They're probably still looking for us. We should wait here for a while."

Finn's gaze flitted around the café. Her loose hair and striking looks earned the fugitives a few suspicious glances from other café patrons, but they soon returned to speaking amongst themselves and sipping glasses of a milky green liquid.

She felt increasingly anxious as her ear caught snippets of nearby conversations. It seemed as if all anyone wanted to talk about was a series of atrocious murders. Three young bohemians at the adjacent table chatted with morbid excitement about two bodies of artists' models that were found at the Jardin des Plantes this morning. Finn glanced at Claude, who was staring down at the scratched wooden table with worried eyes, and shivered despite her sweat-dampened clothes. People are being murdered, mutilated, and turned into morbid works of art? Had she escaped from the asylum into a world even less sane?

Claude was also listening, but his heart still raced from the adrenaline of the day's perilous events and from the anticipation of being alone with Finn.

There were so many questions he wanted to ask her, until he knew everything about her. He observed that she seemed reserved and gentle, having spoken only a few words in her soft, accented voice with her green eyes downcast. She tossed her long hair to one side and sat stiffly in her chair with her hands fidgeting in her lap. Her movements were simultaneously skittish and graceful, as if she were accustomed to being watched but secretly resented it. In the moments when she tilted her face into the light with her hair tumbling over her shoulder, Claude thought he had never seen anything so beautiful.

"Mademoiselle, I wish I had been able to introduce myself sooner," he began nervously, then the words rushed out. "My name is Claude Fournel. I am studying to become a painter, like my father, and I knew the first moment I saw you that I needed you to be my muse."

She smiled softly in reply. She had been right about the boy with the raven hair, she thought. A romantic. She wondered how long he would be able to hide her from the authorities, or if he had even thought of that. She wondered how quickly he would tire of her. "Margaret Rose Finnegan. I'm called Finn at the asylum," she replied quietly.

She continued gazing around the café, wishing to absorb every colorful detail after seeing nothing but the drab walls of the Sainte-Geneviève for so many years. Impulsive fool or not, Claude had freed her from that institutional purgatory, and she was grateful to him for that. Yet when the doctor inevitably recaptured her, she knew he would only increase her torment by any manner of experimental "therapy" he deemed necessary. Claude would face the Préfecture or be declared insane himself, and disappear into the asylum like so many others.

After drinking two glasses of wine to calm his nerves, Claude decided to chance leaving the café. Finn had managed only a few sips before she felt lightheaded, and left the rest of her glass behind. They blended in with the crowds on the *grands boulevards* as he furtively guided her to his instructor's house, intending to hide her in the guest bedroom with the jade-colored walls.

He paused to buy a narrow length of green cloth with black embroidery from a street vendor for Finn to cover her vibrant hair. A respectable *parisienne* never wore her hair down according to current fashion, he explained. She sighed softly in reply and draped the cloth around her head, tossing the ends over her shoulders. Claude thought the dark veil made her look more like a penitent Magdalene than a Salomé, yet neither the cloth nor the slightly outdated fashion of her white blouse, grey jacket, and long matching skirt with its dusty hem made her look any less otherworldly to his enamored eyes.

Finn hesitated at the base of the short flight of broad stone steps to the doorway to Baltard's residence, pushing the scarf back from her head to gaze up at the bluish-grey Parisian sky before entering another stone façade.

Claude turned to see her gazing up at him once the front door was unlocked. Enchanted anew by her emerald eyes, he wanted to paint her there in the hazy evening light, to capture her every angle, but for now he needed a place to conceal her.

Panic welled in Claude's chest as he invited Finn into her new home. What if she had a hysteria fit? What would he do? Fleetingly he remembered reading an article in a scientific periodical a few years ago about the increasing prevalence of hysteria among the female population, and wished he had paid closer attention to the description of the condition's symptoms.

The duelling pistol weighing down his coat pockets still knocked heavily against his leg as he walked. "I shall introduce you to my painting instructor, M. Baltard, soon," he told Finn. "He will be surprised to see you, to say the least, but he is truly kind once you get to know him, and he is a famous artist. He will help me make you—" Claude trailed off, remembering the heated conversation between Baltard and himself about the Icarus boy, trying to think of a different word, but could not. "Immortal," he said at last.

Rémy paced the floor of his shop, stepping deftly along the narrow passage between the shelves and the piles of books. He tried to distract himself by re-reading his copy of Oscar Wilde's recent work, *The Happy Prince and Other Tales*, with its bright green leather cover and gilded lettering, but Wilde's stories of love and sacrifice seemed more bitter than bittersweet.

Few customers had entered his shop today. Perhaps passersby had noticed the policeman who kept surreptitiously passing his doorstep, and feared that they, too, would become suspects if they associated with the occult bookseller. Another officer had been watching his shop last night.

However, Rémy pondered, the most recent murder victims were discovered nowhere near the Latin Quarter, but rather in the greenhouse of the Jardin des Plantes. It was an appropriate site for Hades and Persephone, Rémy thought darkly. Those personages seemed to be what the murderer considered mythological equivalents to the creation of plants and trees in the Bible.

Rémy had scoured the Salon clippings obtained from Stéphane's parents and researched every artist in Stéphane's appointment book, including Gustave Moreau and Pierre Puvis de Chavannes. None of the Salon reviews mentioned a painting of Icarus, and all of Stéphane's contacts were respected and well-known artists, at least in their own circles. Not one, from what Rémy knew and read about them, seemed a likely murderer.

Rémy read the Salon clippings again. This time another name caught his eye: Alexandre Baltard. This artist was notable for painting what critics considered a rather dark and macabre version of Hades and Persephone, even considering the funereal subject. Baltard's painting had been exhibited at the same Salon where a particular painting featuring Stéphane as a model had been well-received.

Rémy remembered the latter painting well. That was the Salon where he and Stéphane met. In his distracted state at the time, he remembered few of the other notable paintings from that year's submissions. Perhaps the artist Baltard had seen the painting of Stéphane and made inquiries into the model's identity. Baltard was known for his interest in morbid mythological themes, one Salon critic remarked. An interview with the painter might provide a starting point, at least. Rémy grasped his silver-topped sword cane and closed his shop early for the day, slipping outside after the policeman passed by again.

If Stéphane had ever posed for Baltard, he had not written the artist's name in his appointment book. Yet artist and model could have met at the École des Beaux-Arts, Rémy realized, and he could probably find Baltard's address there. Rémy turned south and headed across the Seine towards the renowned academy of painting and sculpture.

After making inquiries in the guise of an aspiring art student looking for a painting instructor to refine his skills before seeking admission to the École des Beaux-Arts, Rémy obtained the address of Alexandre Baltard's atelier. Apparently he taught drawing and painting lessons in his own home, located near the academy.

Rémy arrived at the Rue de l'Abbaye late in the afternoon. He paused on the stone steps, observing the silent house for a long moment. Just as he arrived, another gentleman was leaving: an elderly but robust man in a black suit and top hat.

"*Au revoir*, M. Boisseau," a dark-haired woman, presumably Baltard's housekeeper, was saying.

"*Au revoir*, Calais," the gentleman replied. "I hope you will model for me some day when this is all over. If Alexandre can spare you." His smile faded as he turned and nearly collided with Rémy on his way down the stairs.

"I beg your pardon," Rémy said, tilting his feather-adorned top hat.

The older man glanced dismissively at Rémy's long hair, brocade jacket cinched tightly around his narrow waist, and buttoned leather boots before continuing on his way with a gruff nod.

Rémy turned towards the door. Baltard's housekeeper—and model, he noted, from the brief conversation he overheard between the woman and M. Boisseau—was an attractive petite woman, her dark complexion enhanced by her turquoise gown and large white flowers pinned into her black hair. Rémy judged her to be about the same age as himself, or perhaps a few years older.

She regarded him calmly. "Are you here to see M. Baltard?" she asked in an accented voice, one slender hand placed on the door frame.

"I am, Madame. Please inform him that Rémy Sauvage, private investigator, requests an interview. I just want to ask him a few questions. Forgive me, I have no appointment, but it is quite urgent." Rémy handed her his trade card.

Calais took it and read the lines as she turned away. "I will ask if he is available. Please step inside." She raised a dark eyebrow at the words on the card.

Rémy tried to visualize his card from her point of view, wondering what she and Baltard might think of him. The ivory-colored card was engraved with ornate black scrollwork vines around the words *Le Jardin Sauvage, Dealer of Rare Books Occult and Arcane, Rémy Sauvage, Proprietor* above his Latin Quarter address.

Calais turned back to him with a faint smile and offered to take his hat and walking-stick, but Rémy insisted on holding onto them. He would not be here long, he assured her. She nodded, closed the door behind him, and drifted into a room at the far end of the main hallway.

Rémy gazed around the parlor while he waited. The square room was decorated with claret wallpaper, Moroccan lanterns, mahogany furniture, and other ephemera collected from antique shops and the artist's travels.

He stepped closer to the small painting hanging on the wall above the velvet sofa. Painted in somber tones, it depicted a young man in classical drapery carrying a lyre. His face bore an anguished expression while he turned his head to watch a maiden being dragged into a dire-looking chasm by phantom hands.

Orpheus and Eurydice, Rémy knew immediately, recognizing the scene from Ovid's *Metamorphoses*. The mythological musician who descended into the Underworld to retrieve his wife after she was fatally bitten by a snake. Hades and Persephone were so moved by his ethereal music that they allowed Eurydice to follow him out of their realm upon the condition that Orpheus not lay eyes upon her until they both returned to the living world. The scene in the painting depicted the moment Orpheus turned too soon, and Eurydice was lost to him forever.

Orpheus, a symbol of enlightened creativity, had become a popular subject among Symbolist painters and their followers, although the painting's emotional content and sweeping movement betrayed its Romantic origins. Rémy peered at the signature in the lower right corner of the painting. *S. Fournel.*

"M. Sauvage?" The housekeeper had returned. "M. Baltard will see you now. This way, please." She led him to the room at the end of the hall, a spacious office and library decorated with dark wood furniture, gold and cream damask curtains, and dark teal wallpaper with a subtle gilded pattern. Rémy glanced around the room, thankful for the open windows alleviating the stifling air, and resisted examining the leather-bound volumes and yellowed folios behind the glass doors of the bookshelves.

"Come in, M. Sauvage," a rough-shaven man said irritably. He glanced at Calais, who quietly withdrew from the room and shut the door behind her. "Alexandre Baltard," he introduced himself, rising stiffly from his desk to return Rémy's bow of greeting. He sat down again and glanced at the trade card on his desk. "A private investigator who owns an occult bookshop, M. Sauvage?"

"My other line of work," Rémy replied calmly.

Baltard grumbled inaudibly and shuffled through a pile of newspapers and letters on his desk before gesturing impatiently at the green upholstered chair next to Rémy. "Very well. This has been a wretched day, so please ask whatever questions you have and leave me to my work. I suppose you have come to interrogate me about Claude?"

Rémy sat in the offered chair and narrowed his eyes in confusion with a slight shake of his head. "Claude?"

"My foster son." Baltard rolled his eyes and adjusted his reading glasses. "I expect he will find himself in trouble with the authorities any moment now. Would you care for a drink, M. Sauvage?"

"I—No, thank you—I am sorry, Monsieur, but do you think your Claude may be connected with the recent murders?"

Baltard looked at Rémy with a surprised expression. "The murders? Heavens, no. I was just talking about that dreadful news with my colleague, in fact, but, no, not Claude. Claude is a dreamer and a romantic fool, but I doubt he is capable of hurting anyone. His father was my closest friend," Baltard added. "The artist Sylvain Fournel. You've heard of him?"

"Of course."

"That's him, there. His self-portrait." Baltard jerked his head to indicate a small painting hanging on the wall in a modest gilded frame. In three-quarter view it portrayed a handsome gentleman with thick dark hair and a sparse beard, wearing a black suit and a cravat the color of burnished gold. The portrait was rendered in loose, effortless brush strokes except for the translucent layers forming his aloof but gentle blue eyes.

"I have seen engravings of M. Fournel's work," Rémy said slowly. "The painting in your parlor, the one of Orpheus and Eurydice—"

"One of Sylvain's, yes. Claude inherited his imagination and talent, but—" Baltard glanced over his shoulder as if Claude might be eavesdropping. "His work is still hardly comparable to his father's. I am doing my best to teach him, though. Blood from a stone. Anyway, inspector, are you here regarding the Genesis murders, as the journals are calling them now?"

Rémy nodded and tapped his ring on his cane. "Four victims in three days. All artists' models."

"So I've heard. Sometimes I wonder what this world is coming to. First the city of Paris decides to build Gustave Eiffel's abominable steel contraption for the exposition. I signed the petition against its construction, for all the good that accomplished. Have you seen the tower so far? Even when it's complete it will be nothing but bolts and girders!" Baltard shook his head. "If that is the modern Paris we want to show the rest of the world, I am not sure I want to be a part of it. Especially when a mad killer starts slaughtering models. Between that eyesore and these murders, perhaps no one will dare traveling to Paris for the world's fair!" He fell silent with a heavy sigh, noticing that Rémy was eyeing him oddly. "Forgive me. I digress. Yes, I knew Hélène Laroche, the second victim. She modeled for me a few years ago."

Rémy swallowed, his next question momentarily catching in his throat. "What about Stéphane Desnoyers? Did you know him?"

Baltard furrowed his brow in thought and shook his head. "The First Day victim? No, he never worked for me."

"Yes. Icarus," Rémy replied quietly. "Actually, Monsieur, I also am interested in today's victims."

"Ah, yes. Hades and Persephone. No, I did not know the models."

"Monsieur, forgive me, but I happened to read that you are famous for creating a certain large-scale painting of that very subject at the Salon of 1886."

"Infamous, really," Baltard replied with a cynical chortle. "I received scathing reviews from everyone except the Symbolist poets. The painting never found a collector." Baltard narrowed his eyes, suspicious. "Why do you ask? Are you suggesting that I had something to do with the Genesis murders because I exhibited a *Hades and Persephone* once?"

Rémy lifted a hand defensively. "I suggest nothing of the sort, Monsieur. Yet, from what I have read about your work, and from the engravings I have seen of your paintings, your style is rather—macabre. Please, Monsieur, do not be offended! My own tastes are quite similar," he added, observing Baltard's growing agitation. "I just thought you might have some insight into the case. I believe the victims are prepared in a certain location, such as an artist's atelier or an operating room, and then posed in predetermined locations just before sunrise," the occultist continued. "From the killer's knowledge of iconography and the visual composition of each murder scene, I suspect the murders might be the work of an artist, a prominent collector, or a religious cult involving at least one artist as a member. As for the pattern of Bible verses, ancient myths, and locations within the city, I unfortunately have not quite figured out the murderers' next move. If I only knew where they intend to strike next, with four days of the creation story left—" Rémy's voice broke.

"M. Sauvage, I cannot help you," Baltard said calmly. "There are few artists in Paris who have not painted mythological or biblical scenes, and hardly a model who has not posed for them." He paused for a moment, watching the younger man begin to fall apart before his eyes. "M. Sauvage, how long have you worked as a private investigator?"

Rémy lowered his gaze. "Since the death of Stéphane Desnoyers," he admitted. "However long ago that was." The days of grief and sleeplessness and rage had blurred together into an incoherent nightmare. "He was a beloved friend of mine."

"I see. My condolences on the loss of your friend. It must be some comfort, then, knowing that so many intelligent men seek the murderer. You have solved other mysteries, M. Sauvage?"

"Well—" Rémy thought, blinking back tears while he searched his memory. "I have been more of a scholar until now. My interests lie in the occult, in mysteries of alchemy and the supernatural realms, but I apply reason and logic to all my investigations. I seek the possibility of life after death, but nothing I have ever seen or read has convinced me of its existence. No medium or mystic has ever proven the reality of, for example, the spirit world or the Philosopher's Stone. Those are the types of mysteries I pursue, Monsieur."

"Well." Baltard leaned back in his desk chair. "You are young, M. Sauvage. I am certain that life has countless revelations in store for you. In the meantime—" He nodded once at the newspaper on his desk. "Regarding the afterlife, you might want to refresh your memory about more of the Bible than merely the first chapter. Again, I am sorry about your friend."

Rémy exhaled slowly. "Stéphane never hurt anyone in his life," he heard himself say, not caring whether he sounded unprofessional. "He did nothing to deserve being murdered and mutilated and put on public display. And these other victims—" He gestured to the newspaper. "What can they have done in their brief lives for them to deserve a death such as this? Their only crime was allowing artists to appreciate and study their God-given beauty. Yet God allowed this to happen. So if you don't mind, Monsieur, I shall put my faith in other sources for a while."

Baltard fidgeted with the papers on his desk. "May I recommend taking some rest, M. Sauvage? You obviously have been working extremely hard on this case, and you will never catch the murderer in the ragged state you're in." Baltard stood, shoving his chair back from his desk. "Do you have any further questions? If not, Calais will show you out."

Rémy shook his head and rose from his chair. "My apologies, Monsieur. I'm afraid I am not quite myself today. I should not let this madman get the best of me."

"If I may offer you one more piece of advice, M. Sauvage? Let the police handle this. The inspector interviewed in a newspaper article I read promises that the authorities are doing everything they can. I am certain he knows what he is doing, and, if you'll forgive me for saying so, the police will not let emotion get in the way of their investigation."

Rémy nodded sadly in agreement. "The presence of emotion does not always indicate the absence of logic," he replied quietly. "I thought that surely a Romantic painter, of all people, would understand that there is no shame in mourning the fallen and remembering one's humanity during dark times. Thank you for your time, M. Baltard. *Au revoir.*" He strode to the door. Then he brightened as he thought of something, his hand lingering on the door handle, and turned to meet Baltard's narrowed eyes. "Monsieur, you mentioned that you never sold your *Hades and Persephone.* Is the painting still in your possession?"

"It hangs in my atelier. Go and see for yourself," Baltard grumbled, still scowling at Rémy's reprimand. "Take the spiral staircase to the top floor. Calais will see you out when you're finished."

"Calais. Unusual name," Rémy remarked.

"She comes from Tahiti, in the colonial islands. I met her in Calais. She has lived with me ever since."

"Ah." Rémy thanked the artist and headed upstairs.

As he turned the last spiral of iron steps leading into the bright studio, he nearly collided with another figure preparing to descend: a young man with raven-black hair and angelic features. Stéphane was haunting him already. Yet Rémy's eyes soon adjusted to the light, and he saw that the young man's eyes were a watery blue, and his complexion somewhat sickly and pale.

The stranger had a concerned expression in his weary gaze. "Are you all right, Monsieur?" he asked Rémy, then smiled gently. "You look as if you've seen a ghost."

Rémy realized he had flattened himself against the curved iron railing at the top of the stairs and was staring at the young man, open-mouthed and wild-eyed. He recovered quickly from the shock and regained his composure. "My apologies. For a moment you looked like—someone I knew," he said. He climbed the remaining steps into the atelier and took a sweeping glance around the art-laden room.

"I don't believe we've met, Monsieur," the young man said, slowly following him up the stairs to the atelier.

"My name is Rémy Sauvage." He bowed, crossing his cane across his chest. "I am investigating the Genesis murders. You must be Claude Fournel."

"*Oui*, Monsieur," the other man replied with a polite bow, his voice cautious.

"I believe I have seen you at the recent Salons. You look like your father."

Claude's features brightened. "You knew him?"

"Only by his fantastical paintings, and his portrait downstairs in the library. I never had the fortuity to meet him in person." Rémy pushed a lock of hair out of his face, feeling the heat of his blushing cheek. "I don't suppose you have any information or insight into the murders, M. Fournel?"

Claude shook his head. "I wish I could help you, but I know nothing, except that M. Baltard once worked with the Venus model. He is quite upset about her death."

"I understand. M. Baltard has kindly permitted me to view his atelier. May I take a look around?"

"Of course. Our lessons are finished for today. I have some business to attend to downstairs, so if you will excuse me—" Claude began descending the stairs. "It was a pleasure to make your acquaintance, M. Sauvage," he called over his shoulder.

Rémy wanted to ask Claude more questions, but the young man seemed scatterbrained and distracted, probably due to whatever legal trouble in which he was immersed, as Baltard had mentioned. He wished he had pressed him for more information.

Rémy contented himself with studying the paintings in the spacious studio. Most were painted by the master, with a few works by his students. Baltard displayed everything from rough sketches with subjects barely recognizable amid thick layers of paint to imposing canvases of dreamlike mythological scenes and delicate brushwork.

Then he saw it: Baltard's *Hades and Persephone*. The painting was indeed macabre, although it was more spectacular in person and infused with more detail than any engraved copy could convey. Thorns and flowers whirled in the painting's turbulent landscape, surrounding a swarthy figure paired with a young golden-haired beauty. However, Rémy saw no other similarities between Baltard's painting and the description of the Hades and Persephone victims in the morning newspaper.

Judging from the rest of the canvases in the room, mythological subjects were as popular as ever among the circle of remaining Romantics and their admirers among the Symbolists. As for biblical scenes, Rémy found a depiction of Salomé dancing before King Herod, with Saint John the Baptist's sword-bearing executioner lurking in the shadows. Everyone was painting Salomés these days, Rémy thought. Any excuse to paint a beguiling woman and a fantastical orientalist background, emulating Gustave Moreau in endless attempts to escape from reality.

Rémy peered closer at Baltard's *Salomé*. The painted figure in the jeweled costume undeniably bore the lovely face of the Tahitian woman who had admitted him into Baltard's home. Her distinctive features and proportions diverged from those of the typical European model, and lent Baltard's paintings the illusory but exotic aura favored by artists who fantasized about warmer climates and mysterious women. Rémy took another turn around the room, paying more attention to the female models' faces this time. Previously he had searched only for Stéphane's, but he did not see him anywhere in Baltard's paintings. There she was again: Calais as Circe, as Ariadne, as Delilah. She was everywhere.

The paintings confirmed his suspicion that Calais meant much more to Baltard than merely being his model and housekeeper. He hoped for her sake that his other guess was correct: the curmudgeonly painter downstairs was no murderer.

Finn was warily adjusting to her new surroundings on the second floor of Baltard's house. She had met the older painter briefly. She could tell he wanted to be kind to her, and, like most people around alleged lunatics, he was wary of upsetting her lest he provoke a hysteria fit. She could also tell that he was too furious with Claude for bringing her into his home to pay much attention to her.

She unlaced her scuffed black boots and lay on her side in a tangle of sunbeams and bedsheets, her face turned towards the window and her copper hair stretched out across the pillow. She wondered how long she would be allowed to remain here in this fine home and this comfortable room, and how much time she could spend with Claude before Baltard sent her back to Dr. Veyssière.

Earlier that afternoon, she heard the two men arguing in the hallway through the closed door of the guest bedroom. She knew the door was unlocked, and that she was now in a place where she could wander freely without a ward attendant hovering nearby or earning a beating or worse if she stepped out of line, but she could not calm herself to feel relaxed and content, here in the soft bed in the small jade-colored room.

Perhaps she was still lying in her bed in the asylum. She had finally lost her mind, and dreamed of an imaginary portal one night, and managed to escape through it into the safety of an alternate world. It was only a matter of time before she was captured and forced to return to a place where turning latches were followed by the scrape of sliding metal bolts or the clink of straightjacket buckles, and people entering her room meant her harm. Any moment now, she would hear the key turn in the lock, and the door would creak open, and the silhouette of the doctor's broad shoulders would fill her doorway—

The door latch turned.

Finn remained completely motionless save for her fluttering heart and one visible green eye, frightened and searching. She always turned her face away when the doctor entered her room. She shuddered and curled into a fetal position.

"Mademoiselle? Are you all right?"

It was a female voice, rich and accented. Finn turned her head and saw neither Dr. Veyssière nor one of his leering ward attendants, but instead a lovely dark-haired woman with a genuine smile. She was carrying a silver tray.

"I am Calais, the housekeeper. I heard that Claude had you hidden away up here. I thought you might be hungry." She set the tray on the nightstand, then peered down at Finn's face. "Ah! She *is* pretty, isn't she!" she said to herself, then sat on the edge of the bed next to Finn. "So you are going to be Claude's muse. Don't be afraid. He is handsome and kind, even if he is moody and prone to drinking. Oh—never mind me."

Silence.

Calais tried again. "I know where Claude found you. Listen. My name is Calais. I am called that because no one in France can say my real name properly. Calais is the city where I met M. Baltard. My younger sister and I were brought to Europe as part of a colonial exposition. They promised we would see the world, and would not be away from our family and home for long, but—" She sighed. "Here I am, years later. My sister and I were put on display in a miniature version of my village, like animals in the menagerie at the Jardin des Plantes." Calais paused for a moment, images of vibrant fabrics and teal waters briefly flashing through her mind before the bright colors faded back into her memory. "You know what that feels like, don't you, Finn? Being on display?"

Finn nodded, her heart still fluttering like a caged sparrow in her ribcage.

"Claude told me about the doctor at the Sainte-Geneviève. He said the doctor would put you on stage and show men how he could cure you with passes of his hands, like a shaman, and kept you locked up in a room the rest of the time." Calais slid an uncomfortable pin out of her hair and leaned over to set it on the nightstand, gasping softly when she noticed faint purple bruises on Finn's neck and shoulder. "Civilized men," she muttered. "What more can they do to us?"

Calais reached over to take Finn's hand in hers, noting the contrast between Finn's striking pallor and her own cinnamon-hued skin. She could feel the girl's heightened pulse. "Finn? Let us stay together, you and I. We are both two foreign women trapped in Paris, aren't we? Do not worry. You will survive. I have."

Finn squeezed Calais's hand in silent gratitude.

Calais looked up at the white plaster ceiling. "When Claude asks you to pose for him, it will be like being an exhibition again. But the artists will not hurt you. All you need to do is stand on the platform while they draw or paint your picture. Sometimes they give you jewels and dresses to wear while you pose. Sometimes they do not want you to wear anything at all." Calais was watching Finn closely, trying to decipher any messages concealed in her empty gaze. "Are you thinking about Claude?" She smiled again, trying to put the girl at ease. "All he thinks about is you."

Finn tried to smile back, but her figure and expression seemed frozen in place.

Calais moved to raise herself from the bed as easily as her corset would allow and looked at Finn's worn clothes. "I do not know how Claude wants to draw you, but how about I find you something else to wear? You would look beautiful in green."

Finn nodded and reluctantly released Calais's hand.

Calais visited Baltard in his library before heading to the atelier wardrobe to find a gown for Finn. She knocked, then entered without waiting for him to invite her in.

"Are you all right, Alexandre?" she asked, seeing his drawn face as he sat listlessly at his desk. She bustled to one of the windows facing the garden and flung aside a heavy gold curtain, momentarily illuminating her dark hair and throwing her shapely figure into shadow.

Baltard blinked irritably at the late afternoon light.

"It will be dark soon," Calais said in a low voice. "I just met our guest. She seems a little—disoriented. But I do not see why this doctor thinks she is mad."

"Don't get attached to her, Calais. She will not be staying long."

"Why not?" Calais sat in the green chair across from Baltard and laced her arms across her chest.

The painter sighed heavily and glanced up from his letters. "Calais, what do you think will happen when Claude starts exhibiting his paintings of Mlle. Finnegan? Someone at the Salon is bound to have seen her at Dr. Veyssière's hypnotism demonstrations. Plenty of artists, collectors, and critics attend those demonstrations, whatever their intentions may be, and muses are recognizable, Calais. The recent murders have made me aware of that, and you should be aware of it, too. It will ruin Claude's career *and* mine if he exhibits a painting of an escaped mental patient!" Baltard's voice was increasingly harsh, but he paused to take a deep breath, trying to calm down. "The last time Claude was infatuated with a young lady, all he did was draw her portrait."

"That pale creature who worked at the milliner's shop? I remember. He drew her as a siren."

Baltard snorted a laugh. "He gave her wings, claws, and everything. Then he could not understand why she wasn't interested in him after he showed her the drawing. He sulked for days." Baltard frowned and rubbed his eyelids. "As much wine as Claude drinks, I suppose we should be grateful he hasn't yet stumbled home from a brothel with syphilis."

"Alexandre! Enough."

"I am not getting us entangled in this, Calais. I'm sending for Dr. Veyssière tomorrow morning. After everything I have done for Claude, he can ask no more of us. I tried my best to properly raise Sylvain's boy, but perhaps I was never meant to be a father."

Calais remained silent for a moment before replying. "As I was never meant to be a mother?" she asked quietly.

Baltard stared down at the newspapers on his desk. "That is different. You know we cannot—" He heard an exasperated sigh and the creak of Calais's chair as she rose to leave. "Muses are recognizable, Calais," he repeated, trying to change the subject. "Models can become known, admired, and idolized until their deaths."

Another creak of the chair as Calais sank back down again. "Alexandre," she said gently. She knew him well enough to recognize that he was more exhausted than angry. She reached down and touched one of the newspapers. "With this madman loose, do you think anyone in Paris will concern themselves with an escaped hysteria patient?"

"Well, we shall find out from tomorrow's journal headlines, won't we? I imagine Dr. Veyssière will notice an empty room in his hysteria ward," he snapped. "At any rate, that girl will be on her way back to the hospital by then."

"After one night, Alexandre? One taste of freedom? She will never be the same!" Calais twisted her black hair over her shoulder as she sprang from her chair and paced to the door. "What if someone had forced you to send *me* back to the colonial exposition after we had one night together?"

"Calais—"

"That is *not* my name." She fled from the room, slamming the door shut behind her, and strode to the spiral stairs. She realized she was absentmindedly tugging at the tourmaline pendant of her necklace, which Baltard had given her as a gift years ago. His stubbornness was maddening, she thought, but she had not intended to speak sharply to him. Nevertheless, she knew Baltard did not understand the cruelty of shuttling someone as fragile as Finn back and forth across Paris the same way Calais and her sister had been relentlessly shipped across France.

Claude passed Calais on the spiral staircase later that evening, but she ignored his inquisitive gaze. "Calais, Finn is not in the guest room. Is she—"

"Go to her," she said without looking at him. "I helped her prepare for the atelier. I warned her what to expect." She continued her descent.

"Calais?" Claude gazed after her, confused by her sharp tone, then warily climbed the steps, tugging at his thin black necktie with one trembling hand and sliding the other along the smooth banister. His mind felt like a violin string vibrating at its highest frequency, a barely perceptible but constant tension that he could not sustain.

Finn was even more beautiful at twilight. She was there in the center of the room, performing a strange dance amidst the easels, paintings, and plaster casts. Calais had dressed her in a fanciful rendition of classical drapery. She wore a long gossamer gown in colors that shimmered from peacock blue to viridian green, with loose sleeves slit from shoulder to elbow, and it was tied at her waist and shoulders with emerald ribbon. A few thin ribbons and feathers were laced into her unbound hair.

This celestial being turned to look at Claude, and he felt himself fall under her mesmeric gaze once again. For a moment he was afraid to move, lest this living version of the ideal beauty he had envisioned through a thousand paintings and myths and dreams vanish into moonbeams. He wanted to ask how she was feeling, if she was comfortable in her new room, but such mundane questions had no place here.

He drifted through what seemed like heavy, electrified air towards the diaphanous vision and took her hand to lead her to the canopied platform and pose her like an ancient goddess. His personal deity. She stepped up backwards onto it, grinding her toes into the thick carpets covering the wooden surface. Claude released her hand and backed away, letting her drift into the shadows of the canopy. He found a stool and his painting supplies, then set up a small canvas on the easel closest to Finn.

"Step into the light a little further? There. Hold still if you can. I need to paint some oil sketches."

Finn glanced around the studio, her anxious hands twisting into the gauzy fabric of the costume while she tried to focus on the images adorning the walls around her: reveling centaurs and bacchantes, languid harem girls with hookahs, rebel angels falling from fiery skies.

Calais had opened the windows of the atelier once Finn was dressed. A faint breeze now fluttered the thin white curtains, bringing the muffled sounds of occasional carts and carriages passing on the street below. She could see Claude's bright eyes over the top of his easel, darting from her face to his canvas as he worked.

This is a strange sort of sanitarium, she thought with slight amusement.

The anatomical models were there, like the plaster casts and the skeleton in the corner. The stage to demonstrate her illness was there, but it was covered with pillows and exotic fabrics. The audience today was small, and the doctor was missing. The other patients were there, too, but they were all locked away in paintings on the walls. *Is Claude trying to trap me in a painting like the others? Will I hang on a wall like one of Dr. Veyssière's framed specimens?*

Dr. Veyssière could sedate her, but his medications could not help her forget all her years secluded in the sanitarium, day after day of eyes and hands and medical devices searing into her mind and body. She had been rescued at last from the evil sorcerer by this handsome knight, this starry-eyed prince who smelled of linseed oil and varnish, only to have to perform for him, too, whether she wanted to or not.

At least Claude was infinitely preferable to the doctor in both temperament and appearance. With his ashen features, the moonlight and shadows seemed to transform him into a white marble statue that had weathered too long in the elements, and the blue sapphires of his eyes gleamed from dark hollows.

Claude worked quickly, trying to find the accurate shades of paint for Finn's hair. It was a rough sketch, but he wanted his palette correct before he attempted to capture her features in detail. She stood, slightly swaying as if entranced by music only she could hear. Often she stared at the opposite wall, where Baltard's *Death and the Maiden* hung between the windows.

Finn's green eyes were listless, but Claude knew they shielded painful secrets. He recalled a passage from *Notre-Dame de Paris* in which Victor Hugo likened the human heart to a sponge: once soaked with despair, an ocean may pass over it without it absorbing another drop. Claude had felt the same way when the sickness claimed his parents. However, Finn's life in the asylum and whatever madness consumed her mind seemed to have left her in a constant dissociative state and imprisoned in an endless nightmare.

Suddenly Finn began to sob, wrapping her arms around herself and digging her tense fingers into her ribcage. Claude dropped his brush onto the easel and rushed to her. He caught her around her waist as her knees buckled and she fell heavily against him, throwing her arms around his neck. Tenderly he pulled her off of the platform until her limp feet touched the floor. She clung to him and wept into his collar.

"Finn, what's wrong? Is it too much like the hospital?"

She nodded.

"I'm sorry. I'm so sorry. But it's only me in the audience this time." Claude looked down at the white expanse of her throat. His stomach twisted horribly again, and for a terrifying moment he thought he might lose control of himself and try to kiss her neck, her collarbone, her shoulder— Then he noticed that what he thought were shadows on her body were actually bruises: thumbprint-shaped intrusions on her perfect skin.

"Finn," he said after a moment. "M. Baltard says I cannot keep you here, but I will never let you return to the Sainte-Geneviève. Dr. Veyssière and his men will never touch you again. Never. And I'll never ask more of you than to inspire me with your radiance."

Claude released her, making sure she was steady on her feet once she let go of his neck. He thought he perceived something different in Finn's red-rimmed eyes now. He hoped she was beginning to trust him, rather than staring straight through him as if he were just another leering observer at her hysteria demonstrations.

"This may be the only time we have together," he said. "But that is enough modeling for tonight." Claude retrieved his brush from the easel tray and scrubbed its bristles clean, hoping to avoid a lecture from Baltard. He looked again at the half-finished sketch. He had found the colors he needed, but so far the study resembled a portrait of Finn if she were posing underwater or in a shattered mirror.

Finn materialized at his side. He watched her eyes dance over the canvas while she silently inspected his work. "You deserve better," he said. "If I could, I would make you Salomé, Venus, Ophelia. I would show the world the mesmeric power you have over me. It is more powerful than anything Dr. Veyssière could conjure."

The Messenger was pleased. The Brotherhood was now nearly four spectacular sculptures closer to replenishing the lost beauty of Paradise. Almost halfway to the obliteration of this corrupt, sickening, mundane world and to the dawn of the glorious new one.

He was somewhat perturbed when one of the artists dared to mention that arranging the sculpture at the destination site would be particularly difficult this time, but the Messenger insisted. His mother and her consorts in the spirit world, now accompanied by the magnificent guides the

Brotherhood had sent them, had revealed the site to himself alone. It was fate that their work would be exhibited there. It was embedded in the very map of Paris, for the Eighth Day Brotherhood had already written itself into the city's history.

The Messenger watched the Fourth Day artist work. He was quite pleased with their Apollo. The model was a striking youth with sun-bleached hair and summer-bronzed skin, almost the same color as the metallic gold paint used to suffocate the oxygen from his body while he lay on the preparation table.

His arms were stretched above his head, bleeding from the puncture wounds where a golden lyre had been grafted into his hands. He would be draped in golden fabric, and once the golden spikes were embedded into his golden head, the Messenger knew that their Apollo would be undeniably resplendent.

It was also fate, he thought, that the Fourth Day artist happened to be such a skilled metalworker. Thus the decorative arts were placed in the service of the Brotherhood alongside painting and sculpture. Such an exceptional collaboration.

He turned to the adjacent preparation table where a young woman as pallid and lovely as the moon itself had been painted silver and dressed in a matching gossamer gown. She had finally stopped struggling, and her hands were now permanently fused to a silver bow and arrow. Her gilded face glimmered with silver spikes.

Great artists were destined to live forever. Indeed, not even dismemberment and beheading could silence the prophecies of Orpheus, who lived on as an oracle after his death at the hands of furious Maenads. The Brotherhood's immortality was inevitable, especially with a mesmerist in their midst. The Messenger's thin fingers twitched around his scalpel, impatient for his artists to complete their work. Once it was complete, the finished sculpture and its sacrificial emissaries would guide them into the Fourth Day of the New Creation.

August 4, 1888

"And God made two great lights; the greater light to rule the day, and the lesser light to rule the night: he made the stars also. And God set them in the firmament of the heaven to give light upon the earth, and to rule over the day and over the night, and to divide the light from the darkness: and God saw that it was good. And the evening and the morning were the fourth day."

—Genesis 1:16-19

Inspector Percier exited the Paris Observatory, black notebook in hand. He glanced back at the seventeenth-century building for a moment, squinting into the summer light, and strode to regroup with his men.

Originally built as an observatory for Louis XIV, the Sun King himself, the structure resembled a Baroque château with a modern dome attached to the east tower, which housed a massive telescope. Art was inescapable in Paris, and even the walls of the Observatory displayed relief carvings of astronomers' tools, measuring devices, and celestial bodies. With its bright limestone façade and rounded clear-glass windows, the observatory did not seem a likely place for murder.

This morning, Percier could sense that his officers' collective mood had changed since the morning they gathered with grim expressions commingled with fascination and disbelief around the winged corpse of Stéphane Desnoyers at the Panthéon. *Had it only been three days ago?* Percier rubbed his sore eyelids with his thumb and forefinger. The weary officers who reported to the crime scenes had grown increasingly anxious and somber. Even Alain, who had been so eager to assist him with mythological research, appeared to be losing sleep.

Alain raised an eyebrow when Percier approached. "Did you know that the four walls are oriented to the four points of the compass?" the young man asked. "I read that somewhere."

"Thank you, Alain, I'll file that little piece of information away," the inspector grumbled.

Percier's own temperament had changed. Although he did not want to admit it, a veil of shame had descended upon his psyche. He had just examined victims five and six. A fourth day of inexorable death. Six people were dead, and Percier had not arrested a single suspect. He was not convinced that a single one of his suspects was capable of serial murder and sadistic torture, not even if they operated as a group.

The press was a thorn in his side as always. Yesterday one journal had ridiculed the Préfecture's efforts to solve the crime, publishing a scathing editorial and a lithograph caricature of Percier and his officers as Odysseus and his soldiers being transformed into swine by the sorceress Circe, who was depicted as an anonymous figure hiding her identity beneath a hooded cloak. Not to mention the fact that his desk was buried beneath pages of false confessions and useless information from attention seekers and frantic civilians.

Now Percier's dark-shadowed eyes met the agitated gaze of the astronomy student who had stumbled upon the bodies early this morning. The stout young man nervously shifted his feet, scratching one hand through his short brown hair while the other fidgeted at his side.

"Monsieur Delamort? Inspector Marcel Percier. May I ask you a few questions?"

The young man nodded. "I already told the other policemen everything I know. I came to use the telescope before sunrise this morning as usual, but I noticed that the observation dome was already partially open. I assumed one of my colleagues had arrived early, but when I tried to unlock the main door, my key would not fit in the lock quite right, and the metal surrounding the keyhole was scratched, as if someone had tampered with it. I began to worry. I thought maybe someone broke in to steal our equipment or research, but then I went up to the refractor, and I saw—the bodies." He glanced apprehensively at the stark curve of the dome against the azure sky.

"Go on," Percier urged him.

"I just—stared at them for a moment. I could not believe what I saw—" His speech deteriorated into a stammer. "At first, it was—hard to determine.

The sun was shining through the opening in the dome. Someone—posed them there like statues—glittering in the beam of light like that—"

"Try to remain calm, M. Delamort. You said the bodies were in direct sunlight?"

"Yes, Inspector. Whoever did this made sure that the morning sun would be shining directly upon them like a spotlight. They seem to have calculated the angle—"

"I see. Has anyone suspicious visited the Observatory recently?"

Delamort shook his head and kept fidgeting. "Visitors come here every day. We have no record of everyone who enters and leaves the building."

"Hmmph. Well, that might be something to consider from now on."

"Yes, Inspector." Delamort shook his head. "I never thought I would see more bizarre things on earth than in the sky, but I have never seen anything like—what the murderer did to those two people—"

"It's all right. I realize this has been a traumatic morning for you, M. Delamort. Would you like to speak with a physician? I can have one of my men escort you to a nearby hospital, perhaps the Sainte-Geneviève?"

Percier refrained from mentioning that his men were heading there soon to bring the victims to the morgue. He, too, had been shocked by the condition of the bodies. The male and female models were posed back-to-back on the observation room floor, their limbs gracefully arranged in the Genesis cult's demented version of Apollo and Artemis. Their skin was painted metallic gold and silver, and their skulls were collapsing from the weight and force of spiked halos nailed directly into the bone. As always, those maddening numbers were embedded in their foreheads, 1:16-19 this time.

"No, thank you," Delamort replied. "It was just—a shock."

"Very well. I have no further questions. Thank you for your cooperation." Percier turned to leave, then paused as he thought of something. "Wait. One more thing, M. Delamort. Is there any significance to this particular date on the astronomical calendar? Perhaps a full moon, the alignment of the planets, a comet or eclipse, or anything else that might excite an insane occultist?"

"Ah—if I recall—" Delamort rolled his eyes upward in thought. "There is no particular significance to the date, Inspector. The moon is currently waning. Sun in Leo, Moon in Cancer, Scorpio rising. The fourth day of the eighth month, eighteen eighty-eight."

Delamort's last phrase caught Percier's attention. "And the fourth day of murders," he said, thinking aloud. "The fourth day of August. The eighth month. Eighteen eighty-eight. The murders began August first. We assume the killer intends to continue them, according to the days of creation in Genesis."

Alain, eavesdropping from the circle of officers, leaned closer into the conversation. "Then there are two more days, Inspector, since the seventh was the day of rest?"

"Precisely. We can only hope the killer takes a day of rest. So, M. Delamort, astronomically speaking, there is nothing special about the first seven days of August this year?"

"Not to my knowledge." His eyes widened. "Unless—"

"Yes?" Percier wiped his forehead with his handkerchief. The day was already growing uncomfortably hot.

"No—nothing special about the eighth day, either."

"The eighth?"

Delamort blinked. "Sorry, Inspector, I tend to think in terms of astronomical charts and ledgers. I was just picturing the numbers in my head. Eight, eight, eighteen eighty-eight. But there was no eighth day of Creation, of course. Am I free to go, Inspector?"

"Yes, yes." Percier dismissed the young astronomer with a wave of his hand as a growing unease settled into his mind. Seven days of Creation were described in the Bible. Yet if these murders were the work of a demented cult whose members were determined to desecrate the days of Genesis, what if they indeed had a fixation with the number eight? Percier's heart sank. How many more days of slaughter or sacrifice did this cult intend to commit? How many more gruesome dioramas would he be summoned to investigate?

When Percier finally heard Alain's attempt to get his attention, he wondered how long he had been staring into the hazy Parisian sky, lost in thought. He was already dreading the next sunrise.

As the hour approached nine o'clock on Friday morning, Baltard's atelier filled with young men setting up their easels and awaiting their morning lesson. Claude, arranging his easel in a corner of the studio, was even quieter than usual. His pallid features looked supernaturally white in the morning sunlight that streamed inside through the tall windows behind him.

A cheerful young Belgian named Thierry took the empty stool next to Claude. He immediately noticed something was wrong—not only with his hollow-eyed companion, but also with their instructor. Before each lesson, Baltard usually greeted his students while posing his models on the raised wooden stage. Today, however, the master paced back and forth before the platform with a somber expression, his hands clasped behind him. He responded curtly to his students' greetings. No model had been posed upon the arabesque carpets and colorful silk pillows covering the platform.

Thierry set his leather case of paints and brushes on the stained canvas covering the floorboards, wiping the sweat from his brow as he sat down. "*Salut,* Claude," he said. "Is everything all right? You look as though you haven't slept in weeks."

Claude finally tilted his head to meet Thierry's pleasant bright eyes with a sideways glance of his own, appearing as cold and impassive as a marble sphinx. "I have not been sleeping well," he said vacantly.

"I am sorry to hear it," Thierry replied politely. "Perhaps Calais is ill? If she is the model today, she's late." Thierry thought he caught a whiff of sour wine, and guessed that Claude had taken to drinking again. He shrugged and concentrated on arranging his brushes on the easel tray, wondering how the indolent Claude managed to remain Baltard's obvious favorite, foster son or not.

Baltard's three other regular students muttered quietly amongst themselves, impatient to begin working. Olivier, dark and aloof with a touch of arrogance, was regarded as the most talented of the five young men. He always claimed the workspace closest to the subject, which today appeared to be nothing. The two youngest students, Jean-Louis and Auguste, were discussing the Genesis murders.

"Did you read *Le Petit Journal* this morning? The police suspect the murderer might be an artist! Someone who paints or sculpts mythological subjects," Jean-Louis was saying.

"Well, it wasn't *me*," Auguste jested. "The murderer is probably just some religious fanatic."

"I heard that the police are talking to Joséphin Péladan and all his associates," Jean-Louis replied.

Auguste glanced at him. "I thought the Rosicrucians studied eastern mysticism and occult magic, not madness and sacrifice."

"I know. The police have found nothing, but anyone could become a suspect—"

They cut short their conversation upon realizing that the atelier otherwise had fallen silent.

Baltard had ceased pacing and stood before the empty platform, staring vacantly at the floor. "It seems Calais will be late this morning. So, we shall begin with some anatomical studies." He walked to the corner, opened the cabinet door, and dragged a life-size plaster skeleton on a wheeled stand to the center of the studio. "Turn your easels this way if necessary. Change of medium. Draw a charcoal study of the human skeleton, paying particular attention to rendering accurate proportions."

The students replaced their canvases with drawing boards and large sheets of paper, and the studio assumed a hushed silence save for the scratch of charcoal. Baltard drifted from easel to easel, correcting the young artists' dimensions or advising them on their shading. If anyone noticed that he was particularly critical of Claude's work today, no one mentioned it.

Claude's mind wandered as he confronted the grinning skull and delicate bones while dreamily sketching their monochrome portrait. Indeed, he had hardly slept after what seemed like an interminable nightmare about gargoyles transforming into mythical beasts and pursuing Finn and himself through the labyrinthine streets of medieval Paris, nearly catching them at every turn.

He had tried to read for a while in one of the velvet chairs in the parlor, but his relentless mind kept spinning with hallucinatory dreams. Finally, he had drifted off to sleep in his chair while contemplating the small painting above the sofa. It was his father's *Orpheus and Eurydice*, the dreamlike vision of the Thracian poet and his ghostly bride suspended in ominous starlight above the Underworld.

Sometimes Baltard claimed that he kept Sylvain Fournel's work prominently displayed to remind himself why he had agreed to look after Claude for the past decade. Claude still was uncertain whether he was joking or not.

His thoughts returned to Finn. *Has she awoken yet today? What if she thinks I have stolen her from one cage only to keep her in another?*

"Claude, your vertebrae are too long," Baltard said sharply, tapping the spine drawn on Claude's black-dusted paper. "Start over."

Claude nodded and clamped a clean page to his drawing board, praying that the hours until his next chance to paint Finn would pass quickly. He understood that Baltard had every reason to be furious with him. He rubbed his purple-tinged eyelids with blackened fingertips and resolutely put charcoal to paper, starting with the ribcage this time. If he could lose himself in his work, maybe it would take his mind off an unbearable mood that flitted constantly between remorse and exhilaration.

The grim iconography created by his hand sweeping across the paper conjured even darker thoughts. The escape from the sanitarium seemed distant and unreal in the morning light illuminating the atelier, where art lessons proceeded as usual, and he was surrounded by lighthearted men like Thierry who afterward would go about their carefree lives with clear consciences.

Claude's mind snapped back to the studio as Baltard, his hands clasped behind his back with false composure, circled his drawing board again and peered intently at his work. When his teacher could find nothing wrong with the delicately shaded skeleton on the page, he grunted his approval and flicked a handkerchief from his pocket. "Good. Now wipe that charcoal off your face. You look like a cadaver." He dropped the cloth on Claude's lap and paced to the center of the room to address the class. "Gentlemen! Good work." He glanced at the gilded clock on the wall above the wardrobe. "Take a break. Start preparing your palettes if you wish. The model for the figure study should arrive soon." His gaunt face and flat voice were unconvincing.

The five students glanced uneasily around the room while they shook the tension from charcoal-blackened hands and stretched their fingers, their eyes lingering on the familiar large canvases hanging on the light blue walls.

As he often did, Claude found himself staring at Baltard's *Hades and Persephone*. For a moment his overworked imagination replaced Persephone with Finn being spirited away by Dr. Veyssière, while the quaking ground opened a nightmarish pit of wailing souls below her feet. Claude shut his eyes and tried to shake the illusion from his mind, but the rumbling and weeping did not cease, and he realized it was the distraught sound of someone charging up the spiral stairs.

Finn burst into the atelier in a blaze of crimson hair, almost collapsing against the railing of the stairs. She was dressed in her grey asylum clothes once again.

"Calais has been kidnapped!" she cried.

Claude rushed to her side, nearly knocking over his easel. "Finn! What happened?"

92

"They've taken Calais," she stammered through her tears. "I could not stop them. I saw them too late, when they were already driving away. This is all my fault." She wept harder as the students reacted with gasps and stunned expressions.

Baltard grasped her by the shoulder. "*Who* took Calais?" he demanded roughly.

"Dr. Veyssière's men!" she rasped. "I recognized the hospital carriage as it drove away. They're taking her to the Sainte-Geneviève. I don't know how they found out I was here, but maybe—they thought—they were supposed to take her instead—"

Baltard released her and stared straight ahead with sightless eyes.

Claude felt a feverish shiver pass through him despite the day's warmth. His frantic eyes met Baltard's while he circled Finn's shoulders with his arms, trying to comfort her.

Baltard, conscious of his other students' stares, set his jaw as if he were turning to stone and glared at Claude with a stormy expression. "Today's lesson is over!" he announced loudly, not taking his eyes from Claude's. His students gathered their equipment with stunned silence and furrowed brows. Olivier muttered something about the foolishness of hiring madwomen as models, but kept his curious gaze upon Finn while he swept past her and descended the spiral stairs with the other young artists at his heels.

Baltard simmered with rage. "Claude Fournel," he said in a quieter tone. "You are to take Mlle. Finnegan, or whoever this lunatic is, back to the Sainte-Geneviève immediately and exchange her for Calais. If you cannot bring Calais home—do not return to this house at all."

Rémy closed his shop after reading the front-page articles rushed to the presses for the morning journals. This time the victims had been found in the observation dome of the Paris Observatory, their painted-shut eyes oblivious to the sunrise. The Genesis killer—or cult, as Rémy began calling the perpetrators—had murdered two models for Apollo and Artemis to re-enact the creation of the Sun and the Moon.

He—and the Préfecture—should at least have seen that coming, he thought.

Rémy was determined not to squander another day doing nothing.

Pacing furiously while tapping his cane on his shoulder, he racked his brain to figure out the Genesis cult's next move. He was too late to save the Fourth Day victims, but he knew that on the Fifth Day of Genesis, God created the sea creatures and all flying creatures. What ancient mythological figures might correspond with the Fifth Day of Christian lore?

Occasionally he paused to write a few words on a piece of paper lying on his bookshop counter next to a plate of stale bread and dry cheese. Rémy had scarcely eaten for days.

His long fingers swept the pen from the desk again. *Odysseus and sirens,* he wrote. *Harpies. Poseidon. Scylla and Charybdis.* What other sea and flying myths were there? What other tales of birds and flying creatures?

The Genesis murders were getting more ambitious. They had committed two double murders. The next could be a myth involving even more than two characters. He flipped through the Salon clippings despite having nearly memorized them by now. *Hylas and the Water Nymphs* by Vincent Morel was mentioned in one review, and Achille Lemieux's *Sea Nymph Abducted by a Griffin* had won a prize a few years ago. The latter subject included both an aquatic creature and a flying one.

Rémy had the feeling that one madman was the ringleader of the cult, someone educated and creative enough to plan murders involving various mythological creatures, and clever enough to evade capture.

Tossing down his cane, Rémy grabbed a Paris map from a pile of scrolled papers and unfurled it across the counter. Taking up his pen again, he began marking the crime scenes thus far. *Icarus at the Panthéon,* he thought. *Stéphane. Venus in the Medici Fountain at the Jardin du Luxembourg. Hades and Persephone at the Jardin des Plantes.* He took a step back and studied his map. Those three locations were almost points on a straight line from one garden to the other. The Panthéon was closer to the Luxembourg, but still fell upon the line between the Jardin du Luxembourg and the Jardin des Plantes.

Then there was the fourth scene: the Observatory, far south of the Panthéon. Rémy marked it with ink, studied the map again, and threw down his pen with a frustrated sigh. Nothing made any sense. Yet he knew the cult's work was incomplete. He looked closer at the monuments printed on the large map.

"Icarus. The Panthéon. The creation of light," he muttered to himself. "Icarus flew too close to the sun. Too close to the light. And fell to his death in flames. The Panthéon—once a church, now a place to honor the great men of France." Was Stéphane's murder a statement about the vanity of worldly accomplishments? That did not explain the rest, if the deaths were intended as warnings.

Rémy groaned, exhausted, and began pacing his shop again, massaging his aching temples with his fingertips. "The Second Day, Venus. The goddess of love and beauty, born of the waves. The victim found in a fountain with statues of lovers. The loves of the gods. Hélène Laroche's body cut to pieces. The division of the waters. The Third Day, Hades and Persephone. The rulers of the Underworld. The harbingers of winter and spring. Found in the Jardin des Plantes, posed with vines and thorny branches. The Fourth Day, the Sun and the Moon. Apollo and Artemis at the Observatory." Rémy angrily slammed his fist into a bookshelf as he passed it, wishing he had anticipated that location along with the mythological figures.

"The Fifth Day," he continued to ponder. "Sea creatures and birds. A murder location somewhere along the Seine?" Rémy dug his fingers into his white-blond hair, throwing his head back and staring at the dark paneled ceiling. He felt as if he were going mad. Paris was rife with fountains, and the river carved a line through the center of the entire city. As far as he knew, the Fifth Day location could be anywhere.

Claude and Finn sat in the hired carriage, their expressions as drawn and somber as if they were on their way to a funeral. Finn had calmed her weeping and was now sniffling quietly. She knew it was no use apologizing again, but she felt sick with guilt about Calais's abduction by Veyssière's men, no matter how many times Claude tried to reassure her that it was not her fault and merely a misunderstanding.

Her sleepless night at Baltard's house did not help her mood. Claude had escorted her from the atelier to the guest bedroom. He wished her goodnight at the doorway before retreating into the darkness of the house, which seemed as silent as a tomb compared to the sanitarium by night. She found herself lying awake and staring at the door latch, silently preparing to escape into her imagination if Claude attempted to enter the room. He did not.

Still, Finn thought angrily, she had no more common sense than he did, impulsively running away with him. Now an innocent woman, one she might have one day considered a friend, was probably in danger because of her poor judgment. Would Dr. Veyssière release Calais when Finn returned to him? Perhaps. It was certainly Finn he intended to capture instead, but he might have devised a new experiment or treatment for which he needed a subject who would not be missed by the authorities. Calais already may have disappeared into the Sainte-Geneviève.

"Claude, I need to tell you something," she said. "I'm not a lunatic. At least, I don't think so. I—don't really know any more."

Without a word, Claude reached down and took her hand.

"If I ever get out of the asylum again, I hope we—"

"You will. Finn, if these are our last moments together until then, I don't want to remember you looking so sorrowful. This is my fault. I will beg the doctor not to punish you for running away with me."

"That will not help us. We will both suffer. I *know* Dr. Veyssière." She lifted a hand to wipe a tear from her cheek, then froze. "I know Dr. Veyssière," she repeated. "And he knows me. All his men should know what I look like. So why—?" The color drained from her already pale face.

"Finn? What is it?"

"Claude, what if there was no misunderstanding after all? What if they took Calais on purpose?" She covered her trembling lips with her hands, her green eyes wide with horror.

"Why would they?"

"I do not know, but I doubt he will just hand her over to you." She turned to him with an earnest gaze. "Claude, I will turn myself in. I'll pretend to throw a hysteria fit and I'll ask my friends in the asylum to do the same. I will do anything I can to keep the doctor busy, but while he's distracted, you need to help Calais escape, the same way you escaped with me."

The fiacre stopped at the dreaded asylum. Claude's eyes lingered on Finn's face for a moment.

"Go, Claude," she pleaded.

"I didn't steal you away to lose you again so quickly," Claude replied. He brushed her face with gentle fingertips, then hurried to climb out of the carriage. "I will come back for you. I promise."

Finn watched him leave, giving him time to pay the driver and flee into the alley beside the sanitarium. Wrapping one arm around her torso and rocking herself gently, Finn bit down on the knuckle of her bent forefinger until the surge of panic subsided and she felt calm enough climb out of the carriage.

A wave of despair washed over her at the sight of the sanitarium's main doors. It seemed that fate was on the doctor's side, since that unforgiving entity seemed determined to entomb her forever in the Sainte-Geneviève.

Claude waited until nightfall. Anxious and distracted, he sipped on wine at a nearby café until he deemed it dark enough to show his face at the gates of the Sainte-Geneviève. He expected that the guards had heightened their vigilance after Finn's recent escape. Perhaps they were expecting him.

He wished he had remembered to bring his father's duelling pistol this time. Instead, he would have to make do with whatever makeshift weapons he could find in the asylum, possibly some surgical instruments from the operating rooms.

He peered carefully around the bars of the iron gate to the service entrance, his gaze automatically settling upon Finn's former window. He pulled away from the gate upon hearing the approaching footsteps of a guard making his rounds on the gravel path of the courtyard.

Where had they imprisoned Calais? How was he going to find her? Claude pondered the dilemma for a moment, leaning against the stone wall and pushing his disheveled hair back from his face. Dr. Veyssière probably had Finn back in his clutches by now. Despite her warning, Claude at last decided that he would enter the hospital by the front doors, on the opposite side of the building from the courtyard gate where he had escaped with her. There he would ask the doctor to release Calais, plead for mercy for Finn, and turn himself in before anything worse happened to the two women he cared about so deeply.

Claude felt like a man on his way to the gallows when he walked down the polished wooden floors of the main hallway to the dimly lit reception desk. The elderly nurse's inquisitive stare made him feel as if he were already on trial. When he attempted to explain the situation, he refrained from asking about Finn or mentioning her. First he needed to make certain that Calais was safely out of harm's way.

The nurse looked confused when Claude described Calais. "My apologies, Monsieur, but the doctor has admitted no new patients today," she explained, her spidery hand drifting slowly across the pages of the registry.

"A runaway girl just returned to us, mercifully, but she does not fit the description of your missing lady at all. Maybe you should try the police?"

"No—" Claude's mouth felt dry. Finn had been certain that Veyssière's men were the ones who abducted Calais, but there was no record of her even entering the building. *Why else would someone kidnap an artist's model?* A feverish chill racked his body as he suddenly recalled the dreadful headlines and his fellow students' conversation in the atelier. "I need to see Dr. Veyssière at once," he insisted. "It's urgent. Please. This woman's life may be in mortal danger!"

The startled nurse regarded Claude as if *he* were mad. "It is quite late, Monsieur, but I will see what I can do," she managed to reply. "Dr. Veyssière keeps odd hours, after all. Please wait here." She left the reception counter and bustled down the hall around the corner.

Claude waited a moment, his feet shifting impatiently, but soon he became too agitated to stay. As he dashed off to follow the nurse, he collided with a slender man striding around the same corner of the hallway.

"I beg your pardon, Monsieur," Claude said, flustered, and kept hurrying down the corridor.

"Wait," a smooth voice called after him.

Claude slid to a halt and briefly turned to face him. "Forgive me, Monsieur, but I must see the doctor immediately. Oh! But you are—"

"I *thought* you looked familiar," the man said with an odd grin, leisurely sliding his elegant hands into tight black gloves. "Sylvain Fournel's boy. Claude, isn't it? We met at the Salon last year. My name is Étienne Lacroix."

"Of course! I remember. I admire your work very much." Despite Lacroix being scarcely a decade older than Claude, the painter had already made quite a name for himself with his elaborate and decadent canvases. "Forgive me, M. Lacroix, but I must—"

"You are too kind, M. Fournel." The wolfish grin widened. "I assume you're visiting Dr. Veyssière for the same reason I am?"

"I—don't know—" Claude stammered.

Lacroix laughed gently. "To ask about drawing some of his patients, of course." He gestured down the hallway. "Come. I was on my way out, but I would be pleased to introduce you to the doctor myself. I remember seeing some of your work once. You have an enviable talent, like your father." Lacroix chattered on as he took Claude firmly by the arm and walked him the rest of the way to Dr. Veyssière's office, passing the befuddled nurse on her way back to the reception desk.

"Doctor," Lacroix called calmly, with a brief knock on the office door before entering. "Look what I've brought you." He guided Claude inside the office, then closed the door and languidly leaned back against it.

Claude took a sweeping gaze around the office. He found himself amid a sea of anatomical models, bookshelves, mysterious galvanized devices, specimens in jars, and insects in display cases. Finally, he located the doctor at one corner of his desk. With his hawkish features and slick black hair, he resembled a natural history specimen himself.

"Claude Fournel," said the doctor, rising from his chair. "I ought to call the police and have you arrested for assaulting my staff and kidnapping my patients. Plenty of witnesses saw you with Mlle. Finnegan!"

"Kidnapping!" Claude protested. "Then what do you call it when your men carry off a sane and innocent woman?"

"What are you talking about?" retorted the physician.

"What happened today, of course! Your men came and abducted Calais, a Tahitian woman, from my instructor's home."

Dr. Veyssière sighed. "Is that what Finn told you? It sounds like she must be raving again. That is what happens when you take a madwoman away from her necessary treatments. She needs my mesmeric cures every day."

"I'm sure she does," muttered Lacroix with his lopsided grin, still blocking the door. Claude had almost forgotten he was there.

"Étienne, may I speak to Claude alone?" the doctor asked irritably.

"Of course, Doctor. I was just going to suggest that you demonstrate your new treatment using chloroform. M. Fournel should know that Mlle. Finnegan will be well taken care of here at your illustrious sanitarium."

"*What* new treatment?" Claude whirled to face Lacroix. "And how do *you* know anything about Finn?"

"Étienne, perhaps you had better stay. Have a seat, M. Fournel," ordered Dr. Veyssière, gesturing to a wooden chair across from his desk. Claude found himself obeying the doctor's commanding voice. Perhaps there was some truth to the doctor's mesmeric claims, Claude thought, reluctantly sinking onto the uncomfortable chair.

Still smiling, Lacroix nodded his pointed jaw at Dr. Veyssière's window while he paced around the office with his hands clasped behind his back, then strolled back towards Claude and stood in front of him. "I was right here when you abducted her. The doctor and I watched you through the window," he said.

Claude heard a clink of glass, and glanced at the doctor, who seemed to be searching for an item on one of his display tables.

"Would you like to know why we didn't stop you, Claude?" Lacroix continued.

Now the doctor was holding what appeared to be an empty sack of black cloth.

"Because we knew you would return. Both of you. And this time you will stay."

At Lacroix's final words, Dr. Veyssière stood behind Claude's chair and began covering his head with the black chloroform-soaked hood clasped in his hands.

"No—" Claude struggled, lashing his head from side to side and attempting to rise from the chair. Then he felt Lacroix grasp his wrists with an iron grip, subduing him while the doctor yanked the cloth down over his face. He was aware of a chemical odor, pitch blackness, and then nothing at all.

The Messenger was somewhat perturbed. One of the members of the Eighth Day Brotherhood seemed reluctant to work with the new model that the Messenger had selected. Perhaps we should make another example out of any dissenting artists? Transform them into, say, Prometheus tormented by charred skin and spilled organs? No? Excellent.

The Brotherhood continued its work.

The Messenger rubbed his hands together with joy. How marvelous their Perseus and Andromeda would be! These two beautiful souls would look perfect amid their stony brethren in the gothic tower.

Attaching feathers with wax had been appropriate for Icarus, but the artists decided to use tar this time. In the ancient world, Perseus needed only winged shoes to fly like the birds God had created on the Fifth Day. Their Perseus, however, was covered in luscious feathers seared onto the young man's living flesh a few at a time. Soon they would live among gods and heroes again, in their glorious new Creation.

As for their Andromeda, her body glistened like the sea monster she so feared while she struggled, chained to a cliff, awaiting her rescuer! As delicately as possible, the artists fastened iridescent scales and shells to her body with tar.

At last, the Messenger motioned for his artists to dim the gas lamps and place the operating tables side-by-side in preparation for the séance. They gathered in a circle around the grotesque sculptures. Hands stained with blood and tar reached to grasp the others extended towards them.

"I shall now open the portal to the spirit world," the Messenger announced. "I can sense their approach—" He closed his eyes, breathing deeply and letting his mind slip into the familiar trance, his head rolling slowly from side to side. "The spirits are pleased with our work. They expend great spectral energy to communicate with us," he said at last, his silken voice cutting through the sedative-infused air. "Doubting their wisdom only weakens their resolve to contact you through their chosen vessel. Yes, the spirits and I sense your doubt. We wish you to come no further on the Brotherhood's journey if your conviction has faltered. Your disbelief will be your downfall," he continued, an edginess creeping into his tone. "Your doubt will leave you writhing in your grave. You will remain buried alive, no matter how skilled the mesmerist may be at placing your mind and body into the ideal state of lucid somnambulism when the Seventh Day ends."

One of the séance participants cleared his throat.

"Silence!" the Messenger commanded. "The spirits surface from limbo and commingle with the souls we have committed there tonight. Our Andromeda's spirit has pierced the veil between worlds and expresses her elation and gratitude. Yes—gratitude! As always, our sacrifice is ecstatic in the immortality and exquisite beauty we have bestowed upon her through the brilliance of our art, and for allowing her to become our phantom guides in the next world. Andromeda wishes to tell us—that we have proved our appreciation for her anatomy's perfection and transmuted it into fine sculpture, purifying her as within the flames of an alchemist's crucible!"

He paused and tilted his head, listening to the bodiless voices his spirit-medium mother had taught him to receive.

"Perseus's spirit now wishes us to remember our true purpose here, gentlemen," he continued, speaking slowly and haltingly as he translated the phantom words. "Which, of course, is to complete the work that God began. To become gods ourselves in the new Creation. We are *artists*. We have been the true historians and chroniclers of history since the ancient days of poets and bards. We begin with our imagination and we set our ideas into motion. We forge and perfect it through the toil of our hands and the splendor of our minds. Perseus's spirit retreats—" His grip became agitated, tightening around the similarly stained hands on either side of him. "Now what, gentlemen? Do we simply rest upon our laurels? Of course not! We continue to create. We evolve. That is where we differ from God. That is why artists must be the ones to complete the Seventh Day. These are the messages I have received from the spirit world."

He fell silent, lips parted, and drew a ragged breath. To all who attended the séance and dared to open their eyes, a dark mist of ectoplasm appeared to emanate from the black hollow of his mouth. The spectral substance drifted to the height of the ceiling and dissipated, fading into darkness.

The Messenger opened his eyes and released the hands he was grasping, heaving a heavy sigh. "The spirits exhaust me," he gasped. His voice remained high and reedy. "Yet, my brothers, much work remains." He motioned to two empty coffins. The simple pine boxes, recently scrubbed clean, lay open and waiting in the corner of the room. "Let us transport our sacrificial sculptures to the destination site."

The ritual was complete. Once both sculptures were chained to the tower, he thought gleefully, the subjects would be suspended in that climactic moment of the myth: Perseus's imminent rescue of the maiden. Yet the mythological hero's time had run out, and the relentless sun would rise upon the Fifth Day.

Rémy awoke with a start. After a fitful night he had finally drifted off to sleep at his bookshop counter, his head pillowed on his crossed arms and his stringy locks of pale hair streaming down his back. He saw through the gilded glass of his shop door that it was still dark outside. In a moment of heart-wrenching panic he glanced sharply at the tarnished silver and enamel clock atop the nearest bookcase. It was nearly dawn, and he had not yet discovered the location for the Fifth Day murder!

Frantically he looked down at the map still spread across the counter. He needed to find a location associated with sea creatures and birds. Perhaps somewhere on the Île de la Cité. The vessel-shaped island was surrounded by the Seine and situated directly in the heart of Paris.

He picked up his pen and drew a faint *x* on the island on the map, noting that it lay just north of the Panthéon, the first crime scene. *In that case…* Rémy began connecting the marks he had drawn earlier on the other crime scenes. He traced a straight line from the first to the second to the third. Then he drew another line from the fourth location to the possible fifth on the Île de la Cité. The lines formed a rough cross. Rémy nearly laughed. He knew where the Fifth Day victims would be taken. The answer had been staring him in the face the whole time.

Then he was at his front door, pausing only long enough to straighten his rumpled clothing and rummage in his desk drawer for a set of lock picks. The thin leather case had been pushed to the back of the drawer along with a few practice padlocks. The set had come in handy more than once during Rémy's occult research in clandestine places and private collections.

As long as he could avoid the policemen patrolling the Latin Quarter, it would not take him long to reach his destination on foot. He peered out through the glass of his shop door, wishing he could ask the officers for assistance without getting arrested himself. Satisfied that the street was clear, he left his bookstore sign turned to 'closed,' stepped into the narrow street, and locked the door behind him.

Rémy made his way towards the Seine, avoiding the *grands boulevards*. The main thoroughfares such as the Boulevard Saint-Michel were too risky. Instead he would take the Pont Neuf and traverse the Île de la Cité from the Place Dauphine.

As it turned out, Inspector Percier's reach extended that far. Rémy nearly collided with a young officer when he dared to turn onto the Rue Dauphine from a narrower street.

"Wait." A robust arm raised to halt Rémy's stride. "M. Sauvage, is it? You're the bookshop owner," the younger man said, noticing the brief flare of alarm in Rémy's eyes.

"I am," Rémy replied, attempting to keep his voice steady. The policeman looked familiar. He had a mustache and blond hair, a sandy shade darker than Rémy's. Of course—Rémy had seen him at the crime scenes with Percier. He hoped the man would not decide to search him, especially while Rémy carried a set of lock picks in his pocket.

"Another officer's supposed to be keeping an eye on you. May I ask where you're headed at this hour, M. Sauvage?"

Rémy's mind raced. If he had guessed the correct location, the police would only suspect him more. "The Palais-Royal," he replied, naming the former palace directly north of the Louvre, now transformed into elegant shops and a rose garden. "I need a quiet place to think."

"Very well. I'll stop by your shop later to ask how you enjoyed your stroll," replied the officer with a slight smirk.

"Of course." Rémy nodded goodbye and hurried north across the Seine, cursing his own stupidity and foul luck. The young man was probably on his way to alert Percier, who would soon determine whether Rémy made an appearance at the Palais-Royal, but he had no time to feign an outing there.

He reached the Île de la Cité and turned from the Pont Neuf onto the Quai de l'Horloge, swiftly traveling along the edge of the vessel-shaped island that would not be visible from the *rive gauche* or the Préfecture de Police. Then he could turn south again past the public hospital of the Hôtel-Dieu and reach his destination.

Rémy was certain he would find the Fifth Day victims at the monument renowned for its stone gargoyles portraying every flying creature imaginable, while also being surrounded on both sides by the Seine—the cathedral of Notre-Dame. After reading Victor Hugo's *Notre-Dame de Paris,* Rémy, along with countless other aspiring occultists, studied every carving on the building trying to decipher their alleged alchemical secrets. He had memorized every carved relief and every fanciful gargoyle from Viollet-le-Duc's mid-century restoration.

Rémy reached the north tower during that dark hour just before dawn. He doubted the murder victims would be staged inside the cathedral's gothic nave. The previous bodies all had been exposed to the sky somehow, either in outdoor locations or through the opening in the dome of the Observatory. He suspected he would find the Fifth Day victims—still alive, he prayed—arranged among the gargoyles above. He climbed the few steps to a balustrade of stone trefoils, finding that the wooden door to the tower stairs scraped slightly inward on its iron hinges before catching on its lock. Glancing over his shoulder to make certain no one was watching, he pulled a lock pick out of his pocket and slid it into the keyhole.

"You needn't bother, Monsieur," said a drowsy female voice that seemed to come from the pavement at his feet. "Lock's already broken."

Rémy jumped a little and looked down over the balustrade to see a vagrant middle-aged woman crawl out of the deep shadows of the architecture past the protruding stair tower, swaying on unstable legs as she stood and stared at Rémy with red-rimmed and watery eyes beneath a tangle of greying hair.

"I was sleeping just there, in that doorway," said the *mendiante*, clutching her tattered red shawl around her despite the warm night. "An old man woke me up and told me to leave. I thought he was a police officer at first, but he was wearing no uniform. I moved myself to the other side of the tower, where you find me now, but those men carrying coffins inside kept waking me up," she said.

"Coffins? How many men?" Rémy fished a coin out of his pocket and pressed it into her dirty hand. "Quickly, tell me everything you know," he demanded.

"Thank you kindly, Monsieur! I don't know how many, I didn't count them, but there were enough men to carry two coffins."

"What else?"

"I just told you everything I saw! I didn't go inside after them, though, not even after they left. They were dressed like gentlemen, but there was something evil about them, I could smell it on them—"

If she continued to speak, Rémy did not hear. He was already shoving the broken door open with his shoulder and bounding up worn stone steps to the top of the tower, gripping his sword cane tighter in his hand. So the Genesis cult transported its victims to the crime locations in coffins. If they had already left the cathedral, Rémy thought, he dreaded what he would find at the top of the winding stairs.

Gasping for breath, Rémy emerged at last onto the dizzying height of the cathedral tower. The wind was high and fierce even in August. He had visited the towers several times in the past while searching for sites described in Hugo's novel such as Quasimodo's hideout, Frollo's alchemy laboratory, and Esmeralda's sanctuary cell. Yet now the cathedral seemed as alien as the surface of the moon, colorless and silent, save for the callous wind. Paris was a constellation of gaslights below, the Seine a cold and distant sea. Few figures milled about on the parvis, the former domain of medieval *saltimbanques*, gypsies, and acrobats. Even the massive shutters of the bell towers' gothic arches resembled sightless eyes, as if God himself had turned away from the horrors staged atop this eminent place of worship.

Rémy stepped carefully along the narrow walkway around the north tower, seeking gargoyles that resembled birds or sea creatures. He knew where to find at least one, and there it was: the treacherous stone beast styled as a griffin. His heart sank when he realized there was something different about its silhouette against the night sky. He drew closer to the gargoyle, approaching what appeared to be a human figure chained around it.

A young man's body was nestled between the stone creature's wings. Rémy gazed upon the corpse, horrified. The youth wore a metal helmet on his head, and a mirrored shield and costume sword were attached to his hands with neat rows of small iron nails.

Worst of all, half of the man's skin was scorched. His flesh was blistered and peeling around the tar that had been used to attach various birds' feathers to his legs and arms and across his entire back. Golden straps were bound around his ankles, creating the impression of winged sandals. The numbers 1:20-23 were engraved into his forehead, just visible below the brim of the helmet.

Rémy felt ill, but fought to keep a clear head despite his nausea. So the Genesis cult had chosen Perseus for their Fifth Day myth. With two victims transported in coffins, that meant Andromeda would not be far away.

He soon found her. A woman was chained to another winged gargoyle as if waiting for a sea monster to emerge from the Seine. "God—" Rémy could not believe what they had done to her. And the *smell*— He gagged, but at the same time he thought he heard a guttural noise that had not emerged from his own throat. He looked at the woman whose windblown dark hair concealed her facial features save for a faint motion of her cracked and dry lips.

She was still alive!

Rémy was afraid to touch her and cause her even more pain than the burning tar and sharp-edged seashells had already done. He carefully pushed her dark hair out of her blood-streaked face, wondering how she had survived such torment, and cried out in anguished surprise when he recognized her at last.

"Calais! Who did this to you?" he heard himself shouting. His trembling hands acted of their own accord, wrenching at chains and jostling the mutilated body in futile attempts to release her. "Calais? *Who did this?*"

Never opening her eyes, Calais muttered something in a language Rémy could not understand, and then fell silent. A few tears cascaded slowly down her face. She did not move again.

Rémy stumbled away and gripped the tower's ledge for support, his hands leaving sanguine streaks on the stone. He stared at the gargoyles, wishing he knew what secrets their chiseled eyes had witnessed, these unmoving creatures who saw everything that passed in their city below. Medieval churchgoers believed that gargoyles frightened away intangible evil spirits, but they could not defend their sacred domain against diabolical men of flesh and blood arranging dying victims across their ridged backs and scaly wings.

Rémy looked up. Sensing a feast, carrion birds were beginning to shriek and circle overhead. Nearly sobbing, he released a final scream of frustration into the indifferent wind. He had failed Stéphane again. He had arrived too late, allowing the Genesis cult to achieve its Fifth Day of carnage. He stared incredulously at the heavens while the sun began to rise.

August 5, 1888

"And God said, Let the waters bring forth abundantly the moving creature that hath life, and fowl that may fly above the earth in the open firmament of heaven. And God created great whales, and every living creature that moveth, which the waters brought forth abundantly, after their kind, and every winged fowl after his kind: and God saw that it was good. And God blessed them, saying, be fruitful, and multiply, and fill the waters in the seas, and let fowl multiply in the earth. And the evening and the morning were the fifth day."

—Genesis 1:20-23

Claude watched a blood-red curtain rise upon a grotesque ballet.

On the stage, lithe bodies of men and women dressed as gods and goddesses danced around a marble altar through scattered pools of blood, their feet clad in red-drenched slippers.

Fog began pouring in from behind the proscenium arch on one side of the stage, followed by the black chariot of Hades, drawn by a steam-powered horse and accompanied by numerous shades writhing like larvae behind translucent screens in the background. The dancers surrounded the chariot and gracefully reached down to remove the lifeless body of Persephone and carry her to the altar in the center of the stage.

Hades wore sweeping black robes, a Roman breastplate with intricate metalwork, and a silver mask. He descended from his chariot to the crescendo of the high-pitched score performed by a phantom orchestra, then strode solemnly towards the altar.

Claude wondered if anyone else in the audience seemed disturbed or apprehensive. When he looked around, he realized that he was sitting alone in an endless black auditorium. No chandeliers glittered, no jewel-laden ladies whispered behind their fans, no gentlemen in fine clothes coughed politely into gloved fists.

Claude understood that he, too, was part of the spectacle. He resumed watching the stage and saw that Persephone on her altar had transformed into Finn strapped onto a hospital gurney. Hades lifted his silver mask, revealing the flinty features of Dr. Veyssière. Standing above Finn, he lifted a ritual dagger in one stiff hand as if to plunge it into her heart while nymphs pirouetted around them.

Claude opened his mouth to shout in protest, but no sound came out. He tried to stand, but realized that he was trapped in his seat, unable to budge no matter how valiantly he struggled. He could only stare at the stage with wild and desperate eyes. Then Finn turned her head, her fiery hair spilling over the side of the gurney and her glassy eyes meeting Claude's horrified gaze. "Claude," she said calmly, then closed her eyes.

He heard the doctor's voice next. "*Bring him to me,*" he was saying. Claude imagined he could feel the doctor's magnetic stare piercing his psyche.

With his eyes still fixed on Claude's, Dr. Veyssière plunged the dagger into Finn's heart as the music reached a feverish pitch, a sustained unbearable tone resonating in Claude's ears.

Claude tried to scream again, his body convulsing as he struggled to escape from his seat, but now he realized that his wrists were bound to the wooden arms of the chair with leather restraints.

"I cannot reveal his identity," Dr. Veyssière's voice boomed.

Claude felt as if a dark veil was being lifted from his face. He looked up again and shook his hair out of his eyes. Instead of the stage, he saw a blurry sea of black suits, slickly combed hair, and youthful but serious mustached faces.

"This patient was committed early this morning. He is approximately eighteen years of age, and—Ah! It looks like the sedative is wearing off again." The doctor turned to address the ward assistant holding the black hood. "Jules, please prepare the young man's next dose. Thank you." He turned back to his audience. "As I was saying, gentlemen, this patient is an unusual case. Although he appears to be a relatively healthy native Frenchman, his behavior suggests the type of psychological instability that typically we only observe in women, children, and the indolent peoples of the oriental races. For example, this young man already believes himself enamored with one of our female patients in the hysteria ward!"

Quiet laughter rippled through the audience.

"Furthermore," the doctor continued, "he imagines himself an artist, and has delusions of becoming a famous painter. Our tests also suggest that he has dulled his intellect with excessive consumption of alcohol, possibly including absinthe, and with occasional doses of opium. He suffered a head injury from a fall after a failed attempt to attack me. Indeed, he displays violent tendencies despite his seemingly submissive nature and delicate constitution. Now, gentlemen, what sort of diagnoses would you propose for this patient?"

"Erotomania?" one medical student suggested.

"That is one possibility. Yet I believe this patient suffers from multiple disorders. Other suggestions?"

Claude's head ached. Pain shot down the nerves running along the back of his head and neck when he tried to move. Words emerged as incoherent moans when he tried to speak. He looked down and saw through his chemical-induced haze that he was strapped into a wheelchair placed on the polished wooden platform where Finn performed her hysteria demonstrations. *He* was now the spectacle in the Sainte-Geneviève auditorium.

"Yes, yes," Dr. Veyssière was saying. "This young man's behavior and unprovoked vicious attacks do suggest psychotic tendencies. He also is prone to self-destructive behavior, such as the drunkenness I mentioned earlier. Those are all fine suggestions, gentlemen. However, I'm afraid that with his saturnine temperament, the patient has slipped into a chronic melancholy and homicidal madness. For all we know, we could at this very moment be looking at the face of the Genesis killer!"

The dozen or so medical students exchanged glances and began speaking excitedly amongst themselves.

"...Did you hear about last night's murders? There was a feature about them today in *Le Petit Journal*—"

"Yes! Perseus and Andromeda. The police keep saying they have figured out the killer's pattern—"

"The police are useless..."

They kept glancing at Claude.

"...Artists are all mad..."

"...He *did* try to attack the doctor..."

Claude strained at the leather straps again, but Dr. Veyssière gripped him around his neck, pinching a nerve painfully.

"Gentlemen! Your attention, please. Now, what treatment do you recommend for the patient?"

"Hypnotherapy?"

"Taking him to the police!"

Veyssière nodded sagely. "Excellent. Yes, I will hypnotize him, and the police certainly will be notified. For today, however, I would like to observe him here at the hospital to see what he confesses under hypnosis, since, as you all know, the repressed thoughts and deeds of the subconscious mind can be brought forth while in a mesmerized state. Should this treatment fail, whether he is deemed innocent or guilty of any violent crimes, he will be lobotomized and permanently accommodated in the care of l'Hôpital Sainte-Geneviève. Well then! Our time is up for today. Thank you for your attention, gentlemen. I will inform you at our next lesson how this patient responded to my magnetic cure. Remember always to respect my patients' privacy. I ask that you use discretion when mentioning today's lesson to anyone. If the Genesis killer does not strike tonight, we will know we have our man!"

Amid another burst of polite laughter from his students, the doctor turned to Jules and lowered his voice. "Take him to my office."

The ward attendant—the same man who had reluctantly unlocked Finn's door for Claude—roughly grabbed the handles of Claude's wheelchair and spun him around, pushing him down the ramp to the swinging door at the back of the room while Dr. Veyssière's students gathered their satchels and filed out of the auditorium, still murmuring among themselves.

Claude experienced a terrifying moment of floating through what seemed like an endless hallway of barred doors. A female patient being escorted by a nurse wailed loudly as he was wheeled by, as if he was already being mourned at his own funeral procession. His aching head lolled back to gaze blankly at the rhythmic passage of brass lamps on the pale gold wall.

At last he heard the click of a key in Dr. Veyssière's office door, and Jules shoved the wheelchair inside. His senses feeling slightly sharper, Claude heard an additional set of heavy footsteps, followed by the doctor's voice.

"Push him up to the desk. There. Perfect. Jules, the sedative, please."

The chemical odor and darkness descended again.

Rémy spiraled down from the towers of Notre-Dame, his boots nearly slipping on the stone steps worn smooth by centuries of use. He accidentally kicked a small piece of metal at the bottom of the stairwell and crouched down to examine it. It was a discarded nail, one that might have been used in a coffin. The cultists must have removed the victims from their wooden boxes here and carried the bodies up the narrow, winding stairs.

He was relieved to find the same *mendiante* outside the cathedral, still slumped into the stone alcove where she slept in the tower shadows. He reached down to shake her by the shoulder, pressing another coin into the woman's hand once she roused from her sleep with a surly grumble.

"Madame, when the police arrive, tell them that the woman's name is Calais, like the city. She lived with a painter named Alexandre Baltard on the Rue de l'Abbaye." The bewildered woman blinked, silently mouthing Rémy's words as she repeated them to herself. "And forget my face. You did not get this information from me." Once he was satisfied that the *mendiante* had memorized his instructions before turning back to the shelter of the cathedral, he fled from the Île de la Cité towards the Latin Quarter.

The Fifth Day murders had been staged above what would become one of the busiest squares in Paris as the day advanced. The remains of Calais and the unknown male victim would be discovered soon enough. Someone's eye would catch the glint of iridescent scales and metallic armor in the morning sunlight, or notice the unusually frantic flock of scavenger birds atop the towers of Notre-Dame.

Rémy could not help noticing that the Préfecture de Police lay practically in the shadow of the great cathedral. He wondered if the murderers were mocking the police along with profaning the Genesis story. He tried to will his steps towards the Préfecture to report his discovery of the Fifth Day bodies, but knew all too well that the police might consider this a confession. Inspector Percier already suspected him. If Rémy admitted to finding Perseus and Andromeda in the towers, he would be interrogated about how he happened to find the crime scene so quickly after the bodies were placed there. Then he would be held in custody and unable to continue his own investigation into finding Stéphane's murderer. That would not do.

Rémy decided he would at least write to Percier explaining everything he had learned thus far, and hoped his message would not get lost in the shuffle of paperwork that doubtlessly had plagued the Préfecture since the Genesis murders began.

After crossing the nearest bridge to the Latin Quarter, Rémy paused and looked back at Notre-Dame. As always, the cathedral seemed to crouch upon its island like a sphinx, although the medieval structure now guarded a new secret amid its gothic arches and watchful towers.

He strolled to the Place Saint-Michel and rested near the fountain, scarcely glancing at its familiar elaborate façade of colored marble and rusticated stone. He leaned against one of the winged bronze dragons flanking the hemisphere of the fountain and avoided the sight of the other bronze sculpture in the fountain's central alcove, where the archangel Michael stood in triumph upon the conquered devil, holding his jagged sword aloft and pointing to the heavens. The archangel's muscular winged body suspended between the rose-colored marble columns reminded him of Stéphane hanging between the pillars of the Panthéon. For one excruciating moment, Rémy speculated that the scene must have been darkly beautiful.

Sickened with himself, Rémy buried his face in his hands. He was coming undone with grief and fraying around the edges from the lack of food and sleep. Attempting to gain control of his emotions, he glanced up at the morning crowd of Parisian passersby. He was already surrounded by a sea of summer dresses, lace parasols, shirts soaked with perspiration, black suits, and veiled hats in the latest fashions. Everyone went about their business, oblivious to the fact that two more victims of the Genesis cult rotted in the August heat atop the cathedral across the Seine.

Certainly none of these passersby had the slightest clue that Rémy's life had changed completely within the span of a few days. They had no idea that the archaically garbed gentleman with the seemingly ageless face and long pale hair was completely heartbroken and utterly exhausted.

Rémy's own senses overwhelmed him as the city itself became too much to abide. The blurred flashes of bright color, the clamor of horse-drawn traffic and morning deliveries, the stench of the river, and the oppressive presence of a sweating populace all fought for his strained attention. Yet it was the mere sounds of nearby straining ropes and birds' fluttering wings that struck him with breathless terror.

He tore his gaze from the bustling square and searched the sky for comfort, but found only bruise-colored clouds with edges tainted red by the sunrise. Gradually the knot of panic receded from his chest, his pulse soothed by the sound of water flowing from the bronze dragon's jaws. He unconsciously began tapping his ringed fingers on his sword cane while pondering again how close he might be to catching the Genesis killer. As his mind cleared, he believed he had solved the enigma of the cult's murder locations at last.

Rémy strolled wearily away from the fountain in the direction of his bookstore, keeping a wary eye out for the policemen who shadowed it. *Le Jardin Sauvage* had been closed for days now. With everyone growing more suspicious of occult scholars, he thought humorlessly, perhaps his regular customers were keeping their distance anyway. He desperately needed some rest, but first he needed to consult his city maps and consider his message to Percier. Then he would continue his investigation alone.

He remembered that there was one place he could turn for clues. However, the police would probably arrive at the Rue de l'Abbaye before he did. If so, Rémy would lurk inside a nearby gallery or café until they left. Then, as reluctant as he felt about disturbing a fellow grieving man, he would speak again with Alexandre Baltard.

When Claude awoke the black hood was gone, but he was still confined to a wheelchair in Dr. Veyssière's office, gazing dully at the doctor across the large desk. The doctor was writing a prescription and paying him no attention. Claude turned his head slowly when he heard a sound next to him: a woman softly clearing her throat.

Finn was sitting in a chair beside him, staring straight ahead at the doctor as if entranced. Her body slouched in her seat. She was wearing a dingy white medical corset, laced over her blouse and secured with knotted cords, and a long white skirt with a dusty ruffled hem. Her head was slightly tilted, and below her vacant expression her limp hands lay open and immobile on her lap. Claude stared at her, but she did not seem to notice or recognize him. Her hair was half unpinned, as if she had just struggled with someone, and Claude felt a flicker of rage when he noticed new bruises on her face and arms.

"Ah!" the doctor exclaimed cheerfully. "That last dose was a bit strong, wasn't it, Claude? No matter. Now you are both awake, and we can all talk. Claude, I believe you are already acquainted with Mlle. Finnegan, my betrothed?"

Dr. Veyssière rose from his desk and strolled over to Finn's chair. He stood behind her and placed his hands possessively upon her shoulders, where they lingered like large spiders.

"I was Finn's patron when she danced at the Opéra de Paris. I supported her, raised her, cared for her, and gave her a home. Now she performs for me, and me alone. Isn't that right, my dear?"

Finn nodded, her eyes empty.

"Finn, wake up!" Claude said weakly.

Dr. Veyssière chuckled and began pacing around his office. "With their infantile desires and their insatiable lust for men's seed and procreation, women are easily led astray by a handsome face. They unknowingly bring about their own destruction and ruin the lives of others. Fortunately, Finn has come to her senses after some intensive rehabilitative treatment, and realized that *I* am the one she loves. She no longer even remembers your name."

"Finn! It's me, Claude," he rasped, finding his voice at last. The hypnotized young woman did not respond.

The doctor laughed again. He was in a much more pleasant mood than the last time he and Claude had met in this office. "Claude Fournel, the aspiring artist. You might say that I am a patron of the arts, especially the Opéra and the Salons. Tell me, Claude, what do you think of that painting?" He pointed to a spot on the wall at Claude's left.

Claude tried to turn his head, wincing as pain shot through his nerves again. Dr. Veyssière had indicated a small framed canvas displayed among his medical certificates and diplomas.

"I thought you might recognize your own father's work when you were here yesterday—although I suppose you were rather distraught," the doctor said in a reproachful tone.

Claude did recognize the gruesome subject: Apollo and Marsyas. The sun god played his lyre while his defeated musical challenger, the satyr Marsyas, hung upside down from a tree limb. The satyr's raw muscles were visible and his skin hung from his body in thick flaps as Apollo's consorts flayed him alive. The painting was undeniably his father's work, but Claude had never seen it before.

"*Apollo and Marsyas,*" the doctor said, striding closer to the wall to admire the painting. "The satyr challenged the god of music himself to a duel of instruments. Do you know what happened next? He lost, naturally, and here you see his punishment." He tilted his head, examining the details. "It is a fine anatomical study. Your father was quite gifted. Well, Claude Fournel, nothing would give me more pleasure than lobotomizing you and letting you rot in solitary confinement for the rest of your days, but out of respect for your legacy, I have made other plans for you. I want you to watch this world end while I place the faithful into mesmerized sleep. You will not witness the new Creation, but I shall be there with Finn at my side."

He turned to gesture at Finn, but she was no longer sitting in her chair. Claude saw a streak of red hair out of the corner of his eye as she sprang upon the doctor with the chloroform hood. She snarled and pressed it into his face with both hands, blotting out his shocked expression in the moment before the chemical knocked him unconscious and he collapsed to the floor.

Finn could not resist giving him a swift kick in the stomach with her boot, glaring at him coldly. "I should *kill* him," she said, her delicate hands clenched into angry fists. She rushed to Claude's side and unbuckled his restraints.

"Finn! You're— Never mind. What was he raving about? Something about a new Creation?"

"I'll explain later."

"Finn, I'm sorry. I should never have let you return to this place."

"Claude, there's no *time* for this! We need to get out of here before he wakes up." She grabbed his hand and pulled him out of the wheelchair.

Claude stepped a few unsteady paces before he found his footing again. "Wait." He darted back to grab a set of keys from the doctor's desk and dropped them into his coat pocket. "We might need these."

The hall was mercifully quiet as Finn carefully opened the office door. "We need to avoid the guards. Come on, I know a way through the auditorium."

They ran, cutting through the empty auditorium to the entrance hallway. With Claude's dizziness and disorientation, however, they were not quite fast enough. They heard a ward assistant's shout as they approached the front

116

doors.

Finn glanced over her shoulder. "He'll raise the alarm!"

Almost knocking down a bewildered hospital visitor, they burst through the doors into the dazzling summer light. Jules and another of Veyssière's men were at their heels.

"Which way?" Finn cried as they plunged into the crowd.

Thankfully a passing fiacre blocked the ward attendants' view of the escapees. The carriage stopped next to them as the chestnut horse whinnied in protest. To the couple's surprise, the passenger door swung open and a man gestured to them with a desperate expression on his face.

"Claude! Get in. Hurry!" he ordered.

Claude took a moment to fully recognize their rescuer: the eccentric blond man with whom he had nearly collided on the spiral stairs of Baltard's atelier. He took Finn by the hand and guided her safely inside the carriage, then climbed inside as Rémy commanded the driver to convey them swiftly away from the sanitarium. Rémy looked just as shocked to see Claude now as he did then. They all sat in stunned silence for a moment while Claude and Finn caught their breath.

Finn spoke at last. "Who *are* you?" she demanded warily.

"My name is Rémy Sauvage. I will introduce myself properly another time. You must be Mlle. Finnegan." He looked at Claude. "Alexandre Baltard said I might find you here, although I did not expect both of you to be fugitives. The driver has instructions to take you home immediately. Claude—Calais is dead."

Claude drew back as if he had suffered a physical blow leaving him ashen and breathless. Finn's tired eyes welled with tears. She stared down at hands in her lap until Rémy gently offered her a handkerchief. She wiped her eyes and crushed the cloth angrily in her fist. "I *knew* I should have killed him when I had the chance!"

"Dr. Veyssière did not kill Calais," Rémy replied quickly. "She was abducted by the Genesis cult to become one of the Fifth Day victims. Andromeda. I found her at Notre-Dame cathedral, but—I was too late to save her." He lowered his gaze. For all his scholarly knowledge, Rémy suddenly realized how little he truly knew about the world.

"The Genesis cult?" Finn stared at Rémy, horrified. "But—how did they find Calais at the asylum?" She gasped, recalling what the doctor had said about mesmerized sleep and a new Creation, and repeated Dr. Veyssière's words for Rémy. The scholar fell silent, mentally filing the new information into what he already knew about the Genesis cult. Their occult knowledge was more complex than he had anticipated.

Claude stared vacantly out the window, barely hearing a word spoken after Rémy delivered his fateful message. *Calais is dead.* The words made no sense to him. It seemed impossible that the lovely Calais was no longer of this world. He had seen her smile and felt her gentle hand on his shoulder only yesterday. Yet now she was gone, and Claude must avenge her. He needed to be strong, for Calais and for Finn. For M. Baltard and for himself. His imagination envisioned a radiant archangel in a hellish landscape, slaying legions of demons bearing the doctor's face. Claude clenched his fists. "Dr. Veyssière drugged me and used me in a demonstration this morning while I was delirious," he said tersely. "He told a group of medical students that *I* might be the Genesis killer. The police will be looking for us."

Rémy became lost in thought for a long moment, pondering this new information and ignoring Finn's red-rimmed stare of burning curiosity. "I see. I myself am a suspect, being who and what I am," he muttered.

"A suspect? I thought you said you were investigating the murders."

"I am, Claude, but not exactly with police cooperation. I hope my assistance is evidence enough that you can trust me."

"Take us back to the doctor, then. I will avenge Calais myself!"

Rémy understood Claude's simmering anger, but the last thing he needed was the boy acting rashly. "No," he said firmly. "I know how you feel, Claude, believe me. The Genesis cult slaughtered someone dear to me, and I want vengeance as much as you, if not more, but take some time to grieve. Speak with M. Baltard and do what you can for him. He is devastated." The carriage turned onto the Rue de l'Abbaye and slowed as the driver approached Baltard's home. "Tonight we should meet somewhere in secret. Where can a murder suspect and a couple of escaped mental patients hide in Paris?" Rémy asked dryly.

"The Café Hugo," Claude replied. "On the Quai Malaquais, near the Pont des Arts. The café is dark inside, and crowded in the evenings. No one will notice us."

Rémy nodded. "I know the place. Stay with M. Baltard while I gather some maps from my shop and keep investigating. Meet me at the café at nightfall, both of you. We need to discuss a plan."

Claude and Finn found Baltard slouched in his parlor chair, leaning his head on his fist. An abandoned book dangled from his fingertips. Claude tentatively approached his instructor, unable to see Baltard's face behind the hand that concealed it. When he looked up at them at last, they could see that he had wept his tears for Calais. His eyes were bloodshot and his body drained of all energy.

Finn stepped closer to stand beside Claude. "I am truly sorry about Calais," she said, tears springing to her eyes at the sight of his sorrowful face. "I know Dr. Veyssière's men took her. I looked everywhere I could at the asylum, but could not find her anywhere."

"Monsieur, I mourn her too," Claude said. "The doctor is completely mad. He mentioned taking Finn with him into some sort of 'new Creation.' He must be involved with the Genesis murders somehow."

Baltard was only half-listening. "The police were here all morning," he muttered. "Then they made me go with them to the morgue. I did not want to—I never wanted to see her like that. I don't even remember how I returned home. Then that bookseller Rémy Sauvage showed up as soon as they left. He says he found Calais at the cathedral but he was too late to save her. I sent him to look for you. You were gone all night, and with those murderers loose I feared the worst."

"Monsieur—"

"Monsieur, *Monsieur*," Baltard interrupted sharply. "You have never called me 'father.'" He pressed his fingertips to his eyelids for a long moment, then glanced up at Claude, seeing the shocked expression on the young man's face. Then he noticed that both his foster son and Finn were bruised, disheveled, and exhausted. "What happened to you?" he asked quietly.

"We—needed to flee from the asylum unexpectedly," Claude said, not wanting to add more misery to Baltard's burdened mind. "M. Sauvage arrived with a carriage just in time. We are meeting him later tonight to create a plan to stop the Genesis killer from murdering anyone else."

Baltard's gaze remained distant. "Claude, you were right about the horror of these deaths, but I did not listen. This is not the kind of immortality I wanted for Calais."

"Monsieur—"

"She was meant to be remembered as a goddess, an eastern deity, an eternal beauty through my art. Not as a murder victim." Baltard stood, letting the book fall to the floor into a mangled pile of morning newspapers. Finn helped him rise, taking his arm. He looked down at her, his eyes kind despite his haggard appearance, and covered her small hand with his rougher one.

Finn met his gaze, her green eyes brimming with sorrow.

"Do what you must. Avenge Calais." Baltard stepped slowly to the parlor threshold. He seemed to have aged several years in one day. "I must rest now. Take care of Finn, Claude. Do not lose your muse. I shall never be the same without mine." He paused when he passed the couple and briefly squeezed Claude's shoulder. "Be careful, Claude. I could not bear to lose you, too."

Rémy's eccentric fashions and long hair often made him stand out in a crowd. Yet as Claude had promised, he felt inconspicuous enough at the Café Hugo. He sat alone in a dimly lit corner, where he unfurled a well-worn Paris map across a small round table and anchored it in place with a carafe of red wine. Ivory-blond tendrils cast slender shadows on his face while his gaze shifted around the noisy room. A table of drunken students laughed merrily at the table nearest him, while an old man cavorted with a prostitute at the table beneath the framed frontispiece from an early edition of *Notre-Dame de Paris*.

No one paid Rémy any attention. From time to time he glanced at the two empty wine glasses and chairs beside him. He worried about Claude, whose dark beauty, shadowy eyelashes, and ivory skin reminded him of Stéphane's, and wondered if the young artist ever posed on the other side of the easel. Then, overcome with guilt and grief once again, he took a long draught of wine and purged the thoughts from his mind.

He was relieved when Claude and Finn finally crossed the threshold, their eyes darting furtively around the café until they spotted him. Finn had covered her institutional dove-grey clothing with one of Calais's black lace shawls, and covered her loosely-braided copper hair with a dark green and black scarf. Claude bowed his head in greeting, and Rémy realized he had been even more concerned about the young couple than he thought, despite his preoccupation with capturing the Genesis cult. Finn greeted him with a wary nod as they joined him at the table and gazed down at Rémy's map with morose expressions.

Rémy reviewed the information he had compiled about the case for Claude and Finn, pointing out the locations on the map and explaining their connections to the myths and Bible verses. "As you can see, the crime scenes form a cross when you connect their locations on the map," he explained, tracing his finger along the lines joining the Jardin du Luxembourg with the Jardin des Plantes and the Observatory with Notre-Dame cathedral. "One more day of Creation remains: the creation of beasts and man on the Sixth Day, before God rested on the Seventh. I think you will both recognize the place where the lines converge."

Finn peered closer at the map, then gasped softly. "The Sainte-Geneviève," she said, pointing to the location on the map with her finger. She glanced up at Rémy and stared intently at him for a long moment. "How do you know all this?" she demanded.

"I was studying to become a priest, years ago in Lyon," he said, pouring a small amount of wine into the empty glasses. "Instead, I ended up in Paris and became a rare books dealer in the Latin Quarter. I know how mythology and religion intrigue artists, I know this city, and I know its history. You must trust me."

Claude was shaking his head as he studied the map. "Paris has so many monuments," he mused. "True, the Sainte-Geneviève is near the Panthéon, where this all began, but the cross could be a coincidence." He looked from the map to the wine, but left his glass untouched. "Do you believe the Sixth Day murders will take place at the asylum?" he asked.

"The doctor is definitely involved somehow," Rémy said. "From what you told me about the chloroform hood, he and his men have likely been kidnapping the victims and using chemicals to keep them quiet."

"Of course," Finn said. "He sends his men out to find the victims and bring them to the Sainte-Geneviève in the hospital carriage, but the 'lunatics' inside are actually the artists' models. They disappear into the asylum and—" She shook her head and declined to finish her sentence.

"Then the cult meets there to complete the murders before taking the victims to the site in coffins," Rémy finished.

"How could they do that without the staff and patients noticing?" Claude asked.

Finn crossed her arms and shrugged with tense shoulders. "There are parts of the hospital that the nurses and patients never see, and staff who look the other way," she said. "The doctor pays them well to keep his secrets.

They know how I became his 'star patient.' They know I am not really a madwoman. They know he visits my room at night. Yet they will never speak a word to help me or the other girls."

Rémy's expression was grim. He realized that this young woman's ordeal was far worse than his own, and her thirst for revenge even more powerful. "I have seen the morgue," he said. "The Sainte-Geneviève probably has subterranean architecture that descends into the ancient soil of the city, possibly into the Roman crypts and ruins." He closed his eyes and turned away as a flash of memory interrupted his deduction. "The morgue is where I saw what they did to Stéphane Desnoyers. Icarus. The First Day victim."

Finn's suspicious gaze softened. "You knew the victim?"

Rémy nodded. "We were close friends."

Finn lightly touched his arm, wanting to trust him. "I am sorry about your friend. We have all lost someone these past few days, then." She stared down at the map and continued speaking in her softly accented voice. "I only knew Calais briefly, but I know she did not deserve what happened to her. She was the kindest person I have met in years."

Claude reached for her hand and clasped it gently, still mourning Calais but wanting to be stronger for Finn. His mind kept wandering to Baltard's parting words. Claude had always considered himself the painter's apprentice, but he now realized that Baltard and Calais had loved him as a son. He had held memories of his own father too tightly, becoming too quietly introspective to notice his foster family's affection. Baltard had been harsh sometimes, not to show the adopted boy that he was an unwanted burden, but to help him develop and grow as an artist. Claude was Baltard's legacy as much as he was Sylvain Fournel's. "The doctor will not get away with Calais's murder, Finn," he said firmly. "Nor will the others who did this to her." He released her hand and glanced at Rémy. "I know of one. The painter Étienne Lacroix. He was there when Dr. Veyssière drugged me."

"Lacroix!" Rémy exclaimed, tapping his ring on his sword cane and shifting his eyes in thought. "I know that name. He was one of the artists listed in Stéphane's appointment book. I remember his address. I have read those pages countless times."

"Then find him and stop him. I will deal with Dr. Veyssière," Claude said.

"Claude, I'm coming with you," Finn said.

Rémy shook his head. "That is not a good idea, either of you. Are you even armed?" he asked.

"I have a pistol," Claude replied.

"What kind?" Rémy demanded.

"An old duelling pistol. It was my father's."

Rémy leaned back in his seat. "An antique with one shot, then. Does it even work?"

"I don't know. I've never needed to use it."

Rémy sighed, unimpressed.

"I have a dagger in my boot," Finn interrupted, sounding almost apologetic. Claude looked at her in surprise. "The one with the silver and pearl handle. I took it from Baltard's display cabinet in the parlor when we were at his house today," she admitted with a slight shrug. "I thought I might need it."

Rémy was shaking his head. "No. It's too dangerous," he said. "I will go to the asylum myself. Lacroix may be there already." A perplexed expression crossed his features. "One thing bothers me, though. Thus far, the murder scenes have been arranged at locations related to both an ancient myth and the days of Creation. The Sainte-Geneviève seems an odd choice for the final day."

"True. What does the Genesis cult expect to accomplish from all this?" Claude asked.

"Dr. Veyssière said earlier," Finn said. "He believes that he can send the cult members, and whomever else they deem worthy, into a special form of hypnotic sleep. Then they will awaken into a mystical new world. The doctor said he wants to bring me with him as his companion." She shuddered and took a sip of wine, grimacing at the unaccustomed taste.

"Considering his arrogance, the doctor must see himself as God's new Adam. He claims to possess cosmic healing powers," Claude said. "It sounds like he wants you, Finn, to be the new Eve."

Rémy nodded, lost in thought. "Beasts and man," he mused, holding the stem of his empty wine glass between his thumb and forefinger and twirling it slowly. "What will be the Sixth Day's corresponding myth? There is hardly an ancient tale that does not involve one or the other."

Claude pictured a bizarre bestiary as his mind cycled through the ancient myths. "This time, the myth could be anything," he said. "Perhaps we should contact the police before the cult turns someone into a minotaur, a hydra, or worse."

"We cannot go to the Préfecture ourselves," Rémy replied, his tone sliding into cynical pessimism. "I am a murder suspect, Finn is declared clinically insane, and you, Claude, kidnapped a hysteria patient from the Sainte-Geneviève sanitarium. Meanwhile, the likes of Dr. Veyssière and Étienne Lacroix are well-known and respected gentlemen. If the situation comes to our word against theirs, Claude, whom do you think the police will believe?"

Claude leaned back in his seat with a frustrated sigh.

"We could send them a message, at least?" Finn suggested. She did not want to voice everything that was on her mind. Rémy was clever, she thought, but he seemed like more of a scholar than a fighter. Could he defend himself against the doctor's guards or the cult members? If they joined him in infiltrating l'Hôpital Sainte-Geneviève, how could she, a slight young woman, and Claude, an ambitious but gentle artist, stop a cult of insane murderers? She feared that she would only get in the way, but she could at least distract Dr. Veyssière and give Rémy and Claude some time to investigate—or a chance to escape.

"Finn, I have already written my theories in a letter to Inspector Marcel Percier at the Préfecture. He is in charge of the investigation. Assuming that M. Baltard's courier delivered it as promised, and the police have read it, they know everything I know except for the murderers' connection with Dr. Veyssière," Rémy said. He rose from the table and heaved an agitated breath, collecting his thoughts. "The cult could be mutilating its next victims right now. I must hurry to the Sainte-Geneviève."

"Here, M. Sauvage." Claude handed Rémy the keys that he had taken from the doctor's desk. "One, at least, should open the door to the doctor's office."

Finn crossed her arms, scowling bitterly. "I could have given you the key to the gate, if I hadn't left it in the lock when Claude helped me escape from the place."

"It's not your fault," Claude insisted. "M. Sauvage, take this, too." Claude pulled a folded page from his pocket and handed it to the scholar. Rémy unfolded it to see Claude's hand-drawn map of the asylum, with a few new additions, including Dr. Veyssière's office.

"Indeed. Thank you." Rémy re-folded the page, gathered his Paris map, and slid both into his pocket along with the keys.

"Wait. Maybe I should keep the key to Dr. Veyssière's office. I will confront him there," Claude said resolutely, nearly toppling a wine glass as he stood.

Finn's eyes narrowed. "Or kill him, if we need to. Before he hurts anyone else."

"Let's hope it never comes to that," Rémy said, glancing at her. He shook his head and spoke more firmly. "Do not follow me. I insist. This is too dangerous. I do not care what happens to me as long as I stop Dr. Veyssière and his cult from killing again. You two should go home to M. Baltard. He has suffered enough after losing Calais. At least he still has you." His eyes grew distant. "I, however, have no one."

"You have us," Finn said. She stood and looked up at him with a determined tilt of her chin. Gently grasping his shoulder, she lifted herself on her toes to lean close to his ear and whisper a blessing in a language Rémy guessed was Irish. "Please be careful," she added.

Rémy looked into her earnest green eyes and nodded in agreement, unable to speak. A moment later he emerged from the café into the heavy August night, silver gargoyle cane in hand, and strode swiftly in the direction of the Sainte-Geneviève.

Baltard's house seemed unfamiliar and strange without the presence of Calais. Several windows were open to the night breeze. Leaning against the balcony overlooking the foyer, Claude recognized the lingering scent of summer roses, the sumptuous flowers of Calais's favorite season. Without her there to replace them, the roses were already starting to fade in their vases, shedding wilted petals on the ornate carpets.

A floorboard creaked, and a particularly strong gust of perfumed air wafted through the hallway. Claude turned his head sharply, half-expecting to meet Calais's ghost, but instead saw the diaphanous figure of his muse. She had approached silently on bare feet, her skin as fair as her white blouse in the glow of the gas lamp illuminating the hall behind the balcony.

"I didn't mean to startle you," Finn said, noticing his wide-eyed pallor. "I couldn't sleep either." She glanced at Baltard's door. "How is he?"

"I don't know," Claude said. "I don't want to trouble him tonight. Knowing M. Baltard, he would rather have some time to mourn alone. Calais and I were the only family he had."

Finn stepped closer and placed a delicate hand on the railing beside him. "Do you remember your own family?" she asked gently.

"Yes. My father was M. Baltard's closest friend," Claude began in a low voice. "He was a well-known painter. My mother was his favorite model, but she painted a little, too. Mostly watercolors of landscapes and flowers, and portraits of me as I grew up. They taught me everything they knew about art and creativity. M. Baltard says I turned out more like my mother, 'distant and dreamy.' Somehow I think that is not always meant as a compliment." He leaned his elbows on the wooden railing, looking down at the softly lit entrance hall below. "He was kind enough to take me in after my parents died of consumption when I was a child. My mother died first. Then my father seemed to fade away, and soon both of them were gone."

Finn lowered her eyes. "I'm sorry," she said.

"M. Baltard sent me to school, then hired private tutors for me and continued my painting lessons. That is what my father would have wanted, he said. At first I did not like him at all. Whenever he came to visit my father's studio, he always seemed short-tempered and surly. I thought he had no wife because he was cruel and disliked children, but I soon learned that he saves all of his powerful emotions for his paintings. He can be a harsh teacher and has a blunt way of putting things, but I know he wants the best for me, if only for my father's sake."

"Weren't you lonely?" Finn asked.

Claude shrugged. "I've always lived in this district of Paris. I had a few friends in the neighborhood, but we drifted apart, especially since some of them joined the military. Besides, I wanted to let nothing interfere with my work. One day Calais came to live with us, but she became more of an older sister to me. She didn't speak much French when she arrived. M. Baltard introduced her to me as his new housekeeper, but I always knew she meant more to him than that."

"I wish I could have known her better."

The sounds of horse's hooves and a passing carriage broke the silence of the street below. Claude stared intently down at the locked front doorway, his shoulders tensed until the sound faded.

"Claude?"

"Yes?"

"Why did your father own a duelling pistol?"

"It was one of the few possessions I inherited. After my parents' death, our home was sold and most of my father's paintings were auctioned off to collectors. It was difficult to see his paintings go. After seeing them nearly every day of my life, it was like watching pieces of my past drift away and scatter across Europe. A few went to collections in America. The pistol was probably my grandfather's, though, and I was never allowed to touch it. I never saw my father use it. I only heard him threaten to challenge another man to a duel once, but I doubt he was serious." Claude laughed gently. "A much younger artist asked if he could paint a portrait of my mother, and that made him insanely jealous."

Finn smiled softly. "Don't you have anything else to remember him by?"

Claude shook his head. "I have daguerreotypes of my parents and a few odds and ends. Not much remained after the doctors and lawyers took their share. M. Baltard managed to keep my father's *Orpheus and Eurydice*, the one hanging in the parlor. He kept a small self-portrait, too, now hanging in M. Baltard's library. I was able to keep my father's palette and some of his brushes." Claude still gazed down at the foyer, lost in memory.

Finn stepped closer to him and leaned on the railing. Even her own childhood had been less isolated than Claude's, she thought. "In my village in Wicklow, there were always plenty of other children to run around and play with and get into mischief." Another soft smile as she recalled how grass stains and muddy dresses usually earned her a scolding before church or after school. "I helped clean fish and mend nets and repair boats. I think my father secretly wished he had strong sons to help with his work instead of two daughters." She paused. "One day he told us he wanted to become an artist, so he could earn more money than a fisherman and paint on canvas that wasn't attached to a boat. For as long as I can remember, he painted selkies and sea monsters on his sail. Sometimes our neighbors asked him to paint their sails, too. In the evenings he drew pictures of the sea, or portraits of my mother and my sister and I."

Finn remembered how she and Brigid disliked holding still while their father drew their portraits, but he managed to capture their likenesses a few times. He was a strong, weather-beaten man who smelled of the sea, with a short red beard and large rough hands that were stained black with charcoal as he sketched on thin sheets of paper by the red-orange glow of the firelight in their cottage.

For the first time in many years, recalling the image of her father as an artist, Finn realized she missed him. She had always considered him selfish for uprooting her family and moving them to Dublin, where he thought he could find better work and hire a drawing master. The former was true, yet city life meant factory work, dirt, disease, and danger for a young girl. In their cramped and noisy city apartment, Finn missed the sound of the sea, the rocky coastline of her childhood in the southeast, and the emerald hills where she could run freely and breathe clean air. She missed the dances at the public house and trying to make her small feet keep up with blind old Diarmuid Byrne's fiddle tunes.

"One day after coming home from his art lesson in Dublin, my father started talking about Paris," she continued after a moment of reverie. "His teacher believed he had genuine talent, and told him that all the best artists and patrons and teachers can be found in Paris. If he wants to be a real artist, he said, he needs to travel there. So for months we saved our money for his passage to France and for the lessons he wanted to take at the École des Beaux-Arts once he arrived. I never wanted him to go."

When he became a famous artist, Finn's father promised her, taking her onto his knees by the stove one evening, he would buy her and her sister and her mother fashionable gowns and a proper house. Then he traveled to Paris alone, taking everything he owned and his portfolio, intending to impress his new instructors but leaving a void in his family's life.

"He left us for months, but he sent for us at last." Her heart ached at the memories of her family waving goodbye to him at Dublin harbor, and their joyous reunion at the Paris train station after what seemed like an endless journey across land and sea.

Finn realized that Claude was looking at her intently. "We soon realized that life in Paris as an immigrant was not what he had promised. We were poor, living in a garret in Montmartre. My father died of cholera when I was thirteen. My mother and sister may be dead. At least, Dr. Veyssière told me they are. I cannot even remember how long ago."

"Well, he probably lied to you. I'll help you find them, after we deal with the doctor," Claude promised in a somber tone.

Finn shrugged. "Perhaps. I'm grateful for the offer, Claude, but I'm afraid they're lost to me forever." Her fingertips fidgeted on the railing, and for a moment she regretted the loss of her mother's rosary, left behind in her steamer trunk at the sanitarium.

Claude reached out to touch a lock of her hair, but pulled his hand away when she flinched. "Sorry." He paused. "If your mother and sister look anything like you, they should be easy enough to find."

"I don't know." Finn's green eyes grew sorrowful. "My mother worked hard to keep us out of the brothels and cabarets, but we didn't earn enough to pay the rent, so one day she took my sister and I to a ballet audition at the new opera house."

"I see."

"It was a long walk to the Opéra, especially in the winter, and the rehearsals were long, but we needed my patron's money."

"Dr. Veyssière." Claude glanced at her.

Finn nodded. "One day he came into my dressing room after my performance. I refused his advances, so he declared me insane. Everyone believed him."

Finn's mind tormented her once again with the memory of how frantically she fought him, kicking and scratching and biting, until the commotion of overturned chairs and tulle-covered dress forms crashing to the floor drew the attention of the ballet director and several other witnesses. Yet the doctor only wrapped his iron grip tighter around her frail torso and gripped her head in his enormous hand, pressing his thumb and forefinger into the pressure points behind her jawbone to choke and silence her. She remembered a drop of red falling onto her arm as she struggled against his grip. Her fingernails had drawn blood from his cheek. *Please remain calm! The situation is under control, everyone,* he had announced, his voice ringing in her ear. *I am a physician, and this girl has the most severe case of hysteria I have ever seen. I must take her to my sanitarium at once and restrain her before she assaults anyone else!*

"Dr. Veyssière was a respected French gentleman and opera patron, and I was nothing but a madwoman and a foreigner," she said sadly. "You can probably guess the rest of my story."

Claude's grip tightened on the railing. "The hysteria demonstrations?"

Another forlorn smile. "I was a trained performer, Claude. We both knew he was a complete charlatan, but one day while he was trying to hypnotize me out of a 'hysteria fit' and I was tired of being punished for not cooperating, I realized I could make him truly believe he had the gift of mesmerism—" With a sharp intake of breath, Finn wrapped her arms around herself and shivered despite the heat. "What if this *is* all my fault? These murders would never have happened if I hadn't convinced the doctor that he was a powerful man—"

"No! You were trying to protect yourself. You had no idea what he would become," Claude reassured her. "You were right. We should have killed him when we had the chance."

"Claude—"

"Finn, I don't care what you've done in the past, or what Dr. Veyssière did to you. We'll leave Paris if necessary to get you away from him. You will have a new life." He moved as if to take her in his arms, then shyly drew back.

Finn glanced at him. "You don't seem like the type of person who would rescue a damsel in distress or a mad girl from an asylum," she said with a faint smile.

"I wasn't. Until I saw you."

She lowered her eyes. "People are being murdered, Claude."

"I know. I have a bad feeling about tonight. If there will truly be a murder at the Sainte-Geneviève, I think the police should know."

"We can't go to the police. They will not listen to us. Rémy Sauvage was right about that, but I'm worried about him going to the Sainte-Geneviève alone. We should help him, Claude." She withdrew from the balcony into the hall. "I would rather die than spend the rest of my life knowing I could have stopped a murder."

"Wait—" Claude caught her hand and pulled her to him, embracing her tightly, feeling her heart flutter against his chest. "I will go," he said. "Stay here with M. Baltard. You are a braver person than I, but I won't let anything happen to you, because—" He paused, and the words fell clumsily from his lips: "I love you."

Finn disentangled herself from his arms, feeling a sudden rise of panic as the day's events and emotions spun dizzily through her mind. "You know nothing about me, Claude. This is not the time to speak of such things. Not when people are dying while we do nothing. People like Calais! I know I'm the one who lived in an asylum, Claude, but sometimes I think you're more insane than any lunatic I ever met at the Saint-Geneviève!" She shoved herself away from him and headed towards the stairs. "I'm going with you."

"Perhaps I *am* mad, but since we both desire revenge against Dr. Veyssière, and considering what he's done to the only family I have left, I think we should face him together. There is no madness in that. Is there?"

Finn shook her disheveled head, but did not turn around as she strode downstairs with determined steps. Claude remained on the landing for a moment and glanced back towards Baltard's room before he followed her, painfully aware of the weight of the duelling pistol in his pocket.

The asylum by night looked even grimmer than Rémy remembered. He once enjoyed strolling through Paris with Stéphane on summer nights, watching twilight soften the city's edges and lampposts cast its façades into light and shadow as the sky turned a shade painters would call ultramarine, before darkening to midnight blue. The beauty of nocturnal Paris did nothing to quell Rémy's apprehension as he silently circled the Sainte-Geneviève. He contemplated slipping in through the main entrance and inventing a relative to call upon, but visitation hours were over. Besides, he wanted to explore the place.

The darkness was nearly palpable in the narrow street beside the sanitarium. Rémy imagined he could feel its gloom enveloping him as he stepped through the humid night air, like an ominous premonition drifting forth from the recesses of his mind. Walking slowly past the walled-in courtyard, he paused to peer around the corner. He felt his veins freeze and his heart leap at a sudden flash of movement in the alley behind the asylum, illuminated by gaslight shining through the courtyard gate. His breath calmed once he realized it was merely a rat fishing something out of a fetid gutter. Jumping at his own shadow would get him nowhere, he thought, and pressed on.

Then the shadows changed. Instead of stark bars slanting across the cobblestones from the gate, a female figure was now silhouetted there, blocking the light and further darkening the alley. The shadow moved, and then Rémy heard the *rat-tat-tat* of something being dragged back and forth across the bars. The sound made Rémy uneasy, reminding him of clacking bones and clattering teeth.

Shaking off his sense of dread, Rémy decided to take his chances. He did not know what to expect from the Sainte-Geneviève, but after hearing Finn's account of the place, perhaps another patient would be willing to help him. He summoned his courage and turned cautiously down the darker alley.

Indeed, a young woman was standing near the iron gate, idly dragging a stick along the iron bars. She fell into step beside Rémy as he passed, shadowing him silently. Rémy gave her a sideways glance and saw dark hair tied back into a scraggly braid, its particular shade uncertain against the light. She had intelligent dark eyes, a scattering of freckles across the bridge of her nose, and a tight-lipped mischievous smile. She swung the stick over her shoulder as if to mock how Rémy carried his cane.

"Evenin,' *monsieur*. Come to gawk at the mad girls?" she asked in a teasing voice with an English accent. "Or are you lookin' for Finn, too?"

Rémy nearly stumbled over a cobblestone. His startled glance gave him away.

The girl's smile widened. "She's not here, you know," she chattered on, swinging the stick by her side. "She ran away with her young man. She's gone for good. Why, were you expecting a performance? That's all it is, you know. We're all wondering who's going to be the doctor's new star patient." She rolled her eyes at the phrase. "Too bad he's been neglecting the rest of us. He's too obsessed with Finn to pay us much attention."

A high-pitched giggle startled Rémy anew. Peering into the courtyard past the impish brunette, he saw a skeletal blonde girl sitting on a stone bench surrounded by pink roses and vines. Behind her, closer to the building, stood an uneven gathering of headstones within an iron fence. It all seemed an otherworldly vision, like a scene in a William Blake engraving. Perhaps the girl's accent had reminded him of the English poet and artist. Lines from one of Blake's poems began circling through Rémy's mind:

And I saw it was filled with graves,
And tombstones where flowers should be;
And Priests in black gowns were walking their rounds,
And binding with briars my joys and desires…

The girl followed Rémy's gaze towards the blonde. "Poor Marie." She shrugged. "She sits there every day we're allowed outside. We think she's got her eye on the man who brings the coffins to the carriage house."

"Coffins?" Rémy repeated absently. The word lingered in Rémy's mind, until he found himself staring at the wooden double doors of the carriage house in the corner of the courtyard. Dr. Veyssière probably had his coffins delivered from the city undertakers in the nineteenth *arrondissement*. Rémy had become all too familiar with undertakers and their long black wagons while arranging Stéphane's funeral on behalf of the Desnoyers family earlier today. He wondered why the doctor needed the coffins delivered to the carriage house. Certainly the sanitarium must have storage rooms, he thought, although he could not remember seeing any empty coffins in the morgue.

"Coffins in. Coffins out." The girl was watching him closely, her mouth set in a wry smile. "Some of the coffins stay here, though, if the family doesn't come for 'em." She glanced at the pitiful cemetery. "Some of 'em go elsewhere. Lately they've been taking 'em only while it's dark."

"Elsewhere? How often?"

"Every night this week. I hear the coffin wagons leaving and I watch from my window, wonderin' when they're bringin' mine. I don't sleep much. Guess the doctor doesn't want us to know when one of us dies." She shrugged again. "Wouldn't bother me. Seems like that's the only way out. Unless you're pretty like Finn and someone steals you away."

"You knew Finn, then?"

"Knew?" The girl stopped abruptly. "Is she dead?"

"No, but she will be in grave danger if Dr. Veyssière catches her again. Can you help me?"

She resumed her stride, her expression now thoughtful. "Yes. I know Finn. The doctor's star patient, she was. Ran away with a raven-haired boy. Pity. She was one of the nice ones."

"Listen, if you consider her a friend, she needs your help. I need to get inside the asylum and find out what the doctor is planning to do with her and the others."

He looked at her then, and noted the intelligence and wit in her dark eyes. Not mad at all. "Maybe I can help you escape, too," he offered.

The girl shook her head, expressionless. "I've got nowhere to go. I'm not a dreamer like Finn. As the doctor's always remindin' us, this place is better than the street. Safer locked up than locked out. An' since you want in—" She lashed out abruptly and snatched Rémy's silver cane out of his grip, her wiry arms surprisingly strong. The cane disappeared into the folds of her grey skirt.

"You want it back?" she taunted him. "Then come to the carriage house door tonight. Go to the main entrance and tell Sister Thérèse you left something in the courtyard while visiting your niece." She canted her head towards the blonde, whose straight hair was nearly as fair as Rémy's. "Her name's Marie. The doors latch from the inside, but I'll manage. Always do. An' when you see Finn, tell 'er Violet misses 'er."

The black shape of a nun bustled towards them from the center of the courtyard, apologizing to Rémy as she gently placed her withered hands on the girl's shoulders. "My apologies, Monsieur, is this young lady bothering you?" she asked, giving Rémy a disapproving glance nevertheless. "She's been unwell. This is a hospital, you know."

Violet kept her gaze steady with Rémy's and the faint smile on her lips as she turned away, letting her nurse guide her away from the gate with the silver cane still concealed in her skirts. Rémy backed away from the iron bars, shuddering when the pale-haired wraith in the shadows giggled again.

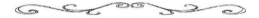

The Messenger was especially pleased with the Brotherhood's Sixth Day sculptures. The spirits were guiding them ever closer to the dawn of the new Creation.

They were fortunate, he thought, to have an underground atelier with ready access to surgical tools and scientific chemicals, and a clandestine one. No one who was not initiated into the secrets of the Eighth Day Brotherhood would understand the dire necessity of their resplendent works of living sculpture.

Tonight's sculpture had required the sacrifice of not only two models— two humans who had willingly placed themselves in the service of the arts by their choice of profession—but also the inclusion of fine taxidermy beasts created by one of the Brotherhood's artists.

Preparing the young man's body was straightforward enough. He was dressed in a classical Greek traveling tunic, and his flesh was lacerated into ribbons using the fearsome claws of one of the taxidermy creatures, a sleek and beautiful lioness.

The preparation of the female model was more ambitious. Using surgical tools and saws, her body was severed in half at the waist, as was that of the lioness. The Messenger watched intently as the animal's hind legs were stitched to the young woman's torso. The slippery river of blood made their work challenging, but the disparate bodies were joined at last.

The artist who designed the Sixth Day sculpture had selected the wings of a swan to attach to the woman's back. They were stitched into her skin with such surgical precision that the wings seemed to surge forth from her shoulder blades. Small wisps of white feathers drifted down into bleeding flesh while the artists worked.

The Messenger could not have been more pleased. Now that the models' souls hovered between two worlds, between life and death, he announced that the sacrifices were ready for the séance. Afterward, they would be transported to the destination site. He could not wait for the world to admire their *Oedipus and the Sphinx*.

Coffins in, coffins out. Violet's words echoed in Rémy's mind like a morbid children's rhyme as he approached the carriage house in the Sainte-Geneviève courtyard. A wilting rose from one of the thorny bushes near the asylum cemetery had been placed before the threshold of the wide wooden doors with weather-blackened latches, a bloom of red against the green patina of the aged wood. Rémy's eye caught the glint of his silver cane beneath it. Its pommel was propped between the doors to prevent them from latching shut and locking. Violet had kept her word.

Violet also had been right about sending him to find Sister Thérèse, who turned out to be the nurse currently on duty at the reception desk. An elderly nun with rheumy eyes and papery skin, she was dozing lightly until Rémy appeared to ask her name and explain the situation of his lost cane. Sister Thérèse told him gently that visiting hours were over, but since he had been kind enough to call upon one of the young ladies, she would be delighted to help him retrieve his walking-stick. She rose and led Rémy through the hospital, her step light and quick on the polished floors despite her slight limp. The halls were mercifully silent, save for one attendant wheeling an empty gurney down the main corridor. Rémy tried not to look too relieved when Sister Thérèse unlocked the door to the courtyard, blinking her pale eyes and taking her leave of him with a nod when he promised he could find his own way back.

The carriage house doors made no sound as Rémy retrieved his cane and slipped inside. As the doors whispered shut behind him, he wondered if Dr. Veyssière kept the hinges oiled and silent for his own nocturnal outings. He blinked into a black abyss, waiting for his eyes to adjust to the darkness and inhaling the earthy smell of the stable, which seemed to disguise a faint chemical odor.

He expected to find a waiting horse and the hospital's wagon, but the carriage house was empty. He peered closely at the opposite side of the building and saw myriad wooden crates stacked along the wall, possibly a delivery of medical supplies, but no coffin-shaped pine boxes. He now saw that a faint sliver of light emerged from between two small doors that covered what he first thought was a large coal chute. The flickering beam filled Rémy with an inexplicable sense of dread. The floor was slick with mud and loose straw beneath his feet as he stepped closer, noticing the chemical smell grow stronger and more intense.

Rémy reached for the iron handles and wrenched open the doors, quickly at first, then relaxed his grip and let them fall quietly aside. He had hoped that opening the chute would provide enough light for him to examine the carriage house floor for fresh footprints, horseshoe marks, wheel ruts, and signs of coffin-sized objects being dragged across the ground. Instead he found himself gazing into a dim underground passageway with a smooth, slanted floor that descended gradually into the asylum's subterranean depths.

He stepped inside. The chute was larger than it looked from the outside, and tall enough for him to stand upright. The row of gas lamps along the walls only intensified the sensation of entering a sepulcher. He stepped forward uneasily, realizing that Stéphane's body must have passed through the same corridor. This must be how the coffins—and the murder victims— were delivered to and from the asylum.

A row of straitjackets hanging from metal hooks mounted on the wall came into focus at the end of the passageway, casting ghostly shadows on the surface behind them. A wheeled gurney with dangling leather straps and gleaming buckles crouched in the corner as if waiting for him. Rémy had discovered the reception area for new patients. His imagination immediately spun dreadful visions: women being roughly forced into straightjackets, breaking their fingers and arms; hair being shorn and clipped tresses joining fallen tears on the cold floor; buckles ominously locking around pale limbs; steel doors slamming shut and keys turning in locks—
Rémy took a deep breath. He did not know if he would survive this night. He knew that even if he found Dr. Veyssière, there might be little he alone could do to apprehend him, but he could at least find the evidence he needed to prove his own innocence and convict Stéphane's murderer. Another flutter of rage twisted through his chest.

He turned away from the reception area and stepped stealthily towards the main hallway, following the signs on the wall in the direction of the crematorium and morgue. He passed the coal chamber, with a blackened chute smaller than the one through which he had descended. He found a storage room with shelves of medical equipment, another with myriad bottled chemicals, and two empty operating rooms before he encountered a locked door. He retrieved the keys from his pocket, not expecting much to come of it—the key ring only held three small keys, after all. The lock released as he turned the last one.

Rémy cautiously pushed open the door to a recently used operating room. The scent of blood still lingered in the air, commingling with a chemical smell. He approached a table covered with large, lidded glass jars, one of which appeared to contain a simple piece of black cloth. Rémy lifted the lid. Instantly a sickly-sweet vaporous odor wafted towards his face. Drawing shallow breaths, he carefully reached inside and examined the cloth. It resembled an executioner's hood without eyeholes—the chloroform hood that was used to capture Claude. Rémy replaced the cloth, covered the jar, and continued to explore the operating room.

In one corner stood a large wooden tub with several bent metal rods protruding from it. He stepped closer and peered inside, recognizing iron filings mixed into the water. "Magnetic fluid—" he whispered to himself. This must be one of Dr. Veyssière's experiments for studying the effects of the mesmeric energy he claimed to channel from celestial bodies. Rémy then remembered that all of the murder victims had been arranged outside, where they could absorb the energy of the moonlight, starlight, and sunlight. After all, Mesmer believed that he could successfully magnetize the sun. "The sunrise—" He needed to reach the roof of the sanitarium. If he was correct about the pattern on the Paris map, the Genesis cult must be staging its scene there!

Rémy fled the room and hurried down the hallway. Although he shuddered at the thought, he needed to investigate the morgue before ascending the stairs. He found the dreaded rooms at the end of their own grim corridor, as he remembered. Summoning his courage, he gripped the handle of the wide metal door and slid it open.

The first large, cold space was empty save for whoever lay under a stained white sheet on the mortuary table at the far end of the room. A few vacant wooden coffins and lids were leaning upright against the wall in the adjacent corner.

There was something unsettling about the shape of the body under the sheet. Rémy slid the door shut behind him and stepped closer, taking shallow breaths of air rancid with the smell of decay. He could see the outline of human legs and feet, but the figure's head and torso became a shapeless mass. As he had feared, the irregular stains were deep red, gradually darkening to rust-colored as they dried.

This was all too familiar. Rémy forced himself to grasp a corner of the sheet. He held his breath and pulled, slowly revealing a bizarre amalgamation of mangled taxidermy animals. The forequarters of a lion and a white swan missing its wings spilled sawdust onto the mortuary table, their glass eyes gleaming. He continued to pull away the sheet. What he saw next sickened him. The lower half of a woman's body, severed at the waist, seeped blood and viscera onto the table beneath sickly-purple skin.

Rémy dropped the sheet in terror and backed away before he realized what he was doing, pressing his hand against his mouth and trying not to be ill. He had found the evidence he needed. He collided with the stacked coffins, knocking several wooden lids to the floor in a noisy clatter.

He stood rigidly, straining his ears for a long moment in case anyone was passing by and heard the commotion. Trying not to continue staring at Dr. Veyssière's latest victim, he swiftly gathered the sheet and covered her remains. Then he heard the sound of pacing footsteps in the corridor. Thinking quickly, he considered hiding in one of the coffins, but instead he adjusted his grip on his sword cane and faced the doorway. He would die pursuing his revenge, not cowering in a coffin.

The morgue door rattled open, and a large shadow nearly filled the doorframe. He was one of Dr. Veyssière's ward attendants who also served as his asylum guards, a man with stringy dark hair, intense eyes, and rolled-up shirtsleeves.

"What are you doing here?" he demanded, in a flat tone that told Rémy he already knew exactly what was happening. He entered the morgue, his gaze scanning the room from the bloody table to the toppled coffins, and glared at the intruder. "Don't you worry," he said, his tone falsely reassuring. "I'll get this mess cleaned up. After I escort you—elsewhere." He took a step closer to Rémy, who brandished his cane and stood his ground. The guard laughed cruelly. "Now what do you expect to do with that?"

He lunged at Rémy, grasping the cane with one thick hand. He attempted to fling the cane aside, but only succeeded in yanking the sheath off its hidden blade. While the man gazed in confusion at the hollow ebony cylinder in his hand, his expression turned to one of shock as Rémy charged at him, leaving an angry slash across the side of his face. Rémy dashed past the attendant, reclaiming his blade's sheath from the floor where the man had dropped it to press his hand to his bleeding wound. Then he sheathed the blade, gripped his cane resolutely in both hands, and swung with all his strength and rage. The heavy pommel hit the side of the man's head and dropped him to the floor in an unconscious heap.

A moment later, Rémy hurried up the familiar square stairwell, leaving the morgue behind. He soon reached the polished wooden door leading to the main floor and twisted the brass latch with a trembling hand. Locked. He tried his few keys, found them useless, and angrily thumped his damp forehead against the door, exhausted. After catching his breath, he reluctantly turned to retrace his steps to the morgue. In his haste he had forgotten to search the guard for any keys or evidence, but the large man would not remain unconscious for long. He expected to hear the guard's footsteps pursuing him up the stairs at any moment. Yet for now all he heard was the ambient noise of the asylum, a woman's distant weeping, and his own elevated breathing in the humid air.

A sudden noise startled him anew. Keys jingled directly on the other side of the door. Rémy held his breath. Then came the click of a sliding bolt, followed by the latch turning. The door slowly opened on silent hinges as a dim column of light widened across Rémy's face and illuminated the stair landing. He raised his cane again, ready to strike whomever appeared before him.

"*Bonsoir*, Monsieur. I feared you had gotten lost after all!"

Rémy managed to breathe again upon recognizing the serene Sister Thérèse. He quickly lowered his cane.

"I thought I heard some commotion down here," she said. "You found what you were looking for, I trust?"

"Ah—*Oui, ma Soeur*. Please forgive my late intrusion." Rémy kept the cane at his side, hiding the telltale bloodstains on the silver gargoyle. "I suppose I should have waited for your guidance after all."

The nurse smiled sweetly. "Here, let me show you the way out. The hospital is all locked up at this hour."

"You are very kind." Rémy followed her down the main hallway to the exit, trying not to glance back at the basement door. He was disappointed that his investigation within the Sainte-Geneviève was over, but the wounded guard would soon set the entire asylum on high alert.

"May God be with you, Monsieur." She opened the door and gestured towards the night. "Do come visit your niece again soon. The young ladies adore visitors."

"Yes—of course." Remembering Finn's story, the cynical tone crept back into his voice as he gratefully slipped outside into the night. "I'm certain they do."

Rémy lurked near the sanitarium long past midnight, looking for a better view of its rooftop cupola and becoming increasingly uneasy as the hours passed. He could not see or hear anything unusual. What if he had been wrong about the location?

His racing mind settled on one place where he could search for clues and interrogate one of the artists involved, provided that the man was at home instead of already mutilating another model. Rémy pulled his map out of his pocket beneath a streetlamp to examine the markings he had made earlier that day. Étienne Lacroix lived in a fashionable neighborhood near the École des Beaux-Arts, not far from Alexandre Baltard's atelier.

He hurried to Lacroix's residence on foot, trying to minimize the scrape of his shoes on the cobblestones, and studied his options once he arrived. Lampposts lined the street, and he did not want to risk being seen by a passing policeman while picking the lock on Lacroix's front door. He needed to avoid awakening any household staff, Rémy thought, and from what he had read, the artist remained a bachelor. An intruder might be fortunate enough to find the house empty.

He slipped into the alley behind the building and carefully picked the lock on Lacroix's courtyard gate, intending to enter through the back of the house. The vine-entangled door creaked open with a gentle push, and Rémy was relieved to see that Lacroix's ground-floor windows were open to the warm August night.

He crept inside through a window, parting heavy black curtains and entering a house that seemed as oppressive and airless as a tomb. He stepped carefully around a painted Ottoman end table and a velvet chair with Venetian red upholstery and a dark wooden frame. Faded Persian rugs hushed his footsteps on the wooden floor. An oppressive odor of dust invaded his senses, irritating his eyes. He wondered again if Lacroix indeed lived here alone.

Stained glass panels further darkened another interior space where a brass chandelier hung from a parquet ceiling above a large, round table. Rémy paused to let his eyes adjust to the somber décor of what he initially assumed was an ornate dining room, but a certain perfumed heaviness in the air betrayed the presence of something darker. Peering closer at the table, he found the evidence of Lacroix's legacy. The array of spiritualist paraphernalia included a hand-painted talking board, a wooden *planchette*, sheets of paper, and drawing tools intended for the medium to write or draw the messages and visions conveyed by the spirits she claimed to contact. Glass lenses and brass fittings gleamed on a boxy camera attached to a nearby tripod. Clearly Lacroix did not want to miss a single communication from the spirit world.

Rémy felt his features contort with fury. If he survived this, he vowed, he would dedicate his career to exposing Orris d'Ombre as a fraud. Spiritualism was typically an innocuous pastime for the affluent and bored, but now nearly a dozen people had been murdered and their loved ones left to suffer because of a medium's parlor tricks, double-exposure photographs, and demented son.

A tall ebony clock against the wall near the head of the dining table reminded Rémy of an upright coffin. He turned away and carefully stepped through Lacroix's house, seeking the stairs to the upper floors where he was likely to find the artist's bedchamber and studio. If Lacroix was asleep in bed, he wondered as he climbed the stairs, did that prove his innocence? If he was gone, did that prove his involvement with the Genesis cult?

The layout of the house was logical enough, leading Rémy to the stairwell. He gripped the black iron railing decorated with metalwork vines in intricate patterns and climbed upward to a curved hallway, its wooden floors silenced by narrow carpets. He crept around a spiraling set of rooms to the double doors of what he assumed was the master bedroom. One door was slightly ajar. A faint light illuminated the room beyond, although no sound emerged from within. Clutching his sword cane, Rémy slowly pushed open the door and entered the room, finally daring to exhale upon seeing that the canopied bed was empty.

The carved jade lamp on the octagon-shaped bedside table also revealed a polished bookcase with glass doors, its deep shelves holding numerous occult titles that Rémy recognized. Several small paintings and oil sketches were arranged salon-style on the dark green wallpaper, and a gilded mirror spotted with tarnish hung above the black marble fireplace. A framed daguerreotype of an elderly woman wearing a mourning gown was displayed on the mantel between a Sèvres vase and a bronze statuette of a sphinx.

Another light shone from a narrow hallway near the far corner of the room. Rémy approached this second doorway cautiously. There was something eerie about the isolated light in the darkened chamber. It reminded him of an Odilon Redon lithograph, rife with shadowy architecture and otherworldly creatures. Indeed, in his own sleep-deprived state, he questioned whether he was awake or dreaming.

The surreal sensibility increased when he peered around the door and saw that the narrow hallway was merely a small space connecting Lacroix's bedroom with an antechamber. Apparently the artist had turned it into a sparsely furnished storage room. Large canvases were stacked against one wall. Other paintings were arranged individually around the room, leaning against empty walls and covered in sheets. Lacroix was nowhere to be seen, but he had left a light shining in this room. Why? If he was not at home, perhaps the Genesis cult was already at work.

Spotting a small desk shoved against another wall, Rémy frantically began opening drawers and searching through Lacroix's papers and letters, seeking clues regarding the Sixth Day location. If Lacroix was involved, however, he had covered his tracks well. Rémy shoved the desk drawers shut.

Large-scale drawings lay flat on the floorboards, showing designs sketched in light charcoal over a faint grid to assist the artist in transferring the composition to canvas. Rémy leaned in for a closer look. In the drawing on top of the stack, a hybrid female creature was challenging a semi-nude young man in a rocky landscape. He recognized the myth immediately: Oedipus and the Sphinx. The sphinx was lifting her lioness's paw to Oedipus's chest, and her feathery wings were stretched out over the mangled remains of the men who had failed to solve her riddle. He knew from having studied the Salon engravings that this drawing was not Lacroix's work, but with its cadaverous figures and tenebrous lighting, it bore a resemblance to the macabre and decadent style for which the artist was celebrated.

Rémy gasped softly. "Beasts and man," he whispered. "The Sixth Day." He hurried to the single window in the room and flung aside the heavy curtain. Darkness lingered outside, but he knew he must race the sunrise to the first location that came to mind when he saw the sphinx: the menagerie at the Jardin des Plantes.

He whirled around to leave the room and flee east across the city, but one of the paintings, half-concealed by a white sheet, caught his eye. The canvas was larger than life-size. Beneath its cover he could see the tip of a white wing and an outstretched hand engulfed in flames, painted against an azure sky. Rémy pulled the sheet aside. *The Fall of Icarus*, signed by Étienne Lacroix. The model was undoubtedly Stéphane.

"How do you like my Icarus, M. Sauvage?"

Rémy had been too transfixed and horrified by the figure's anguished expression to notice the slender man who had drifted silently into the room. His head whipped around to face Étienne Lacroix. "You killed him," he rasped.

Lacroix smiled, pulling off his gloves as he sauntered a few steps closer to Rémy. "So it *is* you. Stéphane talked about you while he was posing for Icarus. I paid him well to keep the subject a secret. I take it he kept it? Even from you." Lacroix sighed. "Alas, I could never exhibit it. You understand why."

Rémy set his jaw, unconsciously clenching his fists. "Did you enjoy your visit to the Jardin des Plantes? The menagerie this time?"

Lacroix raised an eyebrow, a bored expression on his angular face. "It took you this long to figure out the location? Stéphane told me you were a genius." He flicked open the compartment on his large silver ring adorned with a red garnet, lifted it to his nose, and inhaled some of the white powder inside with an abrupt sniff. "The garden is quite lovely by night, in fact."

"I know the truth about the missing artist, Antoine Barre. You killed him, too."

"Of course." Lacroix yawned. "I showed him undeniable proof of the spirit world and a higher existence beyond the visible realm. I invited him to join the Eighth Day Brotherhood and create sculptures that would transform into gods and angels. I offered him eternity, and he refused. I imagine he is watching us with regret through the sludge at the bottom of the Seine where we left him. He was pathetic and unworthy, but I could not allow him to divulge our secrets. He would not have been able to stop us, anyway." Lacroix smiled. "Those two fools we captured at the Sainte-Geneviève tonight certainly could not. They have no appreciation for the Brotherhood's fine work, either, despite the young man considering himself an artist! And the mad beauty with the flaming hair was to be his model, I believe?"

Rémy shivered as the sweltering room seemed to close in upon him, leaving him lightheaded. "What have you done with them?" he demanded.

"All will be revealed soon enough. The chloroform will keep them quiet until the Brotherhood decides their purpose in finishing our work. Your meddling cannot stop us either, M. Sauvage. That was quite a wound you gave Jules, the guard in the doctor's morgue. I imagine he'll have a fine scar. Nevertheless, the loyal man managed to dispose of what you found under that sheet. You saw everything I wanted you see." Lacroix smiled as Rémy fumed silently. "I suggest that you return to your bookshop, M. Sauvage, and enjoy what little time you have left in this world. I seriously doubt you shall be joining us in the new one, a world in which worthy artists shall be immortal! For I alone, the Messenger, have been gifted with the knowledge that on the Seventh Day, when the sun rises upon Orpheus, the incomparable artist-poet of the ancient world, he himself shall emerge from the Underworld, and lead us into the new one on the Eighth Day." Lacroix's icy eyes glinted with madness.

"Eighth Day? So you will continue murdering innocent people—"

"Calm yourself, M. Sauvage." Lacroix backed away, his hands now raised in a theatrical gesture. "*Et in arcadia ego.* Do I need to translate that for you, scholar? In the new paradise, there I shall be, inevitable and indomitable. Do you want me to apologize for turning Stéphane Desnoyers into a fine work of sculpture? Well, I shall not. I know about you and Stéphane. I know what he meant to you." Lacroix tilted his head and sat on the edge of a sturdy table covered in plaster casts and wax-covered wire figures. "If it comes as any comfort to you, he was nearly dead by the time I burned out his eyes."

Rémy's mind snapped. He drew his sword cane and lunged for Lacroix's heart. His rage made him careless, and the painter easily dodged the blow. Lacroix slid off the table, hefted the largest of the plaster statuettes, and dashed it against the side of Rémy's skull. Rémy fell sideways onto the floor, unconscious.

Lacroix straightened his black evening jacket, then reached down to grasp Rémy's narrow face in one hand, slowly turning his victim's head from side to side with a curious eye. "Such Pre-Raphaelite features!" he exclaimed. "Even at your age. Pity I have no use for you."

Lacroix calmly left the room and locked the door behind him, leaving Rémy alone with the painting of Icarus falling in flames.

August 6, 1888

"And God made the beast of the earth after his kind, and cattle after their kind, and every thing that creepeth upon the earth after his kind: and God saw that it was good. And God said, Let us make man in our image, after our likeness: and let them have dominion over the fish of the sea, and over the fowl of the air, and over the cattle, and over all the earth, and over every creeping thing that creepeth upon the earth. So God created man in his own image, in the image of God created he him; male and female created he them…And God saw every thing that he had made, and, behold, it was very good. And the evening and the morning were the sixth day."

—Genesis 1:25-27, 31

Inspector Percier strolled quickly through the menagerie at the Jardin des Plantes, his dark eyes shifting from side to side. He wondered if the confined animals were more agitated than usual, or if they always behaved this way. They paced, fought, or climbed around their cages, seemingly oblivious to the fact that two *homo sapiens* had met horrific deaths nearby. Perhaps the predators were agitated by the scent of human blood.

He approached the small pond where a menagerie caretaker found the bodies early this morning, making him drop the pail of water he was carrying to the lions. The discovery occurred not long after a respectable gentleman in the sixth *arrondissement* reported a burglar in his home. After a brief struggle, the gentleman had managed to trap the intruder in an upstairs storage room until the police arrived to arrest him. Percier gave routine burglaries little attention, but this time the perpetrator's name caught his eye: Rémy Sauvage. Percier was determined to find out what the occult bookstore owner was doing in the home of a famous painter soon after two more artists' models had been murdered.

Thankfully the police had already closed the menagerie to civilians and curious passersby. Some of the officers now surrounding the pond could not disguise their disgust. The more experienced men remained impassive, accustomed to gruesome sights such as the Genesis cult's "sculptures."

Percier pushed his way through to the crime scene. The officers stood aside, watching his reaction while he stared at the macabre display for a long moment. "Have the victims been identified, Alain?" he asked grimly.

"Not yet, Inspector, but the director of the menagerie is having the water birds and fish relocated from the pond."

"Well, *that's* a comfort," Percier grumbled. "Did you ask him about any artists visiting recently?"

"Yes, Inspector. He said many artists come to the menagerie to sketch the animals. Too many to remember. He doesn't know which ones have been here recently."

"Hmmph." Percier removed his hat and stepped closer to the corpses, solemnly observing every detail. He imagined that even the most jaded policeman had to have experienced some initial shock at what the murderers had done to the bodies.

"Oedipus and the Sphinx," Percier mused. Both figures were posed using a framework of wire and wooden stakes resembling the apparatus the murderers had used to create Icarus's wings. The male model's demise was straightforward enough. He had bled to death after being nearly flayed alive, and his skin dangled from his body in coiling ribbons.

A crow landed on the corpse's head and began to pluck at a strip of flesh with its beak. Percier shooed it away with a wave of his hat and leaned closer to the body. His skin was lacerated as if his entire body had been mauled by wild animals, and the numbers 1:25-27 were visible in the torn skin of his forehead. The man was posed at the edge of the pond, one leg propped up on a rock and one arm extended as if he were engaging in conversation with the female victim. His other arm held a traveler's staff, which also supported the body, and he was clothed in a royal blue tunic and costume sandals.

One gore-streaked corpse was bad enough, but Percier could not believe what they had done to the young woman. She was posed on a larger rock submerged deeper in the shallow water. They had severed her body in two. The hindquarters of a lioness were stitched around her waist and a decaying pair of large white wings was sewn to her shoulder blades, transforming her into a monstrous hybrid.

"Taxidermy animals. Not the menagerie's," he said dryly. Percier turned to the nearest policeman. "Find out whether any taxidermists or art dealers in Paris have recently sold a stuffed lion or swan." He peered closer and examined the stitches. "Attached with surgical thread," he muttered to himself. Wooden stakes and wire arranged her arms and head so that she crouched on all fours, her dead eyes wide open. "And arranged on artists' props," Percier said. "There is little blood in the water. Again, the victims were murdered elsewhere and placed here shortly before dawn." He sighed and wiped his forehead with his handkerchief, his head spinning with Bible verses and ancient myths. "If I cannot solve this riddle, I'll end up like the Sphinx's other challengers."

"How's that, Inspector?" Alain asked.

"The people of Paris will tear *me* limb from limb." Whatever was he missing, he needed to find it today. "God rested on the Seventh Day," he muttered. "We can only pray that the Genesis cult will do the same."

"I'm telling you, I am *not* mad!" Rémy repeated for what felt like the thousandth time, although Inspector Percier remained unconvinced.

Percier looked up from the desk near the holding cell at the Préfecture where he awaited Rémy's confession. "M. Sauvage," the inspector began in an irritated tone. "You invaded a respectable gentleman's home and assaulted him. He injured you in self-defense. My men found no evidence of any of these mythological drawings and paintings that you insist were in the room where we arrested you. No *Icarus*, no *Oedipus and the Sphinx*, nothing. I am curious, however, how you knew which myth we would find today." He grabbed a crumpled piece of folded paper from his desk and held it up for Rémy to see. "I am also curious as to why you had a city map in your possession marked with the murder locations, a bloodstained weapon, a floor plan of l'Hôpital Sainte-Geneviève, and a stolen set of keys from that very building. I don't suppose you have any experience with taxidermy, do you, M. Sauvage?"

Rémy grabbed the bars of the cell, his heavy rings clanging against the iron. "I told you, Inspector, I saw the last victim's remains in the Sainte-

Geneviève morgue. I saw the drawing in Lacroix's storage room. That's when I realized the Sixth Day location for beasts and man. I have been doing some investigating of my own. Lacroix confessed to murdering Antoine Barre, the artist who refused to join his cult, and casting his body into the Seine! He convinced the others to commit the crimes using parlor tricks and séances. His mother was—"

"Orris d'Ombre. The spiritualist medium. I know." Percier paused, slowly tilting his head in thought, then continued shuffling through more papers on the desk. "However, the evidence is here, M. Sauvage. The paperwork signed by Dr. Jacques-André Veyssière himself, proving that last night you were committed to the Sainte-Geneviève sanitarium and escaped a few hours later."

"What? That's impossible—"

"According to his preliminary diagnosis, you are homicidal, violent, and prone to fantastical delusions. He also mentions a possible case of erotomania concerning a desired relationship with your tenant, Stéphane Desnoyers. In light of that, I need to ask you some more questions about the Genesis murders."

"Those are all lies! Don't you see, Inspector, he's trying to distract you while he kills again. Dr. Veyssière and Étienne Lacroix are the men you want, not me!" Rémy's voice sounded like a shriek even to his own ears. For one terrible moment, he wondered if he was indeed mad, and his moments of sanity had been mere hallucinations. "I sent you an anonymous letter explaining everything I know. That was before I knew the doctor was involved, but please, if you have read it—"

"M. Sauvage, where were you last night before you broke into Étienne Lacroix's home?"

Rémy leaned his forehead against the cold metal bars. His entire head ached, and his hair was matted with blood around the ragged gash where Lacroix had struck him. "Looking for the murderer. And I found him."

"I am aware of that hospital's reputation, M. Sauvage, but thus far it sounds like idle gossip, and I have a difficult time believing that a renowned physician and a painter of the Legion of Honor are murderers. Besides, Dr. Veyssière informs me that you have some accomplices, an art student and an immigrant woman, both of whom also escaped from the Saint-Geneviève this week."

Rémy's mind raced. This was his chance to stop the next murder. His last chance to avenge Stéphane.

Lacroix had mentioned Orpheus. Orpheus in the Underworld—

The catacombs? He closed his eyes and visualized the Paris map. Perhaps Claude was right, and the cruciform pattern was a coincidence after all. The points on the map merely formed a constellation of crime scenes around the centrally located Sainte-Geneviève—or represented Lacroix's attempt to mislead investigators from the Brotherhood's final destination. The catacombs were nearly on the same city axis as the Observatory, Panthéon, and Notre-Dame cathedral, but that location was entirely underground. The Genesis cult was preoccupied with leaving its morbid creations visible to the sunrise for them to receive magnetic energy from the cosmos, or so they believed. Moreover, Lacroix desired an audience.

Rémy thought harder, mentally scrolling through his encyclopedic knowledge of ancient mythology.

Orpheus the musician. The ideal artist-poet in the Symbolists' eyes. Rémy could think of only one musical location spectacular enough to satisfy the Genesis cult for its Seventh Day composition: the spectacular Opéra de Paris, the Palais Garnier. Of course. Lacroix would place his Orpheus beneath the magnificent bronze and gilded statue of Apollo on the roof of the opera house, ensuring that the sun god himself witnessed the sacrifice of another beautiful youth.

"God rested on the Seventh Day," Percier was saying. "As will the Genesis cult, I presume? Unless you are planning, what, Endymion? At the Observatory again, perhaps?" He shook his head. "I have received countless insane letters, false confessions, and amateur detectives' solutions for the past few days, but nothing has led us to the right place at the right time. I assume your letter is somewhere in the pile."

Rémy sighed, on the verge of despair. "You are correct, Inspector, in connecting the ancient myths with the days of Creation, but the Genesis cult will not stop killing. I know where they will strike next. They have followed the biblical days of Creation thus far, but Lacroix believes himself to be the prophet of a new world remade in the image of decadent art. 'The Messenger,' he calls himself, and Dr. Veyssière is assisting him! You must believe me, I will do anything to help you catch these men for what they did to Stéphane Desnoyers."

Percier wearily leaned back in his uncomfortable chair and rubbed the bridge of his nose between his thumb and forefinger. "I wish I could believe you, M. Sauvage. But I cannot ignore the evidence I found in your possession, nor can I ignore this paperwork signed by a prominent doctor. In fact, I assured him I would send for his subordinates as soon as I finished questioning you, and they will take you back to your room at the Saint-Geneviève."

Anguish, sleepless nights, pain, and hunger finally caught up with Rémy. His limbs trembled as he sank to the hard bench in the holding cell and buried his gaunt face in his hands, still wondering when he would awaken from this nightmare.

Percier stood, approached the cell, and eyed Rémy carefully. His piercing gaze almost revealed pity for the presumed madman. "You will be well cared for at l'Hôpital Saint-Geneviève, M. Sauvage. Have you no one who will visit you?"

"No one. Thanks to the Genesis cult," Rémy said, looking up with bleary eyes. "Inspector, *listen* to me. I believe that the cult captures its victims by subduing them with a mask soaked in chloroform. Where else would they find a reliable supply of that chemical, except in a hospital or laboratory?"

Percier heaved a ragged breath, gazing steadily at Rémy's desperate eyes while the younger man continued speaking.

"We can stop them. Tonight," Rémy assured him. "Release me, and I will show you where to find them before they complete the Seventh Day."

Alexandre Baltard rested on a stool in his atelier, his back warmed by the afternoon sun streaming in through the windows. He gazed at his canvas-laden walls with empty, red-rimmed eyes.

Calais was everywhere he turned. He had lost her, and now he had probably lost Claude, too. Finn, whom he had met only briefly, was likely also gone. A hysteric or not, she seemed to have a kind and courageous heart. Baltard did not react when he heard the spiral stairs creak under an approaching set of footsteps. He knew the visitor was not his foster son returning home.

A lithe male figure emerged into the atelier. The newcomer took the last step with a graceful leap before striding across the floor towards Baltard, who remained slouched on his stool without looking up to acknowledge him.

The grieving painter began speaking in a flat voice. "When Calais was younger, she was afraid of strange lights and phosphorescent sparks. She believed they were spirits of the dead from Tahiti coming to haunt her. Now, whenever I see such lights, I shall think of her."

His visitor remained silent. Waiting.

Baltard slowly turned his head to meet his serene gaze. "I thought you might come here, Étienne," he said.

The slender man smiled. "Of course. I was afraid you would be late for our meeting, Alexandre. Surely you have not forgotten that tonight you have the honor of becoming the Seventh Day artist? Our brothers and I did so admire your preliminary sketches for *Orpheus and Eurydice.*"

"What do you think she felt when she died?" Baltard asked quietly after a moment. "Do you think she thought of those lights? Maybe she will return to earth as one of them. Maybe now she can see her island again. I know she missed the ocean."

"You're getting sentimental in your old age, Alexandre. Besides, your mistress can be near the ocean for all eternity, in the new Creation. We turned her into Andromeda, after all! Remember?" Lacroix leaned over, peering cheerfully into Baltard's haggard face. "Come along now, Alexandre. God may remain asleep, but there is no day of rest for the Eighth Day Brotherhood. Not for a single one of us."

Finn opened her eyes slowly, surfacing from a dreamless, sedative-induced sleep. The last thing she remembered was Dr. Veyssière's carriage emerging from the courtyard gates behind the asylum as she and Claude approached the building in search of Rémy. Claude had instinctively thrown his arm across her body to protect her, but two men in black suits quickly overpowered his slight frame before he could reach for his pistol. When she saw the doctor, she turned to run too late. His cruel fingers snarled into her hair, yanked her head backwards, and covered her face with the chloroform-soaked hood.

Now she lay on a rough, hard surface in an unfamiliar vaulted stone space emanating a musty smell. The golden light flickering on the ceiling suggested that the vault was illuminated by candle flames. Straining her ears, she thought she could hear the sound of water lapping softly against a distant shore. Not satisfied with locking her in a cell, she wondered, had the doctor imprisoned her in the sewers beneath the city?

Finn shifted, feeling wooden planks press uncomfortably against her spine. Her hands lay on her chest, bound together at the wrists. A man's handkerchief was tied across her mouth. She turned her head to one side, seeing only the walls of a pine box. Finn drew a frightened breath. She was lying in a coffin.

Where is Claude?

She looked down and attempted to move her feet. Her scuffed black boots knocked softly against the wooden planks. Her legs, thankfully, remained unbound. Afraid to rise and find the doctor waiting for her, she bent one knee until she could reach the top of her right boot with her bound hands, stretching her fingers to reach the hilt of the small dagger concealed between her boot and stocking, the blade pressing uncomfortably against her ankle. She pulled it out slowly, carefully, terrified of dropping it from her trembling hands or of making a single sound, and turned the dagger until she could sever the thin ropes binding her wrists.

She had almost finished cutting through them when she heard footsteps. Immediately she recognized the heavy tread she had heard outside her door day and night for years. Fighting a wave of panic, she sliced through the final strands of rope and concealed the dagger in her hand, hiding the blade under the sleeve of her white blouse. Then she grabbed the rope, hastily wound it around her wrists, and lay her hands across her chest as if she had done nothing.

She could not help keeping her eyes wide open. Her gaze darted from side to side, unblinking, as if that would allow her vision somehow to absorb more information about her ominous surroundings. Her perspiring hands dampened the hilt of the dagger, but her grip tightened as she imagined slashing it through the charlatan's flesh the way her father had gutted fish.

Dr. Veyssière stepped closer, looming over her as he gazed down at her face. "As lovely as Ophelia drifting down the river. You just cannot stay away from me, can you, my dear?" he asked in a mocking tone. "You never thought you would return to the Opéra, did you? The place where we first met? Well, here you are. You are far beneath the stage, yet tonight shall be your last and finest performance."

The opera house! Finn felt only the faintest sense of relief upon realizing she was inside the Palais Garnier. She had explored this vast building filled with subterranean passageways and secret trapdoors while she was a young ballerina. Perhaps she could still find her way around.

"I assume you returned home to the asylum because you wished to accept my offer of entering the new Paradise at my side, where you belong?" Dr. Veyssière drew back and paced around the coffin. "Soon you shall beg for so gentle a fate, since the Messenger has other plans for you. You will join your young man in the preparation room." Abruptly he reached down to grab her by her arms, yanking her to her feet. "There *is* no day of rest in the new Creation, Finn!"

Finn struggled until her hand holding the dagger broke free of his grip. She lashed out at him, slashing the blade across his face and deeply cutting his left cheek. Veyssière shouted in surprise, releasing Finn's other arm to press his hands to his face and staunch the blood flow.

Finn yanked the handkerchief from her mouth and kept her grip on the dagger. A few drops of blood splattered onto her skirt. She saw an empty coffin next to hers, but no sign of Claude. She dashed through the underground space, but the doctor had recovered and was advancing towards her again—and Finn remembered. She remembered that terrible day in a dressing room of this very building when he had stolen her life and her freedom. The next thing she knew, her stiff legs were carrying her as fast as they could down a vaulted corridor towards the sound of running water.

"Finn!" the doctor roared. "You will not get far!"

She glanced back at him without stopping, her long hair loosening and falling around her shoulders in tangled red curls. The doctor's dark silhouette remained still, she noticed with relief. He was no longer pursuing her. At the same moment, however, her stomach lurched as the stone floor beneath her suddenly disappeared, her boots meeting nothing in the darkness. Finn's scream faded into dank and empty space as she fell though one of the Palais Garnier's myriad trapdoors.

Claude awoke as the distant sound of a woman's scream collided with his nightmarish delirium.

Finn?

In the last fleeting moments of his dream, she was standing in a white gown at the edge of a vast ocean, brackish waves revealing bright flashes of sea-foam green as they churned silently beneath an endless silver-grey sky.

Finn was staring out at the waves with her back to him, slowly turning to reveal a corpselike, drowned face with eerie pale eyes when Claude attempted to approach her.

He coughed and shifted, feeling an unfamiliar pressure on his body. He lifted his aching head and saw that he was bound by thick leather restraints to a white marble slab, as if he lay on an operating table created from the lid of a sarcophagus. His jacket had been removed, and the duelling pistol was missing from his pocket.

A chill sensation seeped from the smooth stone into Claude's back. He inhaled a breath of cool, musty air and gazed up at a low, vaulted ceiling where he half-expected to see a swinging pendulum blade out of a gothic tale. He assumed he was underground, perhaps in a crypt. Carefully turning his head to one side, he gazed around the subterranean vault. His hazy vision gradually focused on a gathering of men in black suits or shirtsleeves near a steamer trunk overflowing with costumes and crates of theater props similar to the ones used in Baltard's atelier for posing classical scenes.

Two men were examining a length of gauzy white fabric. They slowly turned their heads to meet Claude's gaze, resembling hollow-eyed phantoms in the flickering light from the candelabras arranged around the irregular space.

"Ah! He has awakened."

Claude's eyes shifted towards the mellifluous voice, and finally settled upon Étienne Lacroix's grinning expression.

Lacroix stepped closer. His sardonic smile loomed in Claude's vision. "*Bonsoir*, Claude. I wanted you to meet the Seventh Day artist." He turned and beckoned to a figure in the shadows behind him. "Alexandre? Step forward, please."

Claude's eyes widened in shock as his instructor stepped into view. The painter's face was haggard and grey. His rumpled shirtsleeves were rolled up to his elbows, and his step was slow and reluctant. Claude realized that the men now circling him were artists he had seen at the Salons or encountered while accompanying Baltard to the École des Beaux-Arts and ateliers around Paris. Jean-Baptiste Mathieu. Théophile Boisseau. Vincent Morel. Léon Fable. Achille Lémieux, who had been driving the hospital wagon when Claude and Finn were captured outside the Sainte-Geneviève. All of them were known for their decadent and controversial style, which many critics considered a perversion of Romanticism. Painters and sculptors whose work he admired. Claude recognized them all. Yet he could only stare at Baltard's face, which remained stony despite the sorrowful expression in his eyes.

Lacroix continued speaking. "In fact, Claude, you probably know these men and their work. The eight of us are the Eighth Day Brotherhood. I believe the newspapers are calling us the Genesis cult. Not a bad name," he added pensively.

"Eight?" Claude asked quietly, his throat dry, counting seven men in the room.

"Eight, including Dr. Veyssière and his medical arts."

"I knew it," Claude said angrily.

"Dr. Veyssière helped me interpret the messages I received while under hypnosis. His knowledge of animal magnetism is quite extensive. He is the one who sensed the cosmic energy I inherited from my mother, and confirmed that I alone am the Messenger of the new Creation. I have done everything that the spirit world has commanded." Lacroix lifted his gaze heavenward. "According to the Bible, God created the universe in six days. He rested on the seventh. However, judging from the current state of the world, he obviously decided to abandon his work in progress and remain in a somnambulistic oblivion. Thus the Seventh Day has never ended. We live in an incomplete world." His bright eyes met Claude's again. "Tell me, Claude, are you not sickened by this mundane world, by this meaningless, soulless, urban life with its useless, unenlightened population? Are you not disgusted by Eiffel's hideous skeleton of a tower rising over the Seine for the World's Fair? Soon all of that will be gone. It is nearly the eighth day of the eighth month of the year 1888. We shall finish what God began and complete the Seventh Day! On this day, God rests, but man—" He gestured to the somber crowd of artists surrounding him. "Man shall create art."

Claude glared at his instructor. "M. Baltard, how can you believe this nonsense? How could you let them murder Calais?"

"I am sorry, Claude," Baltard replied wearily. "I saw Dr. Veyssière's cures demonstrated. I witnessed the spirits at the séance. I heard the commands of the voices emerging from the spirit world. We all did."

Lacroix nodded, pleased. "My mother, Orris d'Ombre, was a true visionary. She passed her prophetic powers on to me. Now I alone carry out the will of those who commune with the afterlife and know its secrets. Tomorrow night, Dr. Veyssière will place the brotherhood in a state of lucid somnambulism. According to the great magician Éliphas Lévi, we can survive an entire apocalypse while suspended in this state of consciousness. We shall sleep as if buried alive, only to be reanimated and resurrected upon the Eighth Day." Lacroix paused, then leaned his face close to Claude's again. "Tomorrow will be chaos, Claude, as our world changes and transfigures us. On the Eighth Day, then, the sun will rise upon our new Paradise." He turned to Baltard. "Alexandre, prepare your models for the Seventh Day sculpture."

Claude's heart sank. He lunged helplessly against the leather straps, knowing that he would be forced to witness the Eighth Day Brotherhood commit more murders without being able to lift a hand to stop them.

Baltard took a few steps back and wiped his brow with a paint-stained handkerchief, shaking his head. "I cannot, Étienne."

Lacroix tilted his head, gazing at Baltard. "Why not? You dislike the new models I have chosen for you? Will he not make a handsome Orpheus?" He gestured to Claude, who felt a shiver of horror when he realized Lacroix's intent. "Dr. Veyssière will be back soon with your Eurydice."

Baltard kept shaking his head. "Étienne, please. Claude and Mlle. Finnegan are not even models!"

"They are now," Lacroix replied calmly.

"No, Étienne."

"Your reluctance grows irritating, Alexandre. Especially after your reaction to seeing the model I chose for the Fifth Day."

"You never told me you were going to sacrifice Calais!" Baltard shouted, his words punctuated with rage. "You knew she was the one I wanted as my companion in the new Creation."

Lacroix shrugged. "As I told you, she *will* be. You will see her again in a matter of hours. She is already there, waiting for you. Waiting to guide us—"

Baltard flung his arm at Lacroix as if to dispel his words. "Her place was at my side. Not drifting through the ether as an intangible being I cannot hold or touch. Your promises are all lies and illusions!"

Lacroix tilted his head, expressionless.

"I knew it as soon as you delivered the message from 'Andromeda' at the Fifth Day séance. That creature, whether it was a phantom, a demon, or your own twisted soul, did *not* speak with Calais's voice."

"Naturally. An imperfect human undergoes an extraordinary metamorphosis while transforming into a divine being. Her speech will sound refined and changed to match that of ours, since we represent the zenith of human evolution!"

"In that case, there is nothing left of the woman I loved. I am not interested in your new existence if she will not be there," Baltard said, sounding defeated. "Now you want to murder Claude and his muse, too."

"Watch your tongue, Alexandre," interrupted another cult member whom Claude recognized as Vincent Morel, a middle-aged man with cold eyes and a meticulously trimmed goatee. "The Messenger has a more powerful connection to the spirit world than we do."

"Indeed. Thank you, Vincent."

The other artists were drawing closer, closing in on Baltard.

"It is your turn tonight," Achille Lémieux said. "The rest of us have fulfilled our duties. It was you who requested the honor of creating the sculptures for the Seventh Day." The other artists murmured in agreement.

"No! Not Claude," Baltard protested, his voice brimming with desperation. "Étienne, he's Sylvain's son."

Lacroix raised an eyebrow. "And? Had he lived, I would have invited Sylvain to join our cause, and he would have accepted. As a prominent member of the Brotherhood, he would have been proud to see his son immortalized as Orpheus." He smirked. "Besides, no one will miss a foolish boy and a foreign madwoman."

"She is not mad—you are!" Claude shouted, straining against the buckled straps.

Lacroix laughed softly. "Madmen were considered divine prophets in the ancient world. If I am a madman, so be it. But a madwoman is nothing more than a hysteric."

"She was perfect, until the doctor imprisoned her!"

Lacroix ignored him, turning to face Baltard with a bored expression. "Go on, Alexandre. Create your Orpheus," he commanded, handing him a gleaming sliver of metal. Claude lifted his head as much as his restraints allowed, trying to identify the tool. It was a surgical needle. A length of dark thread dangled from its eye.

"I will not." Baltard refused to accept the needle.

Lacroix sighed. "Then *I* will." He took a long stride to stand beside the marble slab. Excitement glimmered in his ice-bright eyes as he leaned over Claude's alarmed face. "Scalpel," he called.

"No—" Baltard moved to stop him, but several men held him back, reminding him in hushed tones that the Brotherhood must complete its work. This was the moment for which they all had painted and studied and planned for years.

Lacroix glanced over his shoulder. "Hmm. The doctor has not yet returned. And he's the one with the sedative. Never mind! Proceed."

Another artist approached Claude, holding a scalpel that glinted in the candlelight. With his slick hair and pointed beard, Vincent Morel looked diabolical while he lowered the surgical instrument to Claude's chest. Sweat poured from the young man's body. "Please don't do this—"

Morel grabbed Claude's collar, sliced the thin white fabric of his shirt from top to bottom, and then paused. Claude's relief lasted a mere second, until Lacroix stepped in next.

Lacroix held the needle aloft. Its reflection glimmered in Claude's frantic eyes. "Orpheus in the Underworld," he mused. "You and your lyre shall become one."

A carriage bearing Inspector Percier, Rémy Sauvage, and two armed policemen rolled to a stop in front of the Opéra de Paris along with dozens of other horse-drawn vehicles arriving for the evening performance. Percier ordered the policemen out first. They eyed their superior with slight confusion, hesitating to leave him alone with the suspect.

"This is under control," Percier assured them. "Stay close."

With a final suspicious glance at Rémy, the officers reluctantly climbed out of the carriage and lingered nearby, ignored by the fashionable Parisians ascending the stairs of the Palais Garnier.

Percier, holding Rémy's silver-topped cane, held the pommel towards its owner in a careful gesture. "M. Sauvage, I am going to take the risk of believing you. Despite what the official paperwork says, I have come to the conclusion that you are not insane. Especially considering the fact that my men cannot find Dr. Veyssière at his home or his hospital. Nor have we been able to locate Étienne Lacroix and several other artists in his circle." His expression did not change, yet he noticed the evident relief on Rémy's face. "Armed men under my command have the building surrounded. Do not try anything that will make me regret trusting you."

Rémy reclaimed his cane from Percier and nodded his thanks.

The two men descended from the carriage into the colorful sea of elegantly clothed Parisians drifting into the opera house. Rémy gazed up at the impressive building in the evening light while the crowd's singular excited murmur hummed in his ears. Inaugurated over a decade ago, the Palais Garnier was a monument to Second Empire opulence. Colored marble, gilded surfaces, and composers' busts decorated the façade. A statue of Apollo lifting his golden lyre between allegorical figures of Dance and Poetry crowned the pinnacle of the roof. Closer to ground level, the building displayed a controversial modern statue of a winged spirit circled by nude bacchantes lost in the ecstatic revelry of their dance.

"Where do you expect to find them, M. Sauvage?"

Rémy thought carefully. "There is a mosaic of Orpheus and Eurydice on the ceiling of one of the grand foyers, but I cannot imagine they will commit any murders in such a public location. The floors beneath the opera house are practically a labyrinth, though. I expect they will have hidden their operation in one of the sub-basements there. Probably an obscure one not being used as a workspace for tonight's performance. I once hired a stagehand to give me a tour of the lower floors and underground lake. You will need several men to explore all the tunnels and passageways, and more stationed near the roof access to the statue of Apollo. With this crowd, we had best not alarm anyone. I believe I remember the way." Rémy rested his cane on his shoulder and took a deep breath that failed to calm his nerves. The evening breeze stirred bloodstained strands of pale hair as he stepped forward. This was his last chance to save innocent lives and avenge Stéphane. "Follow me, Inspector."

Claude clenched his teeth as the curved needle pierced the skin below his left collarbone. Several drops of blood welled forth.

"Stop!" Baltard shouted.

"We proceed with the Brotherhood's plan, Alexandre," Lacroix replied, not looking up as he pushed the needle deeper.

"What I mean to say, Étienne, is that the needle is not the first step. Remember? First we remove a section of skin in the shape of a lyre over his heart. Then we stitch the lyre strings across his chest." Baltard spoke clearly and calmly. "If you must do this, and condemn me to Hell with the rest of you madmen, you can at least follow my design."

Lacroix smiled at him. "*You* do it then, brother." He stepped away from Claude, who inhaled sharply as Lacroix painfully yanked the needle out of his chest.

Baltard had ceased struggling, and the other men slowly released their grip on his arms. He approached the slab and accepted the scalpel that Morel offered him. At last he looked down at Claude, who was desperately shaking his head.

"Monsieur—please—"

"I'm sorry, Claude," Baltard said, raising the blade above Claude's exposed body. "I am truly sorry for getting you, Calais, and Finn into this—"

The scalpel descended. Claude awaited the chill of metal and the searing pain, but instead felt the pressure of the leather straps lift from his arms and torso. Baltard had severed his restraints.

He now gave Claude a rough push, shoving the startled young man onto the stone floor. "*Run*, Claude! Save Finn!"

Enraged men descended upon them both.

"We cannot stop the sacrifice now!" Mathieu snarled into Baltard's ear, grabbing one of his arms. "We've come this far. The Seventh Day is upon us. You will ruin everything!"

Claude dodged Morel's grasp and collided with a workbench covered in art supplies and tools. Spotting his father's pistol in the scattered brushes and surgical instruments, he grabbed the weapon and spun around. "Stop!" he commanded, aiming the pistol at Morel. "Or else." Morel took a wary step back, lifting his hands defensively.

"Or else what?" Lacroix demanded.

Claude noticed with horror that now Lacroix was standing behind Baltard and holding the scalpel to his throat, with Mathieu and Boisseau each restraining one of the painter's arms.

"You've only got one bullet." Lacroix pressed the blade lightly against Baltard's neck, drawing a bright drop of blood. "Six of us against two of you."

Claude heard a familiar heavy footstep behind him. His heart sank even further as he awaited the dreaded voice.

"Seven of us," Dr. Veyssière said. "Drop the pistol, Claude."

Claude did not dare lower his weapon or move a muscle, frozen in indecision until he heard the clink of glass and the rustle of fabric behind him. He darted aside and turned the pistol on Dr. Veyssière just in time to escape the chloroform hood.

The doctor's face remained impassive as he eyed the pistol, but he made no further move to apprehend Claude. He turned and strode casually towards Lacroix. "Messenger, I regret to inform you that Mlle. Finnegan is dead. She suffered a head injury after taking a dreadful fall through one of the trapdoors."

"Pity," Lacroix replied. "We shall fetch her remains, Doctor, and incorporate her into our sculpture nevertheless." He grinned at Claude. "How delightful! Our Orpheus will bear a genuine expression of grief for his lost Eurydice."

"I don't believe you," Claude rasped, frantically pointing the pistol from Lacroix to the doctor and back again.

"Yes, you do. Your hand is shaking," Lacroix replied calmly. "You'll never hit your target like that. Doctor, please disarm the young man—"

Claude pulled the trigger.

At first, Finn was aware of a sickening pain emanating from her skull and her left arm. She had landed on a rough, cold surface where her body lay half-submerged in greenish, murky water. Her lips quivered while she pulled herself out of the water with her other arm and tried to move her injured limb, wondering if it might be broken. Gently she touched her fingertips to her cheekbone, feeling swollen skin and a bleeding gash around her eye socket.

That instant her memory returned. She looked upward with frantic eyes, expecting to see Dr. Veyssière's angular face leering down at her while he crouched on the edge of the trapdoor like a spider ready to pounce. She saw no one.

Lowering her gaze to view her surroundings, her eyes soon adjusted to the dim light. She was at the edge of a mysterious, misty body of water: the opera house's underground lake. Green water lapped softly against tarnished-looking walls, the noise accompanied by scurrying rats and more water pouring into the cistern from above.

She stood, unstable at first on her battered legs. She worried that she had lost her dagger when she fell, but found it a short distance away and slid it back into her waterlogged boot. She leaned against the wall and looked up at the opening through which she had fallen, feeling like a prisoner in an oubliette.

One autumn day when Finn was a child, she had slipped and fallen into the well near her family's cottage. She remained there, cold and afraid, struggling in chest-deep water until her throat grew hoarse from calling for help. Finally, she saw the silhouette of her mother's head and heard her voice: *Margaret Rose Finnegan, what are you doing down there?* Irritated but relieved, she quickly lowered the rope and hauled her frightened daughter back up. *If your father were here to help keep an eye on you, this wouldn't have happened, but he's gone off to Paris to become a famous painter,* her mother said wearily while Finn, wrapped in shawls and blankets, warmed herself by the hearth. Now, however, Finn heard only the water moving in the sinister lake as it traced its reflected patterns on the vaulted ceiling.

She considered retracing her steps, but that might lead her directly back into Dr. Veyssière's grasp. He had probably left her for dead, unwilling to retrieve her body himself. That was just like Dr. Veyssière, she thought with a scowl. Always unwilling to dirty his own hands while his ward assistants carried out his orders.

She glanced upward again. What if the doctor had merely gone back for help in recapturing her? He might return at any moment. As her vision cleared, Finn thought she saw a darkened doorway at the opposite side of the lake with a small boat moored beside it. Perhaps it would lead to a way out, or a way to help Claude. She mustered her courage and slid into the cold water.

Swimming with a possibly broken arm was excruciating, but she reached the doorway at last, feeling half-dead by the time she climbed out of the water. She shoved her wet hair out of her face and realized she was still bleeding from the gash around her left eye, which was swelling shut. Shivering, she stepped into a silent black corridor that seemed to swallow her ghostly figure. The sound of her drenched skirt scraping along the ground behind her intensified the sensation of emerging from a watery grave. She had taken only a few steps when she heard footsteps in the darkness. She froze, her eyes wide, but could see nothing. They had found her already, she feared.

The sound grew louder, followed by the slow tapping of a cane and the flicker of a lantern, its warm glow illuminating a man's gaunt face and pale hair.

"Rémy!" Finn stumbled towards him, cradling her injured arm close to her body.

"Finn! Are you all right?" Rémy, startled, gripped her shoulder to keep her from falling. His brow furrowed with concern as he noticed her blood-soaked blouse. "You're bleeding! What happened?"

"I'm fine, it's just my arm, and my face—" Her voice shook as her trembling fingertips hovered over the gash around her eye. "Dr. Veyssière was chasing me and I fell into the cistern." She gestured at the dried bloodstains on his face. "And you, are you hurt?"

Rémy frowned. "I'll be fine. I had an encounter with Étienne Lacroix. This time he will not escape, nor will the doctor. The police have the building surrounded. Where is Claude?"

"The doctor has him, and he's probably in danger. Please help me find him!"

Rémy glanced over his shoulder. "I was searching with Inspector Percier and his men, but I'm afraid I wandered off." He raised the lantern and glanced around the clandestine space. "All these vaults and passageways down here—"

They both jumped at the crack of a gunshot, then stared at each other, horrified.

"Claude's pistol," Rémy guessed.

Finn nodded, still shivering. "Come on!" She grabbed his arm and pulled him in the direction of the gunshot. "Hurry! I used to be a dancer here. I know the way."

Rémy blinked, surprised, but he let Finn pull him along. He followed her ghostly form while his lantern's glow illuminated their path.

The duelling pistol's smoke cleared at last. Claude had aimed for Dr. Veyssière's heart, yet instead of seeing the deranged physician dead or wounded, he beheld another horrifying sight.

Lacroix was staring at Claude with mocking eyes that seemed to absorb the surrounding light and emanate malevolence instead. Anticipating

Claude's target, he had pushed Baltard from behind, yanking him out of the other artists' grasp and shoving him into Claude's line of fire to serve as a human shield for Dr. Veyssière.

Baltard's expression was more bewildered than agonized. His face was contorted with shock and pain as he gazed down at the red stain unfurling across his white shirtfront. He raised a trembling hand towards the wound. The bullet had pierced his chest.

"*Now* look what you've done," Lacroix said listlessly. No one touched Baltard, letting him slide unceremoniously to the floor.

Claude's incredulous expression nearly mirrored his instructor's. He felt his arm quaking with tension and realized he was still aiming the pistol. Forgetting the imminent threat of the other men in the room, he dropped the heavy weapon and dashed to Baltard's side.

"Give them a moment," Lacroix ordered with a faint smile, lifting a hand to command the other artists to keep their distance.

Claude knelt next to Baltard, who had fallen to his knees before collapsing onto one side, breathing raggedly and clutching his bleeding chest. Claude pressed his hands to the seeping wound. "M. Baltard—Father—Forgive me!"

Baltard struggled to move his hand to cover Claude's. "Claude. You finally—" He attempted to smile. "No. I am the one who needs forgiveness. For what I've done to Calais, to Finn, to so many others—and now—to you. You were right. This is—madness—" Sanguine drops began appearing on his lips. "It's all right—Claude—There is still time—" With a final labored gasp Baltard lay still. His head drifted to one side and his hand slipped from Claude's.

"No—" Claude slowly withdrew his bloodstained hands from the bullet wound. He remained at Baltard's side, his knees pressing into the cold floor and his ashen features frozen in a stunned expression. He did not react even when Dr. Veyssière's footsteps approached him from behind and paused at his side.

Dr. Veyssière leaned over, reached out a black-suited arm, and closed Baltard's eyes. "Punctured lung and perforated artery, most likely." He sounded as clinical as if he were preparing to dissect a stranger's corpse in his hospital auditorium.

"It appears we *all* have blood on our hands now!" Lacroix's smile widened as he rubbed his hands together in gleeful anticipation. "Doctor! If you please." He gestured to Claude, and then turned away. "Gentlemen! Let us complete the Seventh Day."

Dr. Veyssière gripped Claude by his torn shirt collar, yanked him to his feet, and dragged him back to the marble slab. "Hold him down," the doctor commanded, although the young man, his mind elsewhere, offered little resistance. The other artists approached the preparation slab, some with surgical tools glistening in their hands. Dr. Veyssière reached for the jar containing the chloroform hood.

"Wait," Lacroix interrupted. He approached the slab with a purposeful stride and gazed serenely down at Claude. "Hold the sedative this time, Doctor. I want him to feel *every minute* of this."

Finn and Rémy followed the sound of the commotion following the gunshot, illuminating backstage passageways with their lantern as they hurried closer. Rémy could not help wondering if echoes were leading them astray, since Finn seemed to be getting them lost in the depths of countless underground vaults, yet her step remained confident.

Rémy thought he could hear distant music, and assumed that the Opéra's evening performance had begun. Hundreds of wealthy Parisians in expensive clothes were settled into plush red seats, masking their faces with gleaming brass opera glasses and pearl-handled fans, obliviously diverting themselves with the night's gossip, fashion, and spectacle. Suddenly he paused, blocking Finn's swift step by flicking his cane across her path. "Wait," he hissed. The lantern softly scraped against stone as he lowered it to the ground.

"Rémy? What are you doing?" she whispered, shoving the extended cane aside with a grimy hand. Her other arm still ached, but did not seem to be broken after all. She attempted to ignore the pain in her impatience to find Claude.

Rémy lowered his arm and faced her. "You don't need to do this, Finn. Those men are dangerous, and I am sure the police are on their way. They must have heard the gunshot. If one of us has to go charging in here, though, let it be me."

Finn shook her head. Strands of wet hair were still plastered to her face. "Claude risked everything to get me out of the asylum." She reached down and pulled the dagger from her boot, tightly clutching its hilt in her determined fist. "Now it's my turn to help him." She tilted her chin defiantly towards Rémy. The lantern's dim light briefly gilded her face with a haunting glow. She strode silently onward with a demeanor that reminded Rémy of Lady Macbeth.

"Finn, wait—"

Rémy jumped slightly as an agonized shriek tore from an unseen throat, the sound cut short as if the voice had been forcibly silenced. Finn emitted a soft gasp but only quickened her step. The ragged hem of her dampened dove-grey skirt whipped around her ankles. Rémy hurried after her, the silver blade slithering from its sheath in his cane. For a fleeting moment his head swam with exhilaration at the thought of burying the sharpened blade in Lacroix's throat.

Looking at Finn and her raised fist, Rémy sensed the years of stifled rage in the tense muscles of her thin shoulders and the small hand wrapped around the antique dagger's handle, her entire body a storm of repressed fury seeking release and vengeance. Rémy understood her determination, but knew that one of them must remain calm before they did anything careless and both ended up transformed into living sculptures.

The darkened vault before them grew brighter with hidden candlelight and louder with the commotion of a presumably gruesome scene still occurring out of sight. Rémy caught Finn's wrist before she could dart around the final archway of the vault and into danger. She did not look back at him, and her arm gripping the dagger was rigid in his grasp, but he felt her relax at last.

Together they peered around the corner of the archway and witnessed a macabre surgery in progress. However, the physician was standing aside while a cult of fanatical artists wielded the surgical instruments. Seven young to middle-aged black-suited men were committing the atrocities, most with vacant facial expressions and trance-like motion, but Rémy also caught occasional glimpses of blazing eyes and clenched teeth. Four men struggled to hold Claude's thrashing limbs down on a marble sarcophagus. Dr. Veyssière was fastening a leather strap over his victim's mouth, silencing the young man's screams. Claude's shirt had been sliced open, exposing his colorless skin to the cultists' flashing blades. Rémy could only imagine how swiftly Claude's heart was pounding inside his slight body.

Lacroix was gleefully making slow incisions on Claude's chest. "Don't struggle," he ordered in a disturbingly sweet voice. "You'll ruin the aesthetic."

Lacroix chattered on while he worked, moving the blade as slowly as possible. "We finally have a proper altar for our sacrifice. True, the asylum is rife with talkative ghosts, but I grew weary of using the operating tables where so many others had died. So many restless spirits demanding attention at the same time. I shall never understand how my mother endured their clamor." He smiled down at Claude. "I look forward to speaking with you after we transform you into Orpheus and send you to the spirit world. You will thank me, like the rest of them, for the beautiful death I am giving you. You shall see. Besides, isn't that what you romantics fantasize about, when you're not pining away for consumptives and madwomen? Dying beautifully?"

Claude attempted to shake his head, snarling angrily into the leather strap.

"Hush, now. I hope your spirit is more eloquent and enlightened than your conscious self. They usually are."

Rémy, too, felt simmering rage upon seeing the man who had murdered Stéphane and so many others without a shred of remorse. Two other men were standing near crates of artists' props, working by candlelight to cut lengths of surgical thread, like two Fates determining a human lifespan. Surveying the rest of the scene, Rémy noticed with horror that Alexandre Baltard lay dead upon the floor with a bullet wound in his chest. The spreading pool of blood around his body reflected the glimmer of candle flames. Had Claude been forced to murder his foster father?

Suddenly Lacroix glanced up from his diabolical work. "Achille! Jean-Baptiste! Go and fetch our dearly departed Eurydice from the underworld of the opera house, will you?"

"As you wish, Messenger," one artist replied. He carefully set the surgical thread and shears on the edge of a crate and strode in the direction of the cistern, followed by his companion.

Finn, still grasping the dagger, pressed the back of her forearm against her mouth. She was trying not to make a sound—not a breath, a footstep, or a heartbeat. The Genesis cult believed she was dead. She moved to peer further around the massive archway where they hid.

Rémy pulled her back, careful not to touch her injured arm. "Wait," he whispered. "If we stop Lacroix first, the others will follow—"

She jerked her wrist out of his grasp and glanced at him in the dim light. "He's yours, then," she whispered back. She shivered, uncomfortable in her wet clothes. "*I* am going to stop Dr. Veyssière and save Claude. I do not care what happens to me after that!"

Rémy nodded reluctantly. So they each desired their revenge. Silently he accepted his role in this morbid underground mystery play.

Finn, surveying the scene, was calculating the distance she needed to cover to reach Dr. Veyssière. Summoning her courage with a deep intake of chill air, she dashed through the archway, heading straight for the doctor with her dagger. If she had looked at the other artists, she would have relished their terror at the sight of her, a resurrected phantom in a bloodstained white blouse and medical corset, with flame-colored hair and tattered skirts streaming wildly behind her.

The doctor turned at the sound of running footsteps. Lacking Lacroix's dexterity, he reacted too slowly to prevent Finn from burying the dagger beneath his ribcage while glaring up at him, her seething hatred finding its target at last.

The unexpected noise broke Lacroix's concentration. With a flick of his wrist, the artist lifted the dripping scalpel from the incision he was carving into Claude's chest and gazed coolly at Finn and Dr. Veyssière. "Our resurrected Eurydice has finally ascended from the Underworld," he muttered reverently, yet a sardonic tone remained in his voice. "Doctor, heal thyself. I know you can. You must, for tonight, reality and myth converge. The world is beginning to change already—"

"Release Claude," Finn commanded. "Do not move, or I will twist this dagger and finish the job."

"No need, my dear," the mesmerist said. The blade slid out of his flesh as he stepped backwards and staggered away from Finn's rigid hand, his own attempting to keep pressure on the wound. "Mlle. Finnegan—seems to be experiencing a hysteria fit," he added in a distant voice. He coughed as flecks of blood began rising to his lips, and extended his other hand towards Finn. "Let me—hypnotize her—"

She flinched and took a step back, unwilling as ever to let him touch her again.

The despised hand fell as Dr. Veyssière stumbled and tried to remain standing. Finn still brandished the bloody dagger, threatening the doctor and anyone else who dared approach her.

"Oh, for heaven's sake," Lacroix lamented. "She's only a woman! Let us put our Eurydice back in her coffin until we're ready for her." He strode over to the doctor, who was examining his wound with a vacant gaze, unable to focus his eyes and increasingly unsteady on his feet. He did not seem to notice Lacroix fumbling through his pockets until he found the doctor's flask of chloroform, which he tossed to Vincent Morel. "Here. Keep the little wasp from stinging."

Dr. Veyssière fell back against the slab where Claude lay. Two of the artists instinctively released Claude's right arm and leg in order to brace the doctor's collapse. Claude took advantage of the distraction and sprang from the slab, wrestling his limbs out of his remaining captors' grasp and yanking the leather strap out of his mouth.

"Finn!" Claude nearly stumbled in his haste to dash between her and the cultists, protectively throwing an arm across her body. He was alarmed by her bloodstained figure but beyond relieved to see her alive. "Let's go," he insisted, trying to guide her to the nearest corridor. "There must be a way out. I'll get you to a doctor—a real one." He felt another wave of vicious pain from his scalpel wounds, and glanced down at his bleeding torso amid the tattered remains of his clothing. He noted with relief that Lacroix's blade would leave him scarred, but not exsanguinated.

Finn tensed her shoulders and resisted his guiding arm. "Shall we let the rest of these murderers go free?" she asked incredulously. She had not yet lowered the dagger.

Two of the Brotherhood's artists helped Dr. Veyssière drag himself onto the preparation table and attempted to staunch the bleeding with their hands. "Keep him alive!" shrieked the elder of the two, his voice growing shrill with terror. "Only he knows how to place us in the state of lucid somnambulism. We cannot reach the new Creation without him!"

The mesmerist's wound was deeper than Claude's gashes. He bled profusely, adding more crimson stains to the marble slab until it resembled the sacrificial altar Lacroix intended it to represent. "The surgical thread—the needle—hurry," the doctor gasped.

The two remaining artists looked confused. The Eighth Day models had never rebelled against the Brotherhood before. The cultists had not been prepared for a fight.

"Enough blood has been spilled. Please, let us go," Claude said, attempting again to guide Finn out of the nightmarish sepulcher. She continued to threaten them with her dagger, her expression stony but intense, her green eyes flickering with fury.

Lacroix, observing quietly while casually twisting the scalpel's handle between his fingers, merely grinned at them. His features looked demonic in the fiery light. "Go then, Orpheus, take your Eurydice! Try to ascend from the Underworld without looking back. Just know that I shall follow you every—step—of the way—" As he spoke he raised the scalpel towards them, twisting it to make the light slide across the blade. "Soon I shall finish my work that began with Icarus—"

"No!" Rémy dashed out from behind the archway, his sword pointed at Lacroix's heart. "You will *not*—"

Lacroix, startled, managed nevertheless to twist his body sideways and avoid Rémy's weapon. The thin blade glanced off his shoulder, slicing through his suit jacket and drawing blood. Lacroix snarled and struck Rémy across the face with his elbow, knocking him to the ground.

Rémy landed on his back with the wind knocked out of him, but recovered just in time to block the glittering descent of Lacroix's scalpel with the sheath of his cane. He kicked the artist backwards and rolled out of the way, bleeding from a wounded lip, then leapt to his feet and lashed out again with his sword. Lacroix's lithe body evaded him, dodging a blow that would have sliced open his torso.

"You're too late, scholar," Lacroix cried, lunging at Rémy with the scalpel again. "We've nearly completed the Seventh Day. The spirits claim that God chose *me* to complete his work! You would defy God himself?"

Rémy dodged the sweeping blows but was driven backwards, finally slamming into the wall behind him. He attempted a desperate counterattack with his sword, but Lacroix knocked the blade out of his hand while Rémy was still stunned from his collision with the wall. The sword clattered to the ground, where its silver gargoyle snarled uselessly at him from out of reach.

Claude was on the verge of leaping forward to assist Rémy when Finn's sudden exclamation caught his attention. She was struggling with Léon Fable, who had struck her from behind, wrapping his arms around her upper body and attempting to force the dagger from her hand. The remaining artists watched in confusion for a moment, glancing from one conflict to the other. Claude could tell that they wanted to help Lacroix fend off Rémy, but were not willing to let Finn and himself escape.

"Quickly, we must finish the sculpture and deliver it to the roof," Vincent Morel said decisively, his eyes burning like embers as he pointed at Claude. "The Messenger says that our Orpheus must join his father Apollo before sunrise."

"Keep hold of that girl, Léon. She will be our Eurydice," Boisseau said.

Claude noticed with relief that the cultists had turned their attention to him instead of Finn. Surgical instruments glistened around him like shards of a shattered mirror. In this moment, feeling pain down to the bone and watching his world collapse around him, Claude at last found his voice. He drew a deep breath and summoned his courage, knowing that his speech could not falter in order for his words to be believable.

No longer afraid, Claude stepped forward into the candlelight. With his arms outstretched, his hands open, and his head held high, he resembled a revenant emerging from a tomb. "I am—Orpheus," he began. "Beloved of my father Apollo, prophet of the Orphic mysteries, oracle of the ancient world, bringer of divine music and prophecy." He paused, furiously searching his memory for his favorite paintings of Orpheus and snippets of the Orphic poems he once read as a young student. "Hear me, and let my song hypnotize you into magnetic sleep, infused with power drawn from the sun god himself. My spirit, suspended between worlds, is drawn to this modern temple of my father, who summons me to speak through this mortal vessel."

As he had hoped, the artists held still while they listened in awe. Léon Fable nearly lost his grip on Finn. Her dagger had clattered to the floor, but she still fought against his restraining arms and kicked at him viciously with the heels of her boots.

Claude's white shirt created a tattered and bloody shroud around him as drops of red cascaded down his pale chest in dark rivulets, creating the effect of sanguine lyre strings. He continued speaking, his voice clear and strong. "I invoke the Moon's pure splendor, the Stars of night, and the swift wings of Fate. I have entered the dark and silent world beneath the foundations of the earth. With my music I charmed Hades, the Lord of the Dead, and his guardian Cerberus. The intoxicating spell of my voice drew tears from his iron heart. Therefore, I must retrieve the muse of my sacred song." He gestured to Finn. "This maiden must be restored from death, my Eurydice, she who possesses rage none can quell. By the power of my art I shall bear her away, and this time I shall not look back, for love is stronger than death."

Listening to Claude's words, Rémy found that he, too, had rage left in him. He spun out of Lacroix's way, retrieved his cane, and slammed it into the back of his enemy's knee. Lacroix fell flat onto his back, dragging Rémy down with him. Rémy lost his grip on his cane, but caught Lacroix's throat in his other hand. Leaning his knee against the artist's ribcage, he reached out for his cane but grabbed the nearest object instead: a sculpted fragment of discarded masonry on the floor of the workshop.

Rémy lifted the heavy piece of marble over Lacroix's head while the artist struggled to breathe. "Stoned to death. Isn't that how Saint Étienne died?" Rémy asked, an exultant tone seeping into his voice.

Lacroix grinned up at Rémy. "Then cast the first one, sodomite," he spat. "Make me a martyr."

For Stéphane.

The rock descended. Rémy struck again and again, until Lacroix's face was unrecognizable and his grinning teeth were broken and scattered. Rémy continued striking nevertheless, unaware that Inspector Percier and his officers had arrived to arrest the remaining artists, thwarting their attempts to flee or hide. Unaware that Dr. Veyssière had bled to death on the marble slab. Unaware that Lacroix had driven his scalpel into Rémy's torso while the scholar was preoccupied with bludgeoning him.

Nevertheless, Rémy's vengeance was complete. He backed away from the visceral mess that had once been Étienne Lacroix and attempted to stand. Exhaustion, pain, and triumph caught up with him simultaneously. He faltered and kneeled wearily on the ground, watching blood seep from beneath his ribs, only dimly aware of the commotion surrounding him.

The police easily subdued the Eighth Day artists and led them away in shackles, ignoring their protests and ravings. Percier stared at Lacroix's gruesome remains. Then he caught Rémy's eye, his expression a combination of disbelief and concern. Claude and Finn, holding one another for mutual comfort, followed the direction of Percier's gaze and finally noticed Rémy's injury.

"Rémy!" Finn rushed over to him, kneeling to examine his wound.

Rémy was slipping away into a shadowy dream in which everyone seemed increasingly distant. One moment he was aware of sitting upright. The next, he was lying on the ground with an angelic young woman cradling his head in her lap, her piercing green eyes gazing down at him through a fiery red halo. The face of a handsome dark-haired man loomed over him with a concerned expression.

"Stéphane?" Rémy asked softly.

Claude shook his head and pressed his hands to Rémy's wound. His own bleeding had stopped, but gory stains lingered in sticky tatters upon the gashes on his chest. "It's over. We'll take you to a hospital," he said gently.

Rémy smiled up at him with bruised lips. His face had grown as pale as his hair, and not all of the blood streaked across it was his own. "Claude. Finn. Yes—it's over now. We defeated Lacroix and Veyssière and the Genesis Cult." He clasped Claude's hand. "Finn has her freedom. You have your muse. Now—I go to mine." Rémy heard Finn frantically calling his name, but her voice grew distant while his eyes slid shut.

June 10, 1889

Revue des Beaux-Arts à l'Exposition Universelle

"This year's Exposition Universelle offers our international visitors an astounding array of modern French ingenuity and achievement from the Galérie des Machines to La Tour Eiffel, which one must acknowledge as a spectacular feat of engineering despite the controversy surrounding its construction. France's far-reaching progress across the globe is evident in the colonial exhibitions such as the Egyptian bazaar, Javanese dancers, and Pavillon du Siam [...]

Nearly ten thousand works of art are on display at the Palais des Beaux-Arts. The juried works of art were submitted by both established artists and notable newcomers [...]

Among the rising young Parisian painters is M. Claude Fournel, son of the celebrated Romantic painter Sylvain Fournel. After studying with his late father and with the recently deceased Alexandre Baltard, M. Fournel has developed a dedicated following among young artists and collectors of the Symbolist circles.

Although M. Fournel's work reveals the guidance of his mentors, particularly in its intricate detail and rich palette, his style has clearly evolved from his early training and transcended to appeal to the subconscious mind, allowing even seemingly mundane subjects to elevate his audience's thoughts to dreamlike and mystical realms.

M. Fournel's most striking painting in the galleries of the Exposition Universelle is a portrait of his wife and preferred model, Mme. Rose Fournel, in the guise of Salomé. Surrounded by elaborate Orientalist décor, this exotic beauty sits demurely on a carved seat, holding her characteristic silver platter. She has completed her dance for King Herod and awaits her bloody reward.

M. Fournel has given his Salomé the alabaster skin and flowing copper hair of his model, and has rendered her teal and emerald gown with such technical mastery that the viewer can imagine the fabric streaming like water while she dances. She tilts her head to one side, as if listening for the sound of the executioner's sword shearing Saint John the Baptist's head from his neck. However, this Salomé's green eyes maintain a somber appearance, suggesting that even the most vindictive *femme fatale* may experience a sense of regret when blood is spilled on her behalf.

Such meditative expressiveness and talent leave us eager to see more of M. Fournel's work, as he is certain to enjoy a long and successful career at the Salons. M. Fournel is also becoming known as a worthy and compassionate instructor with skill beyond his years. He is currently accepting new students for drawing and painting lessons at the atelier of his late mentor on the Rue de l'Abbaye."

Rémy Sauvage folded the journal he had been reading and slid it into the pocket of his green brocade coat, pleased that Claude's paintings had earned a favorable public reception. A warm breeze blew his tangled blond hair across his face. He had stopped at a shady bench to rest his aching feet after an entire day of exploring the wondrous art and inventions of the Exposition Universelle.

His new shop girl, Violet, had assured him that she could handle *Le Jardin Sauvage* for the afternoon. Rémy had hired her upon her release from the Sainte-Geneviève, and found her a clever and capable assistant. She could speak both French and English, and showed an increasing interest in the esoteric subjects of the books Rémy was teaching her to read.

So much had occurred during the past year. While Rémy was recovering at home from his wounds dealt by Lacroix, Claude brought him the news that Dr. Veyssière's asylum was being decommissioned and closed. Not only were most of the mesmerist's diagnoses deemed questionable, the health inspectors were appalled by the sadistic experiments described in his private notebooks, from electroconvulsive therapy to torturous chemical treatments tested on the patients he believed never would be missed by their families. His patients were re-evaluated by legitimate physicians and relocated to other hospitals or released. The latest word was that an architect from the École des Beaux-Arts had been commissioned to transform l'Hôpital Sainte-Geneviève into a scholarly library and reading room.

Rémy had been too wounded to attend the memorial services for Calais and Baltard, but Claude and Finn had postponed their wedding until Rémy was feeling well enough to serve as one of their few witnesses. They were married at Saint-Germain-des-Prés on an autumn day. Finn—or 'Rose,' as she preferred to be called now that she was a true *parisienne*—looked radiant in ivory lace with the sunlight casting diamond-shaped stained-glass patterns upon her, adorning her graceful figure with translucent jewels.

He visited their home often, discussing art with Claude, helping Finn learn to read French, or listening to her retellings of Irish myths and legends. Finn seemed content enough being married to Claude, Rémy observed, yet each time he saw her he hoped to find that the haunted expression had vanished from her eyes, and the guarded tension had eased from her delicate shoulders at last.

Rémy remained alone. Although his bookshop and his research kept him occupied, now he was troubled not only by Stéphane's memory, but also by what he had done to Étienne Lacroix. The deaths of Lacroix and Dr. Veyssière had been committed in self-defense according to the police report, thanks to the intervention of Inspector Percier. Yet taking his revenge had not returned Stéphane to him, nor did Finn seem entirely at peace now that the doctor had perished by her hand.

One day he glanced up from reading at his bookshop counter to see Percier strolling past while intently gazing through his display windows, and Rémy assumed he was still being watched by the police. Instead, however, Percier proposed to hire him as a consultant for the Préfecture on another case involving the occult. This would not be the inspector's last such request for Rémy's expertise.

After closing his shop for the day or leaving its operation in Violet's capable hands, he enjoyed taking long walks through the evening light, often to leave flowers at Stéphane Desnoyers's polished marble sarcophagus in the Cimetière de Montmartre. Occasionally he stopped to visit Stéphane's family afterward, making certain that they did not want for anything. He and Claude had thus far been unsuccessful in locating Finn's mother and sister, but Stéphane's sister Sabine was helping them search Montmartre for red-haired women who resembled Finn.

He reflected often on the Eighth Day Brotherhood. How could eight educated and intelligent men, including someone as practical as Alexandre

Baltard, fall under Lacroix's spell and devise such an unspeakable plot? How could so many men be led astray by a medium's illusions, a mesmerist's grandiose ego, and a painter's silver-tongued ravings? All he could resolve was that perhaps all of the artists in Lacroix's circle were easily drawn towards decadent and nightmarish subjects, both real and imaginary. All longed to escape from the modern world and live in a fantasy realm, and their art alone had not provided a sufficient form of alternate reality to satisfy their fervor.

While strolling around Paris as an observer of city life, the *flâneur* in his element, Rémy often wondered what the Eighth Day Brotherhood had found so distasteful about modern Paris. The city had its railways, its steel towers, its new electric lights, its covered arcades, its museums and spectacles and monuments. However, like the late Victor Hugo, Rémy mourned the loss of the medieval city. Its mysterious and narrow streets had been replaced by *grands boulevards*. The *saltimbanques* and alchemists had faded away, gradually replaced by cabaret singers and modern scientists. Yet Rémy knew that some of medieval Paris still remained, resting beneath his feet and greeting him around certain corners, those brief flashes of hidden intrigue that were part of the remarkable palimpsest of this ancient city.

With the success of the Exposition Universelle at stake, the authorities moved swiftly to cast a veil over the Eighth Day Brotherhood's atrocities. Inspector Percier did his best to bring the remaining guilty artists to justice. All seemed to comprehend the madness of their plan once they had surfaced from Lacroix's and Dr. Veyssière's insidious influence. The prisoners, save for one who committed suicide before his trial, were incarcerated or exiled.

A few weeks later, the media sensation following the flash of a police lantern over a prostitute's mutilated corpse in Whitechapel, London, further effaced the Genesis murders from the newspapers. Paris would have its World's Fair and assume its place on the international stage despite being plunged into the general pessimism of the *fin-de-siècle*.

While exploring the exposition, Rémy had to acknowledge that Lacroix was right about one thing: the dawn of a new age was approaching indeed. Leaning more heavily on his cane than he did a year before, Rémy stood and gazed one last time up at the illuminated pinnacle of the Eiffel Tower. With a faint smile he turned towards the Pont d'Iéna, strolled out of the Exposition Universelle, and disappeared into the crowd.

Historical Afterword

The city of Paris, its related art movements, and its monuments are accurately described to the best of the author's ability. Rémy Sauvage's bookshop, the Café Hugo, and l'Hôpital Sainte-Geneviève are fictional. L'Hôpital Sainte-Geneviève borrows its location on the Paris map from the existing Bibliothèque Sainte-Geneviève, designed by architect Henri Labrouste and constructed from 1843 to 1850. The description of the Palais Garnier's underground levels also has been embellished. *The Eighth Day Brotherhood* is primarily inspired by the Symbolist movement, particularly French artists Gustave Moreau (1826-1898) and Odilon Redon (1840-1916). All artists portrayed as characters in the novel are products of the author's imagination.

View other Black Rose Writing titles at www.blackrosewriting.com/books
and use promo code PRINT to receive a 20% discount when purchasing.

BLACK🌹ROSE
writing™

CPSIA information can be obtained
at www.ICGtesting.com
Printed in the USA
FFOW02n0130150816
26676FF

9 781612 967370